WHAT YOU COULD HAVE WON

Rachel Genn

D0062857

SHEFFIELD – LONDON – NEW YORK

First published in 2020 by And Other Stories
Sheffield – London – New York
www.andotherstories.org

Epigraphs from the following sources gratefully acknowledged: *Eros the Bittersweet* by Anne Carson (Princeton University Press) and 'Seether' by Veruca Salt, written by Nina Gordon. Whilst all attempts have been made to find the copyright holders of quoted passages and secure permission where relevant, the publishers and author would welcome approaches in the case of omission.

9 8 7 6 5 4 3 2 1

ISBN: 9781911508861
eBook ISBN: 9781911508878

Editor: Tara Tobler; Copy-editor: Lara Vergnaud; Proofreader: Sarah Terry; Typeset in Linotype Neue Swift and Verlag by Tetragon, London; Cover Design: Jon Gray; Printed and bound on acid-free, age-resistant Munken Premium by CPI Limited, Croydon, UK

And Other Stories gratefully acknowledge that our work is supported using public funding by Arts Council England.

For Esther and Ingrid –
that they may know their own power

A space must be maintained or desire ends.

EROS THE BITTERSWEET, ANNE CARSON

I try to keep her on a short leash.
I try to calm her down.
I try to ram her into the ground, yeah.

SEETHER, VERUCA SALT

CONTENTS

ANTIPAROS

Up to now, I have only noted decisions that are poor to extremely poor and/or seem to be defences against shame. From the cafeteria, I can see down to the beach: framed by the rendered arch to the café's terrace, her rectangular shelter by the shore is flapping in the wind. It is made up of a faded, jungle-patterned sheet stretched between four bamboo sticks secured in the sand, and stands twelve inches above her face. In that face, by now, the teeth will be chattering in the heat. Only yards from her, the main knot of Greeks are setting up volleyball, laughing in short barks because it is still early. They were up very late. There he is again, pulling himself from the sea, which makes me switch my eyes to the floor though no one can see me from there. I look towards him again and he is dragging his heel forcefully back through the sand to mark the boundaries of the court.

In the corner of the cold cabinet, there is a doughnut with a panther-pink glaze and I know that it has been put out for her. The doughnut has a cold sweat on it – an idiot among the metal saucers of tzatziki. If she sees it she will be positive that they can get to her even in the Cyclades. I have told her that being positive is dangerous, that there's always room for doubt in the mentally healthy; she becomes positive very easily since Burning Man, though the tendency has been there since the beginning. I have not mentioned the video once this morning.

It's clear that this place exists for the best-looking people from the capital. Athenians, in the main, are taut and deep brown and much taller than I imagined. From the shade in the café, I can get a good look at them down at the shore and I capture and hold on to a flash of small brown breasts. I get to admire the sheen on the torsos of these first weekenders from the mainland and feel that my eyes deal with them in fistfuls. I will make a note of that. They are forever emerging from the sea after swimming back and forth to the scrubby little island she calls Dilpa, two hundred yards from our shore. They are into coolly communicating jokes to each other: they like to quip quickly and make an appreciative moan rather than laugh openly; the handyman in particular makes laughter seem foolish. They drink frappés up to midnight. When not swimming or having faraway parties after sunset (where they laugh openly and often), these people are limbering, ankle-deep in sand. Apart from one, the men are colossal and unperturbed by deep water, large insects or the extreme heat. My skin is much fairer than theirs. I have tried nudity, but prefer to wear shorts.

He's coming to serve me as I knew he would, and I turn from the doughnut to feta with fried courgettes plus dill. I pay him and smile but he treats me impatiently, then slams the till and runs back out to the game. There are more players now. The arch is filling up and there's a new arrival to the group. At first I thought him a child but no, too hairy. A dwarf then? Whoever it is gets hold of the Handyman fondly enough to be family, but I don't imagine that this handyman is related to a dwarf. A stick-thin woman with white-blonde hair follows the Handyman and hugs him from behind then takes a moment to twirl his long curls with both hands and, finally, nips his cheeks. She shouts out a rousing slogan (in what? French? Hebrew? Dutch?) that clearly ends in 'Gigi', at which the Handyman bows deeply, holding his hand palm out towards the dwarf. 'Gigi' cannot be his name and so must be a name for the dwarf. A pet name. Here come some dirty blondes, probably Swedes, perhaps brothers, and they join in with their preparations for the game, bouncing hard and high like Maasai which is not easy in sand. They have a caramel-to-toffee tan that brags 'here for the season', and are lithe and I measure their dicks against the other volleyballers'. It's a matter of habituation: a few more days and I will not do this any more. I can talk my eyes out of it.

The Handyman is the centre of everything round here, carrying armfuls of drainage pipes or sides of meat wrapped in light blue cloth and newspaper, watering basil and oregano that thrive in gasoline canisters painted red, gold and green and kept in the scarce shade of the terrace walls. He has no idea that I have watched him perforate a basil leaf in a series of curves with the white shell of his nail then smell his fingers, then rub his fingers through his hair. He keeps the rustic showers pristine with a comically small squeegee. I whistle when I go into a stall. He polishes everything he passes with the cloth that wraps the meat. Gigi cannot be his name, which is why I am happy to apply it as a nickname for now.

There is a party on this island that we are not yet part of. I hear it. It starts with one lonely hide-beater and builds. Nothing so crass as a flyer, an invite or any evidence, though they have MTV and knew who she was the moment she arrived. Dilpa is where it's at: the smaller, rockier island that I can see but only they can swim to. There is a rowing boat and one ferryman, who disappears between his daily crossings, but before he does thinks nothing of stunning octopus on the side of his boat (the sound, a meaty *Hank*) and firing the black ink in an arc so wide that we sunbathers sit up.

For me and her, island life has rapidly become isolating. When night comes, while the real party heats up somewhere else, we sit in a ghost camp where I am encouraged to agree with her take on why we are so good for each other. I am expected to flow with her high, while she explains how the timing of her album was exactly right; I wonder if she thinks that talking about how we are together constitutes our togetherness, that if she shut up about us we'd be repulsed by what we found us to be. I say nothing, just listen, as she points to evidence that means she is still being followed by cameras. If I try to locate the distant music, or look for clues as to where it might be coming from, she insists that I get closer to her to judge a melody or listen to repeats of verses (commitment is never being bored). On her visits to the camp bathroom, I get to see him polishing the laundry troughs in what look like his party clothes. I am instructed to wait for her under the lamp outside, where she rejoins me in a crisp cone of light, thick with insects, confessing, 'I really can't believe that I only want you.' Later, I will suggest less kissing.

The slide began before we got here. In Athens, a couple of strangers had recognised her on the street so that on the ferry from Paros, all she wanted to do was play Zoot/Not Zoot (a title I coined, but now regret).

Sitting on deck, she sensed my reluctance to play.

'Hey! You evil cuz this canary such a fine dinner?'

'Can't we take a rest from it?' I said, tilting my chin at the sun.

At this, her headscarf (it's old and it's French), her glasses, her cigarette, all quivered. She overdid everything for the rest of the ferry ride: telling a staring passenger to fuck off, to gain my approval. As we approached the modest grey-green hump of Antiparos on the trawler, she performed an exaggerated running man. Since we started the Box Set she thinks she's Adriana La Cerva. *The Sopranos* has a lot to answer for. This lack of inhibition will need monitoring.

From the jetty, we took a wide dirt track that headed from the unmarked harbour through bristly dunes on an incline towards a campsite and, having been there before, she couldn't contain her enthusiasm: 'Now ain't dat barrelhouse?'

'Granted,' I said, taking in the view of a shallow bight of sand edged by green waters, punctuated by a smaller wild-looking island across a lagoon. We entered under a bleached sign for The Camping Antiparos and walked towards an unlit cabin with peeling turquoise paint, which seemed to have office status; through the window a wall calendar advertised ventilation ducting. I predicted a couple of days and we'd have to get out of here.

Gigi was the first person we saw. From behind the cabin he appeared with a piece of cream cheesecloth wrapped around his waist, a short kilt making his skin look black in the dusk. Standing with his legs apart like a wrestler, feet turned out and hands on hips. He carried a compact generator and up close smelled of sweat and pine cleaning fluid.

She pointed to the sign while staring at the generator. 'Are you maintenance?'

'You need hat,' he replied, seriously.

'I don't think so,' she said.

'Bamboo hat!'

She looked to me.

'Who's the Greek here?' I chuckled.

'No hat!' he shouted, pulling my hand from my crown. 'Hat!' He pointed to a row of small bamboo enclosures that stood in a row along the edge of the campground.

'Huts!' she cried, clapping her hands, as he went over and opened a rickety door constructed from odd lengths of old bamboo strapped together with binding. Inside was a six-foot-square corral and behind these huts were the boundaries to the camp, live bamboo thickets hissing in the breeze.

'In here, you can sleep, two-fifty drachma.'

'We have a tent,' I said, swinging the nylon pod round to my chest and patting its bulk.

We were given a pitch. Before I had even hammered in the pegs, she had begun her routines, but I immediately noticed the insistence of a beat and became distracted by the faraway noise of a good deal of people. The tent was up just as the sun set and I heard a switch in the distance, from a lone drummer to faint music. Every so often, voices lilted in consensus, and I caught a Greek hooray at something unexpected. The tents around us were empty. She didn't find this mysterious at all and intermittently sang into my face or did an English accent to coax me back to her. She drank the last of the ouzo then demanded the bag again. It wasn't all I had brought but I did not tell her as she is incapable of leaving so much as a salting. While she went to the bathrooms, I noted the mg/kg ratio in the book.

So it was no surprise that our first morning started unevenly. The Handyman arrived outside the tent as I, after struggling through anemones of silk scarves to reach the air, had just suggested a blaming pathology. From inside she shouted that if we didn't fucking arrive late to every fucking campsite we would know where the fucking shade was going to be for the fucking morning. I smiled at him and he shook his head. Without warning, he pulled out our tent pegs in strong smooth movements, helped her from the tent and removed our bags. With the tent emptied, he hooked two fingers around the strut, picked it up by its frame, and toyed with it to highlight its handiness, placing it finally in an empty patch of shade. When he left, we fucked. Something about the shaded heat of the tent and the inescapable stink of pine made it compulsory. I told her the heat put me off kissing, still, she tried to kiss me (NB: impulsivity to compulsivity).

Already, my favourite part of this camp is the cafeteria. If he isn't in his seat at the till, I find myself scanning the beach or scouring the shallow bay for him. I know she won't come out of her shelter. When paranoid, she waits until I say something she wants to hear. I had already told her this morning that a fresh start is always just around the corner but she called me a smug motherfucking yard dog who's just as needy as she is. Instead of analysing why she demolished the remains of the stash from Piraeus, she began acting as if it were always her intention to be well and truly rid of it. The inevitability of failure sits at the back of all this but today she looks blithely forward, talking the talk (the newly abstinent adore hyperbole – *This is the easiest!* – etc.) while I predict that by mid-afternoon there could be a catastrophic failure of will. Before then, there will be the breakdown in decision-making (possible chapter titles: 'Does it hurt to choose?' / 'Why it hurts to choose'). I could tell her that in some respects addicts want the regret, that they are longing for longing, only satisfied when there is nowhere else to go. This is the crux of my book: the very key to *How Cocaine Can Break Your Brain* is that regret is an integral part of the addiction machine. I am gathering evidence.

Making my way back towards the beach, my tray balances a cup and a frappé. The glass is tall and creaks with ice. She asked for coffee but I have a mint tea for her that will help her feel less unstable. My feet are burning, though no one on the beach would know. I check Gigi dividing his glances fairly between the volleyball and her shelter. A smart breeze lifts up the flap of the cloth coffin and I see the chocolate-dark corona around her nipple and my head swings to the Greeks and there he is again, looking, waiting. His colour matches hers. If only he knew that their little superstar was oiled up and nude under the sheet.

I put the tray down beside the sheet.

'You should offer yourself to him,' I say.

I take up my book then find the paper I need, 'Degraded Decision-Making in Long-Term Cocaine Users', from an up-and-coming Italian group. She squints through the flap at the ruffling pages of my maths notebook and I flick a look at the pages to see what she might have seen.

'Psychiatrists do it with squares,' she says.

I pull the book beside me in the sand, just in case.

'Do I look over your shoulder when you're writing songs?'

She blurts a laugh, 'You couldn't write a song,' and I am disgusted at how convinced she is of this.

BOX SET

It was the episode where Adriana was crying and couldn't stop. The day on-screen was clear, New Jersey autumn, and when Adriana scrabbled on all fours through the fallen leaves, the crack of Silvio's pistol shattered the air, and though the camera tilted upward from the forest floor there was no doubt about what had happened. You looked to Henry but he was staring at the patch of screen where Adriana was last seen. You have taken Ade's death like a basketball to the face. Two basketballs.

By the time you get out of bed the next day Henry has already left for the clinic. You switch on the TV, pressing the button on the remote hard like you are mid-argument and you play with an idea. If you put on an old Hermès (perhaps *Les Merveilles de la Vapeur*?) and your biggest glasses, you can go out by yourself, buy season six and get over Adriana, but you know you will never watch an episode without Henry. Not even to punish him.

It is already a real effort to hold off opening the packet that Lucien has left in the hall; your management has given him his own key and he can let himself in while you sleep. You have been out to examine the little package twice: it feels like a miniature coffin, or a novelty soap. The midday news is taken up with Yemen and the reporter plows through to the story of a spate of teenage suicides upstate. You decide for fucking certain that you will talk to Catherine about Lucien's attitude and this burst of assertion means that you can click off the television before the entertainment news and make for the hall and face the closet that holds the package but now you must also face the newspaper that has been left open on the green glass table. It's you in Paris, only days ago. In the picture, you are startled and your mauve sweater is splattered with tahini. It says: 'Astrid eats through pap slap.' You want to stop the slant from anger into sorrow.

Paris had been management's idea, but the Box Set was all you. You couldn't believe Henry had never seen *The Sopranos* (you thought you were the only one) and you took it as a sign. Of course it was Melfi that got him interested and he began by commenting on the length of her skirt.

'Therapy will never open up a man like Tony,' he said. 'ReOrientation is the only way forward,' as he pounded an ice bag, 'backed up with ReThink.'

'Psychiatry's gone to shit,' you whispered to Laddie, a stuffed fox in a cap and cravat mounted on your middle finger through a hole in his stitching. You hung your head over the back of the couch. 'ReOrient this!' You brought Laddie and your finger back in close and whispered, 'What did drugs do wrong, hey buddy?'

Henry returned from the kitchen with a drink and you almost suggested playing popcorn Rorschach. You started planning a joke about that last night in Greece, but you didn't have the nerve for that either.

'It's undisciplined attention that's the threat to his mental health.'

'Not the family of ducks,' you said.

'Perceptions are choices. You should all realize this.'

Henry and Gregor implicitly encouraged everyone to use ReThink. You wondered if he had always done the clinic smile? You couldn't have fallen in love with that, even back then.

*

Back then was when Catherine managed to get you and your band their first paid gig at the Eliot Perlman Wellness Center in Manhattan. Arriving early, you realized you may have been a little high to do a charity gig because when you left the elevator, you felt threatened by the ballroom chandelier and began a little trot to get away from it.

The band squinted together at a banner: *Eliot Perlman Wellness Center Welcomes Non-Invasive Psychiatry Practitioners.* Looking at Catherine, you asked, 'Is this us?'

Just before the set, you began to regret the joint in the dressing room because you found yourself being stared at. Hard. You stared right back, first looking at his head then the suit, the hair. You did not tolerate not knowing and so you were over to him in a few steps.

'Your kind of gig?'

'Absolutely,' he said, looking up and down the line of you. No shame.

'What do you do?' You were sweeping for clues. British? Light gray suit, charcoal shirt. No tie. Good pecs. White lacquered cufflinks. Myrrh in the cologne. Milk-fed.

'I stare.'

You sank a substantial portion of his red wine, placing the glass back into his hand.

'What else?'

'That's what I study. What people fixate on.'

'Oh yeah?'

'Their dwell time.'

There was a definite high-wire recklessness to him. You stayed silent, waiting for him to pitch one way or the other under scrutiny. 'Then I train them to fixate on what really matters.'

This guy had monkey feet.

'Nice work, hombre,' you said, taking the last drops of his wine and leaping up onto the stage, knowing that you were the expert here and had never looked better in your ten-year-old jeans. He might have spooked you, but his attention to you was so complete, so insistent, that you felt he had already put down a deposit. Dwell Time had crouched patiently in your mind. It would be the title of your first album.

'Loose in LA' opened the set, and for once, you held the note you always chickened out on too early, managed a move during Eddie's solo that you hadn't dared since leaving Lotus Falls, and made damn sure you didn't search for Dwell Time in the darkness. The audience exploded after the song but quickly settled down quickly to a couple of mistimed whoops. During the encore you allowed him eye contact. He was the only one not begging for your attention so you pulled the mic close:

'When I was twelve . . . back in Lotus Falls, a guy came to fix our TV.'

Your tired-looking yellow hair covered your cheeks and shaded your eyes. The part you kept purposefully black.

'My mom told him, "Astrid will always have a hole in her bucket." This last song is for him.'

Wild after the encore, you jumped down from the stage and stood before him breathing fast, the sweetness of red wine full in his face; not a single sour note.

'OK,' you said. 'Tell me about it.'

You grabbed his hand and tugged him through the clusters of associates and partners. You snuck him past security, out onto a balcony where neither of you acknowledged the magnificent view of downtown above the handrail. First, he made you laugh pretending to know about Electro. From this you got onto the tedium of cocaine compared to meth, next he had pressed into your hand what he said he had brought for himself. For a good half hour of speaking with him you hadn't been able to tell if he was psychotic. Two hours later you were sitting at his feet.

'A bird boy?' you asked.

'Not his official name,' said Henry.

'But this bird boy can read?'

'He can't move his eyes. His head moves like a bird's to make up for that.'

'Would a person be able to tell?'

Henry thought for a second. 'I have never seen a busier neck than his.'

Your pupils spread like dinner plates at this and you felt the need to set up a recording of your conversation, imagining his answers ticker-taping from a tiny slot in the back of your head, gently parting your hair and coiling between the soles of your feet. Who says busier neck? You were falling for Busier Neck.

'I started imagining a beak for him today.'

Henry tapped his nose briefly on an imaginary piece of wood in front of his face.

Silently you begged him. Don't do that.

'So his gaze is at the mercy of his neck, not his eyes.'

'It's all about where the eyes need to get to next. What's important for him to know.'

The bird boy emerged in glorious detail, the data explained in such delightful and unexpected terms that the ticker halted right there because, just like that, he had made a world for you to hold in your hand, a BirdBoy at its center. His choice of words split you up the middle and from that night on you would be holding in your guts with your hands. You were determined to ignore the unnerving feeling that he had known you were coming. His thoughts were made for you.

You decided to test him. 'What would you call your autobiography?'

'How right I was, how right – exclamation mark, maybe two.'

If he came up with that just for you, you will never let him go. Then he said, 'I think perhaps *Hole in My Bucket* could be volume one for you.'

You smiled lopsidedly.

He hated the work ethic here in the US, despised the lack of holidays and the unspoken dictates of the psychiatry department he was part of, and the ass-licking robots that he worked with, but he was yet to specialize and so was still kowtowing to a cigar-smoking mentor, who made shameless millions in condoms and recycled paper in China and who insisted on calling him 'Hank'.

'What's his name?' you asked.

'Frank.'

You smiled. Full and equal smiles.

Midnight brought the first real lull. You panicked, sure that it was because of the story you had foolishly told about yourself.

'I could stay here forever' – your words were steady as a lunatic's, and when he laughed you laughed right alongside him. You sensed imminence: movement on a planetary scale, as if a new sky was being rolled out and under it; brutality, with the right kind of guidance and determination, might be avoided.

You were upset at his surprise at your love of French literature. (You didn't tell him that it began because Colette's mother, like your own, seemed to have a fund of love for the world she never had to encounter.) Growing up in Lotus Falls you had smoked weed that was homegrown under plastic pitchers but was too strong to enjoy; you didn't say that you thought it had changed you. You needed to confess to this stranger that after what you'd done, no one should push you to get perspective on yourself. You had fooled strangers by asserting your uniqueness but you didn't want to fool him. You let him know you played the flute as well as the guitar and piano, but left out the news that you had remained indoors for a long period when a review of your first band described your performance as *forced and emulatory*, the reviewer concentrating instead on your tiny frame and the *capricious switch* from jet-black to yellow-ocher hair. You had no idea you and your loose-stringed guitar were soon to be plucked from the D Train by Lucien, an A & R man with a Hendrix-sized Afro from E&I Studios who looked as if he needed a bath. Recording the album in Nashville, relief would serve as well as regret to usher you into ignoring what you were really capable of. At the Eliot Perlman, neither of you would believe that you would one day lose the bump on your nose bequeathed you by your Greek grandmother (the miniature hillock of bone planed firmly away by a surgeon sick of your overexposure).

It had become chilly on the balcony in the dark.

You opened your hand on the ruined packet and allowed a pooling of anticipation. In savoring the ache of it you gained unnatural poise. You could wait! Spinning out the want, you asked him coolly, 'What drew you to psychiatry?'

'Dependence, mainly.'

'All the fun's in the waiting,' you said.

'Nothing beats it,' he said, but wholesomely, so that you wondered if he was making you feel idiotic on purpose.

'Or . . . ' you said, 'anticipation is best when it ends.' And hiding your chanciness, you got up and turned toward the bathroom, looking over your shoulder to flash your goofiest grin.

There's a pause after a drug-fueled sleep, just before the mind realizes there's no taking back what's been said. You had woken alone that first night, hurtling toward terror. Undone by something, you fought to fill the wilderness that had threatened you in sleep, feeling a need to keep terrible things at bay with your bare hands. Once awake, you continued to lope under an awkwardness, a mismatch: because you remembered from the night before the ease of talking with Henry, the joy of it, each revelation seeming as simple and smooth as the progress of a coin flipped into a fountain. You watched the flash/flash of a penny turning through water and then – who tells someone a story like that on a first date? – sat down sharply. The panic made you want to snatch that penny before it reached the bottom, to chomp your teeth into the chalky plaster at the bed of the fountain to get it, if you had to.

Catherine calls you on your cell just after you switch off the news, telling you to ignore the papers and look at the sales, but the media, it seems, is unable to let you forget what happened in Paris.

'Adriana's dead and I don't like it,' you state baldly.

'You should have stayed with Ray's program.'

Catherine has never believed that it's an agent's job to provide sympathy.

'How'd you like a photographer groping your cunt?'

She shudders. 'I don't want to think about it.'

'What has the label said?'

'Only if you tour again.'

You think back to the last gig of the tour, the bonfire, the threats.

'Sit tight.' Catherine gave a little. 'I'll work on them.'

You know it's the truth, because Catherine is finally able to leave her husband and buy the house in Silverlake, all because of you.

'But in the meantime, no going downtown. Those scarves are like flares to the press.'

'I guess *Combat de Coqs* is out of the question?'

Catherine wants no more risks.

Since you flew back from Paris, Henry has been in meetings or on exaggerated calls with Greg about ReOrient and the book, leaving you looking out from the apartment, scanning the park and surrounding buildings for the black glint of long lenses and wondering why you thought that finishing the Box Set could help you. You began pawing through Henry's things. The graph-paper notebook had been left on the bedside table and slotted into it was a Xeroxed psychiatry article. Scanning the title, your eyes jumped to Henry's writing further down the page but he interrupted you looking for his good cufflinks, a present from a friend at college. You began reading aloud: *The face does not age as one homogeneous object but as many dynamic compartments, which need to be evaluated, augmented and modified as such.*

Henry's distracted smile hovered above the performance but he had found what he was looking for and was leaving to meet Gregor.

'Why have you underlined that?'

'They love that shit.'

'Who does?'

'NYU. Gregor's patients.'

The notebook felt poisoned and you threw it on the bed. If you can't rewind, ReThink; it came naturally. Henry: the great coach.

'Why do these patients need you?'

'Mistakes need a ReThink.' He made to kiss you on the top of your head and you turned from him so that the kiss was a shock in the cup of your ear, shrinking the skin over your shoulders. He picked up the notebook. When you heard the door, you padded quickly after him into the hall.

'Hey!'

'I'm already gone,' he lilted.

'Lucien's coming over!'

The door closed gently as if by an invisible hand.

After seeing Tony Soprano getting a blow job at the Bing, you began dreaming of Tony as your therapist. Lucien was called round to check the locks. You touched Henry much less. And you became increasingly spiky when Adriana turned up on-screen. You called to Henry in the kitchen.

'Hey, Hank! White jeans. Your favorite.'

Henry had favored your navy over your white pants before his faculty garden party and now, instead of joining you on the couch, Henry sat on a chair, a declaration that he only did things that he chose to.

The horizontal rips in Ade's jeans were equally spaced, a punk-me-by-numbers for the mall. Henry leaned away from your childish tug toward a change of mind.

'I would say white is fine.'

Lightning at night shows the world just as it is but you must scan greedily because it will only show for a second, the rich wide territory behind someone's words. Gone for good was the notion that you would ever have the power to get him to change his mind on anything that mattered to you.

'She's an informant! She has IBS for Christ's sake!' You wanted to scratch out the word fine with something sharp. Pausing the action, you jammed the remote now at the jeans. '*That's* OK?'

Adriana, frowning slightly, was captured at a point somewhere between a fox and a fawn and was dumbly beautiful. You felt your throat constrict.

'It's fine. In this case,' Henry said, all effortful neutrality.

'But not for your party.'

'The navy looked better on you.'

Adriana held still for you on the screen, everything you wanted but paused. She was all yours, captured forever if that's what you demanded and she stayed there, accepting layers and layers and layers of looking at.

In the episodes before Paris, Furio and Carmella had been falling in love behind Tony's back and it was killing you. Henry sighed as a song struck up dramatically; old school Southern Italian, chaotic with melancholy. He began to smirk at you.

'What's so funny?' you snapped.

'Look at the shirt! I can't work out if he's a gladiator or a hairdresser.'

'Who cares about the shirt? He's exactly what she needs.'

'He's a murderer. From Naples.'

'She loves him.'

'They have barely ever been in the same room!' Henry was openly laughing at you, the exasperation he had felt now transformed. You stared at him levelly.

'Whatever happened to the insurmountable joy of anticipation?'

Henry's look was suspicious, as if he thought you were trying to play a trick on him.

'Did I say that?'

Maybe it was this. Or maybe it was when Carmella admitted her love for Furio to Tony, despite the shirt, the ponytail. Here Henry sniggered and you felt raw, unable, you had to leave your seat, you walked blindly to the kitchen, bumbling into the counter, then to the bathroom, only then did you pause. From the living room came sounds of Tony punching through the wall and you considered getting clean, catching the briefest glimpse of how things might be if you were to save yourself.

You could smell it was a hospital before you opened your eyes. From your hospital bed, the team had you sign a contract to attend and complete Hypno Ray's program in Paris. Lucien stayed in the company apartment, near Rue de Surène, and to start with, because of *Dwell Time* album sales, you were given a suite at the Hôtel Costes, where the walls of the lobby were lined with velvet the color of eggplant. On the way to your suite, unwelcome thoughts pushed you to the walls where you put your hand up inside the guts of a thick dark satin tassel. The room Catherine chose for you was exquisite: beetroot, turquoise, gold and white, with dull gold curtains and a highly decorated pelmet. After a few minutes in the room, you ran downstairs to the terrace and scraped an iron chair into the sun as if the light itself would save you. A toned waitress whose hair had a liquid sheen, dressed in scarlet Lycra at 9 a.m., took your order without a word. You could see in her face that the hospital stay had not been kept private. Without returning your fake smile she brought your order of tartines and sliced olives and you commented on her hair, which she didn't respond to either. Out of spite, you asked for french fries. Then you pointed to a flask of vinegar. For the first time, you could feel your anger rallying under Henry and went along with the idea that that's where it belonged. The vinegar looked pink in the light which carved a twist of grief through you because, without drugs, wishing became impossible. It was the food stirring up trouble, that was all. Eating ravenously, alone, you had tilted in at yourself but you must look inward only if you are ready to deal with things. Wasn't this a great hotel? The dining courtyard was a secret even from most Parisians but forcing yourself to feel this privilege made your eyes brim with tears. You finished the bread and looked through the sharp outline surrounding the sky above the courtyard while the thought of your room, two floors above, the colors just right, broke your heart.

It's not long before the Handyman is looking over at her shelter too, but he doesn't yet realise that it is only I who can coax her out.

'Hey Chirp,' I whisper, 'quit catching cups, get out from them dreamers, and see this.'

She stays silent so I speak up. 'Come on, peola, you love this sun.'

'I thought you said no *Zoot*.'

Bingo. I roll up the Italian paper, push it under the flap and speak through it: 'Welcome to the Hellenic butt-nekkid volleyball competition where wigs are curly and asses are furry!' I make a sound that suggests a distant but raucous crowd.

'It's volleyball,' she says sourly from under the sheet, 'and nude guys. The prize is rice pudding. And you're the peola.'

I change tack. 'What's that, ma'am? Yes, there is a dwarf on the team. Who is the dwarf? Ma'am, you just asked the question on everybody's lips back home.' I look over to the Greeks, where the dwarf just about kisses Gigi. The volleyballers cheer as if playing this game was all they ever wanted to do.

'Henry, can we please do this later?'

'But I need help with the rules. You are Greek, aren't you? For instance, can a cat hoof it?'

'G-man, you know *that* ain't in the book.'

'OK, ma'am. Can a cat whack it?'

'Whack it with his foot? Sure, or his hand or his head. But whack ain't in the book either.'

'Shheeeit. Buddy G done did that with his dukes.'

'His arms. That's digging,' she says.

'I dig. Now what other rules are there to this piece of shit homo-erectus pussy-ass game?'

She peeks out then and I get to my knees, pretending I have binoculars. 'Baby, his nuts nearly jus' bust loose! Damn! They gonna take a lickin'. His little pecker be red an' swellin'.'

'Pecker is not in the *Zoot*,' she says. 'I ain't buying that.'

'Gigi is breakin' it up. Check it.'

'Gigi? Who the hell is Gigi?' She pokes out her head and Gigi looks over. 'Either him or the dwarf,' I say.

She takes off her glasses and squints peevishly.

'Oh I get it,' she says.

'Get what?'

'This is all about the party.'

'Ain't you still my barbecue?'

She reaches out for her glasses laying in the sand, pale yellow, patterned like bamboo, but I rake them towards me to pull her out in full view. 'I did not know dwarves did that!' I say in a shocked whisper, holding the glasses to my chest.

'This sho' better be a hummer. Boot me them cogs.'

I pull the glasses further away from her and she warns me, 'Don't play me cut-rate, Jack, or I'll stay home this early black.'

Out of the shelter at last, she keeps her eyes closed until she's put on the giant sunglasses while I keep it rolling.

'I would give fews and two to film these cats. That dwarf's ass? It's tighter than Plymouth Rock when he eats that sand. Them some fraughty issues.'

She lifts her glasses and wolf-whistles faintly. 'Geez. Where his dry goods? I won't be able to clock him in the dim for shame.'

Gigi looks at us and Gigi smiles. Gigi beckons – *Come and play!* – and I know he means her and she comments without any edge at all: 'Gigi is gammin' for that dwarf.'

My heartbeat deepens in my chest.

'You plum crazy? Gigi ain't that way.'

The sun pulses.

'You killin' me,' I say.

I shade my eyes and we look again at the game.

'That gate be swingin',' she says.

PICNIC (NO PICNIC)

Dwell Time had found your apartment and was standing right there in your doorway pointing to a package in a brown paper bag gripped between his thighs. Reacting to your focus, he patted his pocket and you recalled what a terrible gift his attention was. In the few hours since you met at the Perlman gig, you had been strung out with doubt. You had written down your address scratchily enough that it could be misread.

'I didn't sleep,' you said, fully ready to jet-pack out of this.

'Highs are just comedowns you haven't met yet,' he said, stepping back, his palms open and pious, the doorway around him a square halo of clear blue Bed-Stuy sky.

Any humiliation over what you had confessed was replaced this morning by a desire for the easy slick and flow of last night. It was appalling that you were willing to hand over the ten hours of longing just like that. Longing that began with him walking away despite your body from the waist up leaning out the open window of a moving cab.

Deploy emergency craft! had started on a silent loop. You prayed that he had just a little more control than you did.

'What are you doing here?' you asked.

'Jimp sleeps under his lab bench because he works so very, very late. We live one block away from the unit!'

Whatever this guy is telling you, you were the reason that

he was ditching the lab today. You hoped he'd borrowed the jacket. The casual clothes he was wearing sat awkwardly on him, his shoulders under the leather screaming *We do leisure!* Pulling open his jacket, he nipped the jade silk of the lining at the bottom of the pocket until a hip flask nosed into view. You did not want to waste one more second worrying whether Dwell Time was really as precious as he had made himself out to be.

From between his legs, he handed you the brown paper bag with a stiff arm and, unable to stand the wait, he waggled it. As you took the bag and pulled out the book to scrutinize it, the shock of him (it was him) turning up at your place ran fresh through you and you were glad of the book's solidity in your hands.

It was called *The Zoot*. The cover was a pointillist rendition of a black man's face: his eyes were cabasas and there were bongos for his nostrils; saxophones in gold switched back on themselves, edged with their own black silhouettes. These were the waves of his hair. Cymbals formed his earlobes. You sniffed the cover.

'I never saw anyone read like that,' he said.

'Fifties books,' you exhale, wondering if they'd ever make a cover like this now.

It's been analyzed to death since but that book, right away and irreversibly, fused you so that any way out would set you asunder. You're silent as Henry tells you how he almost chose an occult handbook but he's glad now of his choice, and this confirms your suspicions from last night: your fear that this kid-like enthusiasm that he so wants to hide will knock you down and take you over. In letters detailed with piano keys, you reread the subtitle, *A Lexicon of Jive*, and it helped you ignore a worry with a wingspan: this book that belonged to neither of you might possibly become a token of love, but equally could curse you.

He snatched the book from you saying, 'You are going to learn with me.'

You looked into his face expecting self-consciousness but detected zero and you wondered if your head was weaving as it sometimes can when you're bombing.

'Like now?'

'You still high, sister. Damn right, right now.' His voice was raucous, the delivery entirely without qualm, but during this otherwise pitch-perfect performance he kept his forehead and his shoulder leaning against the jamb of the door.

'You want to come in first?' you say, thinking clearly for the first time since he arrived. Ironically, now you could sleep.

'Right on!' he blared. 'I knew you was hicty,' and he chest-bumped you (he chest-bumped you right where your tits were).

You could still feel the meat of his chest though he'd gone sassing down your hall – you were saying *it's my fucking hall buddy* but your nipples were coming up with their own slogans – and you checked out his back while he strutted, holding his lapels, elbows touching the walls of the narrow corridor. Following him you saw that with his build, the shoulder seams of his jacket would struggle under pressure.

He was in your kitchen before you were. Your kitchen was small and very unclean.

'So how long will you be in New York?' you asked him from behind.

'Until my boss runs me out of town,' he answered.

'Is he a sheriff?'

'He's a power-mad cigar-smoking narcissist prone to rages and hazing rituals.'

'So better than a sheriff?'

You saw then that he was afraid but he was never going to let you know what he was afraid of and you swept away the implications of this.

'Lucky for me, I was spotted by a shit-hot plastic surgeon over at NYU.'

'Plastic surgeons need psychiatrists?'

'Frank doesn't give me what I deserve. I have to collaborate with outsiders. And, of course, that takes me away from his lab.'

'And what exactly do you deserve?'

'ReThink is a simple, cost-effective way to re-engage damaged minds by reprogramming eye movements. Frank has the hardware, the eye-tracker. But Frank would be in tremendous trouble without Gregor's plastic surgery fuck-ups to provide him with data.'

At the description of Gregor's patients, a gulch appears in your shared landscape but you won't have it; you leap the cleft clear.

'So Frank's the enemy?'

'Frank is a very jealous man.'

You were glad of the mess of the kitchen so you could make busy with your hands. Silently, you began to put off your imaginary US tour.

'So how is BirdBoy? You see him today?'

'Jimp is charged with testing BirdBoy. It is I who have the privilege of testing the nameless controls.'

'And you're not happy about that.'

'I found him,' he said before you had finished.

The silence that follows gives you a chance to do the right thing.

'What's not to celebrate, right?' you say.

'BirdBoys do not grow on trees. And don't worry about Frank,' he said. 'I have my own plans.'

You were thinking about revenge though the word hadn't been mentioned. You wanted to believe that he was sore about real injustice and not another paranoid disaster. With effort, you reasoned that he felt safe enough to say these things to you because he had already imagined a future which you would be in.

Your quest now was a simple one: you must show him it was you that he'd always wanted. You displayed piece by piece what you had in your fridge while he unstuck his leather elbows from the counter to fold them high on his chest. Who had already spent hours strapping him into the tracker? he asked. Not fucking Jimp under the bench. And why does Frank have a problem with Europeans? It *just so happens* that Frank and Jimp were both Canadian. You lay out fridge distractors: fearlessly crass vintage bullshit. You wanted the Twinkies to do some talking. The trailer park was dead / long live the trailer park! You filled your tote with clues and put the bag over your shoulder asking him if he was all set, but at the end of the hall you pulled up, scared shitless of what else you might reveal if alone with him again.

'I should call Eric. He could bring Stacey?' You reached for the landline.

Henry got to the telephone first, pausing to smile before yanking the set clean off the wall. Outside, you both honked with laughter and you never mentioned Eric again.

Within minutes of walking beside him, you picked up an intense nameless energy. His chat seemed kind of irresponsible and capricious and you noticed it encouraged you to match him in these dangerous qualities. Meanwhile, your blood was being filtered of overnight horror by his takes on what it was to succeed and how understanding language was key. You goaded him, saying that you didn't need to be able to read to fall in love with a song, and succeed in what? He stood still in the street and recited unknown lyrics that force-fed you with tenderness. You laughed with an open mouth. He asked you why. You wouldn't say.

Back in step, your hands touched accidentally and you bummed a smoke to cope with the aftershock. A few tokes in and he brushed the outline of your panties with the back of his hand and you flinched as if stung. 'Woah!' he laughed and tucked the hair behind your ear. You would have to crush him.

Reaching a small park, you both arranged yourselves as if you didn't care what angles the other could see, lying on a bleached-out patch of grass beside a basketball court. You were glad to lie down because it's hard to keep your moving body made of parts complicit in a lie and anyway, the court was way too loud and the newly laid superstuff on the floor of the court was so unnaturally blue that it stayed with you even out of view. You put on your glasses to save you (a Vegas Keno player, jungle green) and continued in this charade while the ball game went on not ten feet away, the rubbery court protesting in squeaks when players changed direction. Beyond your shades, the light somehow became brighter by a good grade, making lounging impossible. You moved, with no explanation, to sit on a bench a little too far away, wishing you had worn a hat and wondering whether, withdrawing in such bright sunshine, you could trust the feelings that were releasing in you. You reassured yourself that you could never feel this way if he didn't too. Teetering was not your thing. Soon after, you were up on the ledge asking yourself if you'd really have to wait to show him what you are all about.

'Startling trousers,' he said, his eyes revealing a moment of intention.

'Thank you,' you said. 'My Mom's.'

Emergency! No one wanted to fool around in mom pants but he saved you with his grin and flicking through the book he asked, 'Where shall we start?'

He patted the ground and you almost asked him if he would be as excited about this book with anyone else. How had you qualified, you wished to know? He opened the book wide at a page. You knew from experience that you must pretend that you cared about logic and sense but the signals from him made that hard to stick to. Radiating both hubris and shame, you opened a bottle; there were already two other drink options on the go.

'How about B? Let's start with barrelhouse,' he said defiantly.

You chugged from a soda can, and you saw plainly that Henry not only wanted to win but wanted to witness great losses as a result of winning. You must have known somewhere you were equal to it.

'Barrelhouse,' he boomed in his best English accent.

'Big! Wide?'

'Nope.'

You bit your knuckles as you asked him to put it in a sentence.

'You is pretty barrelhouse sister.'

'You know I'm going to play the Bowery Ballroom.' Using the future as a shield, you often defended yourself without thought. He made a hurrying hand movement to spur you in the game and your instinct flashed hot: you could not be enough for someone like him. What you wanted, Henry wouldn't give, but he couldn't resist potential. It was what you might become that had brought him here.

He pressed you:

'And barrelhouse?'

'Beautiful! Talented. Talented! Gifted? Young? Black?' You are ashamed that you are weighing up the possibility of more blow in those pockets. 'Good in an argument?'

'Definitely not.'

'In a crisis?'

'Nyet again.'

'Gorgeous!'

'Yep!'

'Don't fuck with me, what does it say?'

But you'd begun to breathe like a bison. A bison who could feel her eyelashes pressing against her shades.

'It means free and easy, sister, free and easy.'

'Not the same thing at all,' you scolded.

He fanned the pages a couple of times into your face until you thrust your chin over your shoulder.

'OK, where to now?' he said.

With your face turned away, you lit a cigarette and when you pulled your chin back over your shoulder he plucked that cigarette from your mouth without asking. From your red sparkling tote, you pulled out a flimsy garbage sack. The first couple of items from inside it were revealed. You were mutely capable, like a magician's assistant who was also the magician, and you cracked harissa olives and brandished an open palm over them. Then to show that you were not afraid of anyone, you pulled out a Twinkie and an Almond Joy; taramasalata and two flatbreads; a can of Coke; a can of Diet Coke; an unopened soft pack of menthol Newports; a small dusty bottle of pink cava and two toothbrush mugs. You threw the sole toothbrush in an arc behind you and it landed on the basketball court (he guffawed – it proved to you a common love of risk), then slunk out a cute, pineapple-shaped ready-mixed piña colada, a starfruit, some ginger cookies, a tin of canned meat with a winding key that came all the way from Lotus Falls, greaseproof paper wrapped around a cold calzone with actual bites out of it (you pretend to cut it with a candle – you wink!), then a useless but blood-red plastic knife turned up, a roll of toilet paper and a bottle-green ceramic candleholder in the shape of Aladdin's lamp that belonged to the previous tenant. The finale was a large box of kitchen matches.

He popped the cork on the cava and looked at your nose.

'So your mother's Greek?'

'Grandmother.'

'I want to know more about the songwriting. You brought those Psych zombies back to life last night. What was that last line?'

You hesitated while you pressed the glasses to your eyes.

'The thing I told you last night. That's not stuff I usually keep for strangers.'

He swigged from the bottle and said 'I'm a vault,' before placing it down in a gesture that said, *and no longer a stranger*.

Thank fuck for the glasses. And the cigarettes.

Before you knew anything about Henry, before you knew there was an accent or a smell or a divine, absurd way of telling tales and connecting with you mainline, there was that declaration in his stare, the oath in it. *I will make things easy again.* Stretching out on the floor with his eyes closed, his brand of not caring already relieved and irritated you. You would never be ready to test whether his nonchalance was real.

'Take off your glasses,' he said.

'Why?' Your mouth twisted like a teenager's. You needed black-and-white answers to difficult questions.

'I like to know what I'm working with.'

You pulled the *Zoot* into your chest then narrowed your eyes to look over the top of them. He leaned over to remove some strands of hair from the corner of your mouth. You shattered with no noise and before you rejoined the game you had to rearrange your puzzled face component by component.

'OK,' you exhaled. 'Gammin'.'

'Eating. From the Jamaican to yam.'

'Nope!' This ache to match him was pathetic and very difficult to hide.

'Playing. You know, fooling?' he said.

'Nyet.'

'Ah! Of course. Hating.'

'Play properly.' You pushed his shoulder viciously then pretended you hadn't.

'Ridiculing? Gimme a sentence?' He straightened up on his elbow.

'You were gammin' for me big time last night.'

'Admiring?'

'Closer, brother, closer.' You furtively caught the push of his lips against the mouth of the hip flask. You were close enough to him to breathe in his mystic's cologne and helpless to stop the flow of what you wanted from him.

'I know!' he said. 'Desperate to get into her old lady's trousers!'

You laughed together.

You stopped first.

The *Zoot* will go with you to the tiny island of Antiparos next summer. The man on the front will by this time be known to you both as Fabio. You will have used it so much in these first weeks that it will be battered and in need of reinforcement but still you'll clap your hand to your mouth when you see what Henry has done because he will have reinforced the shabby book with glossy black electrical tape, rough under the fingers, heavy-duty stuff that was pulled too tightly over the flimsy covers, making them curl. You will not go to Greece without it but you begin to sense the loss of those mild eyes under the cabasas and in fact, you start to take Fabio's fate too much to heart and yearn to see again the saxophones and their inked shadows, believing irrationally that lost in the waves of hair, your future with Henry will become uncertain. Or certain in the wrong way.

BIRDBOY

I was the one who spotted BirdBoy in amongst Gregor's clinic pickings: a lean frizzy-haired teenager with braces, who had never made eye movements in his life but instead moved his head as an eyeball would, with tiny sideways jerks. He was an exquisite freak, a walking *Nature* paper. Frank would have no choice but to be impressed.

It was important to give Frank the correct impression from the start. I'd begin by telling him how BirdBoy's face darted almost letter to letter, how the mechanism of his shuttling jaw initiated the short and long stitches of a glimpse, the deeper sweep of a glance. I had decided how his eye-tracking data would appear before I ever tested him. What I really wanted was to wipe the look from Frank's face, the one that said *remind me what you are bringing to the table?* In short, after months of eating shit in Frank's lab, BirdBoy was on the menu.

If Frank Leary was the king of eye movement research then it was only because of Gregor's vision. It was Frank who first showed the world the importance of dwell time in advertising, and had managed to muscle through to mental health thanks to his uberstudent turned plastic surgeon, Gregor Pinkus. Like me, Gregor chose Frank's lab to conduct research in during his doctoral degree. Frank must have liked the sound of me on paper: Henry James Portland Sinclair. Before I knew it would do me no good, I told Frank I was a pale version of my industrialist grandfather Geraint, that all since had been physicians, but that I was the first to make it professionally in the new world, the first to tread the path to psychiatry. Frank joked that I was the first Brit he'd allowed into his lab.

Despite a rudimentary NYU lab set-up, Gregor had serendipitously discovered that eye movements could be retrained. In Frank's swankier lab, Gregor mapped out ReOrient, excited by data showing the potential of rewiring thought processes by redirecting attention. Gregor wanted to burn off his old boss but he couldn't; he still needed Frank because Frank, backed by private investors, now owned the most expensive corneal reflection system in the United States.

The Regreteers flocked to Gregor at NYU because he was a great combo: a plastic surgeon with psychiatric training. Gregor still thinks that he came up with the name Regreteers. These cosmetic surgery casualties returned through the revolving door of their own dissatisfactions. They messed with their lips, their wet/dry junctions, snipped their labia and scissored through earlobes. This country was infested with people who were both stunned and encouraged by their regret, addicted to it. At first it was only on Mondays that I would skip Frank's lab to help in Gregor's clinic. The patients gathered for their appointments in the waiting room, combing each other for stories of failure before Gregor called them in. In amongst these recidivists sat BirdBoy calmly explaining that he was here for a tattoo removal and had always lived without eye movements.

I took his initial notes, trying to keep calm. Brad agreed to be tested and I saw his raw data a week later, flashed the brain scan at Gregor, listened to his instructions – *We need Frank's kit. Trade him if you have to!* – and then, leaving Brad still strapped in the tracker, I sprinted chaotically from the corridor outside Gregor's office, down onto First Avenue, across town, flailing between sidewalk flows of workers, thinking *I will never, ever trade him.* Frank's office was on the third floor of the Phyllis Altkopf building, overlooking a clipped lawn around a quatrefoil of soil; altogether a synthetic-looking patch, there to naturalise the silvered windows above the animal house that winked suspiciously at me as I rounded each turn on the stairs.

Frank's office smelled of men of his age. Mechanical grease and hot dog brine. All I could think was BIRDBOY: first author Henry Sinclair. HJP Sinclair. HG Sinclair. Sinclair, HJP. Out of breath in the doorway, I didn't care what I was interrupting.

'He moves his head exactly like a bird!'

Frank didn't look up.

'There's a boy at NYU, reads almost perfectly. Get this: no eye movements whatsoever!' Frank raised his eyes and I saw briefly in his yellowed face what a find like this could do for a flabby career. We had overlap, Frank and I: there were similarities between us that neither wanted to own publicly.

'Exactly like a bird!' I said.

'I heard you the first time,' he said.

As usual, Jimp's figures were spread across Frank's desk; here was Frank's devoted stats chimp. My roommate, Jimp.[1]

I already had an idea of the dangers of saying what you thought in Frank Leary's lab[2] but no real notion about how treason was viewed by others in this kingdom. Jimp was an orange-haired, wiry Canadian climber who smiled at me very regularly. I should have known. Right now, Frank had his hands behind his head.

'One thing we discovered,' he said to the ceiling, 'is that the eye is never still for very long so when it stops and rests, you really should give two hoots about why.'

A recorder winked red on the table. Who would get pilot data while crushed against BirdBoy for hours at a time using Gregor's medieval set-up at NYU? Would Jimp be dragging BirdBoy over here from NYU afterwards? A man who slept in the lab even though we only live a street away? I reminded myself that I was doing this for Science; my career.

'I suppose we'll use my tracker for the real experiments?' Frank asked flatly, continuing to look at Jimp.[3]

'Gregor says he's happy to do pilots.' No one answered. I bit inside my cheek. Frank had a sour face as if he was ignoring a fart.

'I know! Hank can run controls,' Frank exclaimed.

Hot dog was taking over from nipple grease and Jimp, nimble with reason, continued to read from his laptop. '"What we know is that saccadic movements of the head or eye form the optimal sampling method for the brain . . . "'[4]

In my rage, I slid Brad's scan onto the light box. Together we toured his defects and it was *me* that helped them imagine the rogue brain cells that had coupled incorrectly to the superior colliculus somewhere in his development. I began to talk about the puppetry of him, but Frank cut me off: 'Remove metaphors or you lose sight of the data.' Jimp nodded.[5]

One night, at dinner with his publisher, after a bottle of Malbec, Gregor used my phrase – 'Analogy is the *only* thing capable of letting the public know what BirdBoy is about' – and I admitted to the publisher that I had recently dreamt of replacing smooth cedar balls in BirdBoy's head, which I painted bluey-white, but that the brush had slipped into the holes of his pupils. The publisher seemed amused. Gregor made my ideas seem like worthy endeavours instead of pulling them to pieces.

I first met Gregor on a grad students' tour of his NYU lab. Almost immediately, I was plotting to get away from Frank and it seemed right to look to someone who knew how Frank's hazings worked.[6]

On the tour of his lab, to keep up with Dr Pinkus, we post-grads had jostled down the halls of the hospital to his 'research closet'. I remember feeling humbled for a moment as Gregor explained that even with the ancient coil and drum set-up in this dusty cupboard, he had been able to do top-drawer research, assessing how his worst Botox cases evaluated their own emotions and bolstering his theory about induced autism. Then there was the high-profile but low-paying government sideline, looking at how remorseful rapists differed in the tracker to sociopaths and matched controls.[7]

A gasp had escaped almost all of us when Gregor showed where the tracks of the eyes scored the surface of a picture, a woman's torso, no head. The track between the mounds of her breasts was scratched straight and deep with a childish scribbling over and around the nipples as if to coax them further into being; most tracks etched a very straight line down to her pubis. Gregor cut in, his expert finger circling around the nipples on the overhead projection.

'Look at these tracks. She's lassoed by each one of you,' Gregor said, 'around her points of interest.'

I sensed the women around me bristle, imagining they would do differently on this task. I whispered to an Asian doctor: 'Interesting parts of a scene receive more attention.'

'Can we have a volunteer?' Gregor picked a tawny Slovenian Med Sci grad who had not balked at the tasks in any of her year-long clinical practicals. Gregor chose lime green for Matea's tracks. It didn't take long to reveal that her eye movements mapped exactly onto the telling black trails that had betrayed the male college students before her.

'Your dwell time snitches on you!' I cried, unfazed by the caged eyes of other doctors.

Gregor searched out my face. 'Exactly! But luckily for us, I have discovered it can be bribed! What's your name, Doctor?'

Gregor would be my ticket out of Frank's jail.

When Jimp took over testing BirdBoy, he began to complain that he did not like Gregor's apparatus. Unsurprising, as you typically forced subjects into restrained head positions. Sometimes we even used straps. This, as well as the constant need to recalibrate the machine, made the test situation highly intrusive for test subjects and myself. As our peer reviewers[8] had recently made clear after our 'premature' short communication to *Science* with the pilot data, it's hard to ask control subjects to lean over and put their head into a steel rack then ask them to read a newspaper as if they are by the breakfast table. During these endless calibrations only Sandy stood out from the scores of controls we also had to run; throughout test sessions she insisted on talking about which bands she was seeing or where she bought her socks, throwing the calibration off more than any other test subject; when focused she had the steadiest baseline of all the controls.

While putting Sandy in the tracker, my belt buckle often grazed her shoulder blades. All those hours in the dark, me fumbling round her head and neck, positioning her in the clunky, out-of-date machine. My finger went in her mouth on more than one occasion. It was unavoidable really. In the embarrassing lull after one of these occasions I told her about Astrid and where she was playing next. She stood up so quickly she banged her head. She was already obsessed with her and wanted to tell me all about why. Could I get her backstage? I strapped her back in, smiling without committing to anything.

In public, Frank exhibited BirdBoy and scooped him around corners of corridors in the department as if BirdBoy belonged to him. Frank revealed the corneal reflection system, showed him how it worked, what it did, the kind of pathetic relaying of instruction and costs that old men must do around machines.[9] I waited outside to hand a student pass to Gregor, late as usual, so he could access the animal house. On arrival, he was not happy about the municipal blue overshoes and complained loudly that the animal house stank of *lamp-dried piss*.

But if there was a dollar sign in science, Brad was it: even social psychologists got excited by him. Hiding behind screens to watch the bird twitch of his face as he assessed the tiny skyline of newsprint was a real thrill for newcomers. Jimp acted as if he had given birth to Brad and as Brad shook hands with the oglers I prayed that no one actually *call* him BirdBoy to his face until Jimp had got from him exactly what I needed. It was his way with data that stopped me from killing Jimp.[10]

Since his book launch, Gregor has become much more like Frank than I'd envisioned.

'I'm going to be on Minerva,' he declared, as if prime-time TV appearances were inevitable.[11] Gregor would be her first guest after the campaign launch of LILACS (Learnings in Life after Cosmetic Surgery).

'Great! What about getting our data?'

'Writing a book on Botox-induced autism gets you on Minerva, kiddo!'

So I will have to collect the control data alone. Sandy and her cohort will do their part. I will suffer the Frank and Jimp show in Gregor's absence but I can still be first author if I write up the paper. Of course, I will secretly work on my book without the help of any of them. Only eventually will I have to admit to Gregor that I was not careful enough, and of course it's so obvious now that I should have taken my work off Jimp's computer before anyone found it, let alone Frank. On the night they discovered it I returned home to two pairs of Jimp's shoes neatly lined up on our stairs. Neither should be outside of a farmyard.

In the morning I will arrive late to work but I will look sharp, entering the department with an unashamed 'Good morning, Frank!' and Frank will mimic my tune – 'We are not barroom buddies, Dr Sinclair!' – whereupon I will descend into the fake light of the animal house, put on the impressively blue overshoes, swipe my card and slip into the smell of piss on a hot bulb, coveting Brad's gaze jittering around the outline of Jimp's head. They will never put me off.

1   Jimp's hair is a long shapeless bob, a couple of inches thick at its bottom. There are large flakes of skin to be found on Jimp. He chooses clothes that declare his origins in Super Natural British Columbia. Jimp looks like a park ranger; there are often mud splashes on his three-quarter-length trousers even if we are hosting visiting academics. His shoes might be mistaken for my mother's. I wrote 'model's own' over his fleece on the glass of the department garden party photo. If you look closely at his face, he seems bloody proud to be wearing it.
2   I don't take warnings from Jimp. His name is Frank, I'll call him Frank.
3   Jimp absorbs my late-night jibes about Frank without resistance so they will always be present when the three of us are together. Computers do statistics, Jimp, not people. I'm sure Frank would love to know that Jimp took a Ladyshave when we went to the IEMR conference in Clearwater last year.
4   You cannot make him first author on a *Nature* paper just because you rely on him for the running of the lab while you meet your stockbroker about Virofodol risks or go over the border to buy Japanese art. I know that you need Jimp to weed out outliers and manipulate your raw data. He should not have immunity just because he is the only person in North America who knows what the anchor button on your stats package actually does. No one else uses that package in the Western world.

5 Pure reason crushes imagination. Gregor has a kind of anabolic influence over me, since Frank and Jimp are doing their very best to waste me, which in their case is a common defence when fragile egos sense a different class of thinker.

6 If you didn't have Jimp, you would have no data. During the Yale departmental seminar, you shot me down from the back of the room. You would only allow sentences of up to twenty words with one embedded clause. Gregor would never ask me in public if I had ever been taught how to use commas or whether I'd ever tried reading my work aloud.

7 Jimp doesn't like it when I say that Science is about kit first, data later. I can tell by the collapse of his face that he thinks it diminishes Frank's genius.

8 Ipso facto jealous cunts.

9 Even now, Gregor claims ReOrient as his, but without Frank's corneal reflection apparatus, without the discovery of Brad, without me to do the work, it could never have been patented.

10 Jimp has no option other than being right. We witnessed an Imperial Palace waitress turn him down at the ICEM conference in Vegas.

11

UNDER THE DREAMERS

You stole the sheet from a kid's bunk bed in a hostel in San Diego, but you didn't feel bad because you figured it wouldn't last three more washes. Ten years later, it pleases you because it fits in the topmost pocket of your backpack. From the first day together on Antiparos, you showed Henry how to do what the islanders did and you stretched that faithful jungle print sheet over four sticks to create a shelter sunk into the sand. You don't care what nude Athenians think of your sheet. Henry's only comment was, 'Hiding is a symptom.'

You look for Henry across the beach, toward the terrace of the cafeteria, trying to focus through the shimmer, but can't ignore the barely perceptible lip of a downturn, a faint horror at what you nearly ordered, and you shiver. You glance to the water's edge at Handyman, but you don't want to make eye contact again. You force the *Zoot*, black spine first, into the sand beneath your bag, because Henry wants a rest from the Lexicon of Jive. He blames you but you can't help it if the campsite handyman recognizes you from MTV.

There's been a far-off beat each evening when the sun goes down and Henry acts like there is a 'happening' that people don't want him to be part of. Henry is not a relaxer: he has to be able to reach his psychiatry papers and make his notes. It would feel like grief if you admitted that on your first time away together, with no other distraction, Henry was attracted to what he might be missing. The mainland blow was finished solo last night and you are about to pay. The video, unable to hurt you yesterday, looms, threatening to replay.

The label said an MTV video was the right thing to do after your accident. Henry was on set and you were excited, that's all. No, you can't say what made you do that right in the middle of 'Dwell Time'. Who knew the director would pan to Henry?

Escaping has always been your thing. You went to San Diego, age fourteen, right after TV Repair Guy left Lotus Falls for good. You moved by train through the uninteresting desert between the only home you'd known and the coast, without any clue as to what was going on inside you. You chose the train so that what had happened couldn't hover. You stole the sheet from the spares closet because of the overdone optimism of the hostel manager and his good moods, he bugged you into stealing from him. In your teens you had imagined an exotic escape in a place called San Diego but the zoo and the military base turned out to be pillars of non-interest in a flat and rule-ridden city. A casual military presence policed the place, nobody had to tell you what not to do. Litter free, it felt like no one's home. You left with the sheet as a souvenir. A faint jungly warning.

You would have liked some childish things in your own childhood, a picture, a zebra, and so you blocked out San Diego and inlaid the sheet into your early years and it gained a preciousness. The preciousness of something owned since age six. You told Henry that you never wasted time on dolls or dawdling over flaps to be lifted in books. Real Life was the story, you said. Lift the flap on that.

In fact, you had puzzled over children playing between trailers as a kid, washing their dollies' hair in rows of fawn Tupperware tubs. Real Life must be capable of supporting the life of the doll, the cherries on the front of a swimsuit, a glass cat, the tail snapped off, in a box under your trailer bunk. There was a space, a magic, a land whose rules you didn't understand where putting a doll's shoes on and off really mattered and where it was expected that her hair was brushed and neat rather than brutally cut off. Leaving the doll under a bulb had nearly set fire to your trailer. When other children played contentedly, in the sheltered, honeyed light of shared understanding, you felt the need to spoil it. Childhood can end in a single hot afternoon.

You are waiting for Henry at the beach, wearing the putty-colored leather gaucho boots, but looking backwards is worsening things. Movement makes distance from the last hit. The need to push against weight. There's an inertia in your joints but you get up. Dust clouds pother when you scuff your way through roots and knots of khaki grass behind the beach, you bend to try and pull a gnarled branch from a thyme bush that the wind has forced low to the ground. There's the spicy smell of the thyme sprig then, and under that, the stable base note of the sand. These details are hoarded until they topple and suddenly you are empty and aware again of having no purpose. You scramble further up behind the solitary shower and into the scrub that marks out the end of the beach. Straight strong sticks are all you need for the shelter but to get to the bamboo patch you'll have to pass the volleyballers and Henry will say you want them to notice you.

Handyman and Co. have set up a volleyball court and once more, you can feel the pull of him waiting to catch your eye. It must be only you and Henry if things are to be mended; you imagined somewhere to make a fresh start with him. As soon as you look up from your task, Handyman waves. You pretend you didn't see, shading your eyes to look at something way beyond him. You begin to dig. Being clean is so simple and feels so good that you cannot believe you spend your time avoiding it, in fact it is so easy you may not bother with it at all. You moan a little when you think of how Henry is the answer, but are convinced that this is proof of the physical effort and the state you're in. You almost shout help. It's conspicuous, you trying to screw sticks into the sand in a faux suede bikini. It's not the faux suede but the bikini. He's right, the nudity of these campers assaults the clothed. *Give me hard work!* you think. Colette would write pages but admitted she could have just as easily pulled a handcart and you know how she feels as you grasp roots tighter and try to crank them loose but somehow the violent agitation of the roots begins a rhythm that shakes free an answer to a question you felt you'd dealt with. You're a Blamer. No way out. Suddenly in a hollow of regret, you can't escape how furious you are that you've finished the mainland blow. You finally find five unsuitable twigs among the low bushes, one in a Y shape that may be an obstacle to getting the sheet up. You whump into the sand because you don't feel strong enough to put up a shelter. A push-up to you is a mythical thing. Since Burning Man, the label has encouraged you to present yourself as a warrior to the press.

It's just a video.
    You waved and you mouthed it. 'I love you.'
    No one heard.
    The director panned to Henry.
    You never asked her to.

You had not predicted anger, and no way had you expected repulsion, captured forever on camera. 'Dwell Time' was always his title, a gift to you; it meant that you were locked in, co-conspirators. Wasn't that the deal? After the accident, after so much doubt. A four-minute music video where Henry features for three seconds. A full three seconds. The memory threatens to skyscrape.

You breathe and look out over Dilpa's pretty gentle hill not five hundred yards away. In the blue-green sea between, a rowboat painted with the name *Petroula* is taking gas canisters across. Tablecloths? A crate. The waves approaching Dilpa are bigger than you've seen on this island. There is a faint breeze now, which makes it hard to imagine the fierce heat that, since you arrived, sparks daily incidents between you.

The morning sun would heat up the tents until the air was almost too hot and thick to breathe, and, too loudly and too viciously to ignore, your neighbors would attack each other. You stared at Henry wide-eyed, sometimes open-mouthed, then the rest of the morning you'd search the beach for the couples who dared say such things to each other. It was a filthy game that you knew Henry loved and it happened to mean laying close to each other while listening. With the argument paused it felt like the right moment to whisper something you'd been saving to tell him.

'Hey, remember?'

Henry's eyes closed.

'In the *Zoot*? Sheets are dreamers.'

'I can't stand it in here anymore,' he said, lifting you off of him, fighting to get out into the air. At his back you shouted, 'Petroula means pebble!' but he didn't reply. In a fascinated agony you watched him grab his clothes from a pile and leave, clawing chanterelles from around his neck – there was real meanness in his haste to shake the scarf free. You weren't going to cry just because you had no supplies. You crouched to see him and Handyman through the zip of the tent. Henry was all freckles but in this heat his cheeks were dark pink with pale centers. The deep brown hand was on Henry's, and you noticed he didn't flinch or brush him off and there was no doubt in your mind that with Handyman, Henry would never claim it was too hot for kissing. You were still as Handyman circled around, pulling out pegs, then suddenly with his hand through the slack slit of the tent he grasped for you and he pulled you out in your underwear. Henry's sharp look let you know that you had spoiled things. The bags were hauled out and Handyman picked up the empty tent and toyed with it, miming his instructions: *No pegs! If you don't have shade? Pick it up and move it.* With Handyman standing there, you put your stuff back in the tent now in its shaded spot and Henry followed you in close behind and got you to straddle him. Then slick with sweat he kept you quiet and came quickly while your Dutch neighbors argued in English.

That afternoon, Handyman did the thing. In front of everyone. He did the knee bend thing and mouthed 'I loff you' to Henry. You only laughed to make things easier for him.

You wish Henry would get his peola ass over here with your order. You need to fix this dumb shelter. The sun is really getting to you, so you grind your bare heels down into the sand while you screw in corner sticks. Two of the thinner twigs snap and shock you which you take on board no problem. Shocks are always dealt with in the future so right now there's a minusing happening that you can't feel but you know is there. Maybe you are wrong about your arms too. Maybe you are strong. Maybe you can be exactly what you have made yourself without the help of anyone else. But after the tent this morning, you are starting to see what he is saying about Blaming and your indecision is becoming more than kooky. Since Black Rock your hairdo has a name and you don't like what it implies. You know it was different before Burning

Man. He tells you these things without asking whether you want to know and when he becomes objective about you it is terrifying. Yes, OK, on a first date, you told him you gave away a baby, but it's just your comedown makes you cycle through these thoughts. In ten years, you've learned the ups and downs of these things: resistance intensifies the cycling. Right now, you are just ground that the thoughts need to cover to exhaust themselves.

You try to see how the guy with the towel has achieved the corners on the shelter for his baby while the baby, oblivious to the need for it to stay in the shade, is roaming in the shallows on all fours, eating sand and looking perversely conspicuous in its nudity. You dig through the scarves in your bag for elastic hairbands. These work better than you expect to secure the sheet to the sticks, but a zebra eye bulges through the tight circle made by the band and it bothers you so much. You want to protect the cartoon eye so you take off your boots with only your feet and slip under the sheet into its cool space, just taller than you are when crouching. Enclosed in the shelter you get rigid in the stomach with excitement. You want to blast off in your jungly rocket, show it to your dead mother, or lay on your back and push your feet against the fine taut material until all four twigs pop out of the ground and the sheet drapes your legs. To get out of the hot sun, you trail the flaccid cotton coffin with two attached sticks over to the cafeteria like a failed New Year's dragon. But you lie on your back and the wind lifts the flap and you are sampling paradise in lazy blinks.

OK, so you waved and mouthed 'I love you.' The bend in the knees? You had no idea that was in you so maybe the Blamer's there too. Hey, cool those jets St Bernadette! You are supposed to be resting after a successful tour. Catherine said you needed this. He says you are a Pathological Blamer because of what you have done to your chemistry and so in that sense, he assures you, it's no one's fault. He says 'Retributive Tourette's' is a thing. It stinks of Gregor. Despite everything, there is nothing yet that forces you to question Henry's role in your recovery.

In the mushroomy light of the shelter, you smile broadly at your four corner sticks (everyone here uses bamboo, not you!). A huff of breeze allows a glimpse of the bay, Dilpa behind, a goat surveying the sea from a plateau, the volley-ball players, naked and shining, all in one breath of wind, and you decide you will tell Henry when he comes back from the café that you are not a compulsive Blamer (though your heart still thumps from the accusation; bespoke and inescapable). Under the sheet, you take off your bikini top and brush away sand that sticks to the dark circle of skin surrounding your nipple and think of early days, when he first saw you naked.

'Wow,' he had said, 'Your areola is much darker than people might expect.' He broke off from the kiss to add, 'High contrast ratio.'

'Cool,' you said, trying to continue, but he had made a point of saying:

'Normal has its benefits.'

The sight of Henry crossing the sand tightens your chest. Henry could snap. Like when you implied Jimp had thrown him out of the apartment, or when people from the lab mentioned his experience with math or his paleness. Catherine had asked whether you were impressed by Henry doing things wrong on purpose like a toddler. You didn't tell her that he disgusted you with his kiss but that you'd sold your rights to complain when you told him your secret. That you have accepted, then endured the kiss, and now want the kiss. If she knew you well she would know that this means you will never leave him. But because she was appalled, you told her how he liked slipping a pad of his finger from the skin of your tit to the areola to show how it skidded to a stop before the nipple.

On Catherine's advice, you left for Greece from Rochester, with the whole country in the grip of a breast implant scandal that had spread from New York State to national news in a matter of days. At the airport, when you asked Henry what he thought about Gregor's involvement, he said you made him paranoid. You rallied, spending the rest of the plane ride trying to make him be kind to you but you have discovered that you can't recall much beyond information he has already planted in you. When something is brought to your attention, it often means your attention has turned it down before (*ReThink*, vol 1, preface). So you ReWind and look again. On film, all you said was 'I love you,' but Henry mouthed furiously 'No!', brushing you away with his hands. You are only now aware how important it all is. The Blaming, the inability to make a decision, the soreness at the very point of commitment to a choice. The strain of comparison, the lack of certainty. You were yourself with him before you tested him out. You dumbass crybaby.

You play the video for a last time, to see what he might have taken from the bend in the knees, and there's a little kick of the heel that you have just noticed and the 'No!' mouthed in slo-mo by Henry is much more than outrage. At his dismissive hands, shooing you, you want to turn to stone, because you never for a moment thought that Henry would do anything but love the whole thing right along with you.

You worry about the coming evening, how all of a sudden the music will be just there where it wasn't before and how Henry will be if you can hear the party again. Teeth chattering under the sheet, you let your eyes close and are away. You are on the sand, crawling toward your own shelter, but you can see two other people sitting cross-legged in it; the light inside it is peach beneath the sheet against a darkening sky. When they hear you approach they shush each other and you let your chin fall to the sand, your hands flat under it. The space in your chest aches with betrayal. Your eyes open under the sheet and the light itself feels sorrowful. You know what's wrong with this. It's been too fast. You have never been ill with him, never watched anything together. You are going back to the Box Set to complete it. You could poison him then help him recover.

You drift again, now facedown and you feel something under you, a mass that is struggling terrifically to get through the sand that is packed tight as rock, your tits are crushed against the hard sand and when you feel the force of a muzzle you freak out, arching up onto hands and knees, trying to appease the animal's frantic mouth with some brittle straw you grab from nowhere, but inside the clump of straw is a thick, rocky seashell. The zebra chomps, the shell against its teeth drives it wild and with a scream that stinks like manure it lunges through your stomach toward your spine.

Terror breaks with a clink of ice and your hands tight full of sand. Finally! But no, he has brought something in a cup and yes, you'd asked for it but didn't want it, you want ouzo, you had always wanted ouzo. Why did he not know what you really wanted? Nothing is more important to you than this now. You're going to say everything: 'What *exactly* about Love is temporary brain damage?' and 'I am not a Blamer, I hate Blamers! It shows weakness, feebleness of mind, lack of dignity. A definite smallness of spirit. Knee-jerk Blaming is not what I am into. I am not some big baby.' You look at his precious notebook and he catches you.

'Scientists do it with squares,' you say then you dip out from under the sheet and it is as if Handyman has been waiting for you. Then Handyman shouts 'Em Tee Vee! I loff you!' and you laugh.

Handyman waves emphatically just as Henry sits down. Because you laughed you dare not wave. You want to scream that you hadn't meant I love you, you had wanted him to know how unpredictable you were. How brave. What you really meant was, *I am too much for me to handle. Help me! Save me!*

It wasn't the wave or the mouthed 'I love you,' anyway.

It was the bend in the knees, Henry said, that was too much.

THE KISSING

I am not the kind of man who gets in deep. I have not decided whether she didn't know this or didn't mind. Neither of us could muster a rush to screw. From my side of it, without closing down options, I tried to impress on her that if the kissing was really all she wanted to do there would be a price to pay, but this was delicate stuff, useful data. She was out of her depth because of the kissing. Even for me it was quicksand. I guessed it was the best she'd ever had and though I found it sometimes unnecessary, if you portioned out the tedium, the lack of build, it was not all unpleasant. With hindsight I see it infected me; mesmerised by the slowed-to-standstill phases screwing counted for nothing suddenly and in fact it seemed outside possible experience. The kiss was it: the tongue the cock, the mouth a sucking cunt. I think the sap accumulation had a stupefying effect. It was laughable to think that this satisfied me to the same extent that it did her, but somehow that pulled me right back in again. Somehow that meant that it did. How did it get to this?

It was the year before Antiparos and her apartment was still dirty and cool and she remained unknown, unsigned. The walls in her bedroom were indigo with white picture rails that I admired very much. I told her this on an early visit. 'Nothing to do with me.' She lit a joint, blowing on it to keep it lit. The gesture was meant to imply I wasn't a priority but I already knew she was treading water and that if anything came within her reach she would be as relieved to go down with it as she would to stay afloat. I would keep poolside.

I don't mind admitting that I had gone to the Perlman for revenge: Jimp loved the old guard and I thought I would find him sidling between paunches at this charity gig. Instead I found her; like him, she considered herself a match for me. After a twenty-word info-exchange, she had jumped onto the stage and dedicated a song to a repairman in her past. Gutsy, I'll give her that. Lithe, certainly. She immediately imagined me complicit in her attack on reality which irritated but interested me. Maturity was not something I could detect in her. Her second song seemed to be some kind of cheery chanson; even so, when the chorus kicked in, I experienced a surprise rush of joy and hope that forced me to sit down. The honour and courage of it meant my sympathy and pity crowded in and I watched her, pinching the bridge of my nose to hide my embarrassment. To the Franks and the Gregors I promised I would make the best of myself without hangers-on. The swell of revenge soon gave way to a sense of betrayal. The stage lighting meant she couldn't see me but I looked at my watch anyway and stifled a yawn. The more she revealed in these songs, the more I saw that I needn't worry; her talents were so unallied to mine, the streams didn't cross, I had nothing to fear from a woman like this. Perhaps this is why I remained so uncharacteristically curious. After the set, she accepted the blow I had signed off from the animal house without question and couldn't wait to unburden herself of a sticky secret. The force was attractive at first.

There's no way of proving it, but I knew from the outset what she would become to people and it was this, not Gregor's suggestions, that kept her under my scrutiny. Here was someone compelled to sing, not choosing to, and this was the elemental attraction she had. There were stiffs at my shoulder, editors from *Psychiatric Annals*, with tears in their eyes because this jaunty, unassuming combination contained an aggregate of experience that was deeply captivating. I looked into my empty glass, and yes, I was cringing at her shamelessness, but there was something else. Wonder was not it, much too strong, but let's just say she was becoming herself right before my very eyes and needed nothing from anyone else. I saw what she could be so clearly, aware also that if she knew what she contained, it would be the end of her. As Frank says, we can all be encouraged to misjudge our own worth.

Gregor might have laughed out loud hearing I hadn't left the Eliot Perlman gig after buying her one drink, might have warned me about turning up on a doorstep because of the ache in those songs. He'd have questioned why I had given her the last of the animal house blow or why I had secretly started underlining tracts from Colette's novellas in translation. He'd question why I had not balked at her secret. Why I didn't throw it back to her like a glowing coal. Why I did not correct her when she made her pronunciation mistakes. Why my laughter at her jokes seemed natural. Why I impressed upon her that she couldn't impress me. Why I kept on with the kissing.

Her apartment became a haven. Of sorts. I could avoid the hazing in Frank's lab but ended up smoking weed with her behind venetian blinds that stayed unopened for days. She sang to me with a cheap wood-effect ukulele or sometimes just played a harmonica which, she let me know, earned five times the amount for a busker than any other instrument they played. I counted how many times she said 'in France' and noted it. The picture above her bed turned out to be a photograph from the emergency room of her own colon, which fit with the story she had told me on the comedown picnic (that she had once not crapped for a month after giving up olestra). I told her that lies didn't impress me either. This was enough to prompt our longest bout of kissing. From visiting her more frequently, I discovered she thought washing to be a particularly American obsession. I asked her whether, living here, she felt cheated out of her Greek heritage (NB: she uses Grandmother as a buoyancy aid when drowning culturally; 'in Greece' also overdone). I worked out that she liked me to think that all she did was less designed, less arranged than it really was. Around the apartment I saw no evidence of abstinences. There was still sugar on the kitchen floor. Herbs wept dryly, unloved, queuing along a windowsill dusty with spores. Habits formed. I'd escape Jimp's statistical prowess in the lab by visiting her apartment though I tried to avoid rigid patterns of attendance since they were powerful omens to her. I knew that by presenting myself intermittently, unpredictably, I increased my incentive value, but this demand for us being together was fast becoming unworkable. She'd pretend to understand how important it was that I was seen around the lab then would cry to come with me, begging 'I want to see BirdBoy!'

Instead of BirdBoy, I had Sandy, who proclaimed herself Astrid's biggest fan and was uncharacteristically star-struck when she finally met Astrid while waiting to be tested in Gregor's closet. While I got what I needed, I left them together.

The animal house was underground. Igor, pale as a grub, saw nothing wrong with my signature despite the fluorescent light. I decanted stand-ins into containers that would survive life outside, from the delicate colours of the Eppendorfs into metal casings in acid green and blue, only ever used for interdepartmental loans. I carried them to quad level clanking in plastic overshoes, and as I passed under Frank's window, I squeezed the plastic tighter so their fat metal casings no more than rumbled against each other in the baggy confines of the thin plastic. In the office, I checked quickly that things were in place. I had made the title of the folder for my amusement but would see how Greg reacted to it. How Cocaine Can Break Your Brain. Keeping it in the raw data subdirectory. I double-clicked on it and got this message: IT IS IMPOSSIBLE FOR HUMANS TO GENERATE RANDOM SETS OF DATA. Jimp had found my book draft but Jimp was not courageous, and so this was as far as he would go and anyway, I had a backup if he blabbed to Frank that I'd been writing it on his time.

I didn't want to be caught in the lab with her so I hurried Astrid out of the closet where Sandy had escaped her fittings to have her shirt signed and had melted into an adoring slouch. I gave Sandy and the technician the afternoon off. 'Great kid! So smart!' Astrid told me as we quit the place. I took my need for vengeance back to the apartment, explaining to her that data analysis was not an instinctual gift bestowed on the Jimps of this world but was predicated on a tiny amount of practical knowledge about the idiosyncrasies of a particular statistical package. It was nothing to do with intelligence. It was in the middle of this she confessed:

'I have a gig tomorrow, the guy from the train is coming to see it.'

I was simply to accept that a skinny-looking ghoul whom she only just met on the D train on her way home from rehearsal might be part of the set-up. She had already admitted to me that she thought he was a hobo and was about to scream when he gave her his card, his name and position in A & R embossed, the company name in shiny azure ink on a dark green matt background. I saved the card to show to Gregor.

She was not as pleased as I had forecast when I told her I was ready to move in. My black rubbish bag contained shirts and suits and a framed sepia photo of four black knees, Xoli and

Thulani, me occluding them in my cream tunic, aged two, up to my neck in savannah grass.

She was often high before I came back from the lab or clinic with her supplies. I would get directly into the frustrating and avaricious shower; the image of her face, meek with stoned indifference, made me shout. Knowing she couldn't hear made me hope that she did.

'You should know by now I never pursue women who want me to!'

I scrubbed myself quickly, I liked being clean. Grinning in anger, I shouted louder.

'And when they pursue me they will know very quickly that it's not what they should be doing.'

While I was drying myself she called out when she saw Gregor on TV.

'How comes he gets to be on TV?'

'You just don't get it, do you?'

I'd already explained that since his appearance on Minerva, NYU were making the most of Gregor's 'outreach'. The book cover was pasted around every communal area in Psych. On every corridor were whispers: 'He'll never get another NIH grant.' Or 'ReOrient is hypnotism with a rebrand.' I had tried to explain to Astrid that this kind of criticism always had roots in envy.

At first, I began giving her stand-ins at home, noting particularly that initial bout length stayed the same. Perhaps this or that particular stand-in was firing repetitive circuits a little too hard. I'd get other compounds to compare. I gave her one before a gig in a warehouse (a free ticket for Sandy) and another before a C-list celebrity birthday in a bakery. Unlike Lucien, I always kept a note of doses and times because living with someone meant observation. It was unavoidable; a byproduct of intimacy. She reported the latest to be the best, 'without any of the panic and a sweet layer of visuals thrown in'. There was a strobing at a certain dose that she said was great for gigs. Astrid was really very eloquent when relaying experience on drugs, and I think I would have been just as good had I had the level of cumulative experience she had. I suggested she write a song. She suggested I did.

They just wanted her to use one name. Astrid was signed to E&I in mid-January. I suggested dinner because this was exciting but no, we were playing a new game from the *Zoot* where each of us tries to catch the other out with a word that isn't in there. The *Zoot*, I realised, had become an extension to the endless kissing. The task this evening was to test the other with a word and work out whether it was authentic or made-up Jive.

'So it's Zoot/Not Zoot,' I asked, and, higher than usual because of her good news, she looked at me like I was Wordsworth. She cheated with jizzle, she said it was a saxophone. I was bored of all of this but I didn't say anything while she jumped up and down on her mattress, thwacking her fingers like the scruffy little honky she was, hooey-ing way too loud because she was so sure that she'd run doubt out of town. Her win twisted in my chest, a cramp like love that she wouldn't get away with again.

After the kiss being its own reward for such a long time, the contrast fuck was bound to be impressive. When the brain no longer receives anything but has been primed to expect something many times over, the net effect on receiving the desired is not real but it is a powerful hallucination. I'm not saying she made no impression on me previously. The singing counted for more than she knew.

She couldn't wait for me to meet Lucien, a lugubrious hipster from her description. He sounded ridiculously shallow with no sense of the classical and he thought he knew about drugs. Cocaine, he argued, she overused, it made her self-indulgent. I said I thought it had never been the right drug for her. It had also occurred to me that it could be a stimulant-induced perseverance that was to blame for the kissing. An oromotor side effect. Perhaps the blow she was getting from Lucien was too pure to mix with these. I acquired some new preclinical dopamine agonists from Igor in the animal house. Gregor strongly encouraged me to start writing up the paper but the more she smoked, the stickier her ardour. She wanted me so much. It is hard to disentangle one's own feelings from those of someone who is infatuated with you, which is why I probably didn't feel the tip into danger.

Irritants began to accumulate in that small untidy apartment of hers. An entire wall devoted to a French writer had always seemed pretentious, but in private I started to waver about what the sure signs of pretension were. I began to grind my teeth in my sleep: the indigo of the walls lost their majesty and seeped sinister intention. The bed sheet was too small for her double mattress and when kissing was over, she'd use it as a prophylactic shroud while she slept, leaving me to study the sheet's faded zebras, with blunted rounded features, their stripes barely fighting for attention, striding ludicrously beside elephants of roughly the same size. Her shoulder blades angled pitifully under them.

'I bet kissing sucks if you're a liar,' she'd say dreamily from under it.

I worked Gregor's clinic, I avoided Frank and Jimp.

From Nashville, she sent me letters in Jive. I stopped opening them after the first one. If I was to free myself I had to work. The *Zoot* did us no good at all. It got us in way too fast. I didn't want her wanting me this much, but when she got back from recording the album she smoked cigarettes furiously while I listened to the first few recorded tracks; how much she cared about how much I cared was difficult to bear. The songs had it, and floated on it, up above and beyond where the usual shit circles, and she begged me to look at her to know that it was because of me that they could float up there on their own. I didn't say it out loud but surplus talent should not be made into love.

Then one morning, I heard her planning logistics on the phone and her braless, cross-legged unstrung coolness caught me out; she was about to go back down to Nashville to rerecord the last tracks. She pulled in her toes while she held up her hand to stop me from asking her anything, then giving a thumbs up, she looked at me to mouth 'They love it.' After the release of *Dwell Time* she allowed us a stroll into Manhattan, but the more they loved her the more she held on to me, wanted to stay home, watch something together. I wanted to scrape her off and reassemble her out there to be admired. Now, when we were not kissing she had started to talk about how much she didn't want to go on tour. If she had to go out to gigs with Lucien, she came back way too high, leaving me to bring her down.

If I worked on the book it made her vicious.

'Forget the book! Let me be famous for both of us.'

'You couldn't be famous enough for me,' I said, but with only weeks to go she was going to miss me and couldn't live without me and I was going to forget her so easily and I'd rather be at work and she was an idiot for thinking that I gave a shit and I was a fraud and a nobody and she did not want to go on tour because if she did I would not love her when she came back. So when Gregor called to get the data averages for the control subjects I was off guard. Sounds like you need me, he said, and in a panic I found myself telling him about the kissing over the lab phone. 'When it heralds fucking, kissing is fucking great,' he said, 'but when the fucking kissing becomes the fucking, you're fucked.'

With Astrid out of town for an extra night, Sandy claimed to be here purely to make a delivery but paid homage to Astrid's home open-mouthed, fingers trailing the walls as she passed through the entrance into the apartment. She had brought a specially compiled CD of songs for Astrid and held it as if she meant to slot it into me and have me perform the songs. I took it and read her careful capitals on the white card insert, *For Astrid love Sandy*, the last d incorporating a heart. It was she who skimmed it onto the sofa, where it stayed while I kissed her, and we fell together over the arm onto the couch like a single felled trunk.

I took the Nina Simone cushion from out of Sandy's arms and guided her towards the elevator at some unearthly hour. I accompanied her to the front door of the apartment building, to the pavement, I assured the concierge that she would get her own cab, she lived in the city. Through the smoked glass door to the stairwell, I briefly glanced back to see her hands cupping her elbows as she sifted the night air for news of a taxi.

You didn't call Henry for the first days in Paris but the stamina needed to not call made it impossible to raise any energy, other than to flip the remote in the hotel room. The great benefits of not failing were just out of your grasp. You would always be lured by the relief of doing what you were not supposed to do.

Paris was doing its very best, kissing your ass even, rolling itself out for you at every intersection; you should be feeling free and this failing spurred a need to keep moving. After attempting to find a pleasing café in the hotel's neighborhood, you sat outside one that you had originally shunned. The tiny cup was drained in thirty seconds and the restlessness bothered you once again but with the coffee filtering through you, inklings of triumph grew, as you strolled down Rue du Faubourg Saint-Honoré, so that by the time you reached Hermès on the corner, you had convinced herself that you had never needed a person like Henry. In the momentary relief, you called Lucien but resisted placing an order because his matter-of-fact tone shot a hole through your confidence and deflated your flimsy progress.

The Hermès window display had modest European dimensions and inside, the boutique's luxury of color in the semi-darkness made it feel like a library. The staff was respectful and silent and you decided: if no one recognized you in Paris, you would return to buy the new-season orange scarf with the corncob motif. This little bargain struck, you felt elated. Out again into the Paris sunshine! Anyone could love you! Another coffee! But the service and the setup were inferior even to the last café, and it brought about a bleakness that took any possible good out of the coffee. Suddenly sick to your stomach, you forced yourself to stop and appreciate a sight – the *orangerie* – a pause which transmuted into a seven-minute stare, the effort Olympian, the effect anesthetic because the desires to be satisfied would always be sabotaged by bigger, better, stronger ones. A certainty circled back before you: the only sensible thing to do was to deal with the wanting; in the future there would be multiple avenues leading out of this but for now, unfortunately, there was only one and you'd already opened the gate to it. You became childishly animated and hopped the cobbles in the road, savoring the gap between yourself and Lucien, a matter of streets. The slice of space a phone call takes.

Even now you can't believe it took you nearly a month to escape the program at Hypno Ray's, finally ditching the group on a junkies' field trip. Lucien had broken rank and delivered to Café de Chambéry and you wandered Le Marais by yourself with his package intact. High on anticipation (you had done nothing wrong yet), you bought an overstuffed pita and sat on a closed shop doorstep, crushing Lucien's package in your jeans pocket against the curved stone of the ancient step. The tahini was escaping your fingers as a bearded man appeared in front of you, in fact at first you thought he was offering you a napkin. A second later and he had his camera in front of you, swiveled expertly from around his torso. His knees, out and to the side, almost touched the stone doorframe and these (Colette would have called them peasant thighs) said that he was not letting you go. He chattered quietly in French, as he might to a frightened child; whispering *ts ts, cha cha cha* in between animal breathing and all the while the hands were working to keep the camera steady. He held it up to his eye, with his left hand forced his palm under your crotch and with a strong upward lift tried to scoop you back a little into the doorway. Someone bellowed ASTRID! and he started clicking frantically. Outraged, you struck out with a straight arm and through the long lens felt the camera connect with the cup of bone around his eye. Then you kicked him crossways in his throat and he tipped onto the cobbles. The air was soon alive with your name. You ran fast, shoulder first, through the crowd and up the closed alley.

Lucien and a lawyer accompanied you from Paris back to New York. Lucien had the goods: season five would show you were willing to work with Henry and were strong enough now to pick up where you left off. You cried for the corncob motif but you were determined to believe that you had been wrong about Henry. About all of this.

Henry clattered in from the clinic and at your mention of Adriana he pretends he does not care. The stories about Ray in Paris that have most satisfied him have turned to ashes in your mouth. You can't get warm in the apartment but you try to escape what you cannot ignore by smiling down at a hot dog vendor in a plastic poncho who is in the wrong neighborhood, willing her to look up and put a chip in the day's smooth horror. Under this, you feel the currents of your certainties. You want to ReOrient. You really do. There is always season six.

You look beyond the hot dog vendor and you lob your intention with a strong arm over, over, over to the park and it digs in heavy and dangerous, like a grappling hook, but the hook fails to anchor and is yanked back; the prongs, reeling murderously just under the surface of the lake, churning and snagging through the putting green and shrubs, whip treacherously between patches of undergrowth and closer to home, ring off the sidewalk, the hook whistling low over the tarmac of Greene Avenue when it sparks off a hydrant at great speed and is thrown into a wide arc around the front of your building. The heft of the hook hammers a Chihuahua in its tiny temple and in the frozen focus of your mind's eye, all four pink paws are in plain sight. The owner falls to his knees while in the alley beside Milford Place the hook catches a shopping cart and drags it up and over the entrance to your building, showering the sidewalk below it with crushed soda cans. Out of the cart, the hook clangs then chimes and bounces gleefully up, up, bounding, it seems, up the stone wall to your floor, until it obliterates both window and frame and reconnects, all four prongs hooking into the space under your ribs.

There's a loud knock at the door.

There was Astrid, stepping ecstatically into the crowd from the stage in her blue spandex jumpsuit. As big as Greg's thumb, she seemed to hover above the steamy crowd in Black Rock. Gregor held the picture too close to my face.

'This better not be the reason why I don't have my data.'

I pushed the magazine away from me, flinching slightly so he wouldn't miss that my appraisal of him had changed, that my trust in him was thinner. He did not get that tan in a bookshop.

I had waited an hour for him and in that time realised how haphazard the med student bar had been made to look. Everything seemed arbitrary, leather cushions were gentle with age, but every last coaster knew its place. Smoking was still allowed even though it was underground. It should stink down here but it didn't. I sat on a saddle stool with my knees grazing the floor, while the returned traveller appropriated the entire chesterfield and with his eyes on me fingered the cracks on the arms where the split leather was thin and sharp. I saw instantly that he was expecting too much of me. My commitment to Gregor now felt toxic, sticky, entangling. He pointed to the magazine. Her microphone tilted at the sky in the foreground as she took the first faithful step off the stage and out into the rolling crowd. Beyond the stage set, the camera lens torqued the sixty-foot rust-coloured wicker man so he grew bending out of the desert, the ribs daubed in cantaloupe-flesh paint through which the mountains peeked, so distant that they were no more than a blue smudge between each glowing rib.

'So Frank finally got Brad into *Nature*?'

Gregor had never squeezed me in this way before, and it was truly sad that he felt he needed to test my resistance now. A shame for him, because things would change if he did. I knew that at some point I would have to kick free of this.

'I've been up to my neck in your clinic.'

'What's with the do-rag covered in chickens?' Gregor scored her headscarf with his thumbnail. 'You don't have time for Nefertiti.'

'*Coqs*. It's French. She likes French stuff.'

'It says here that she was singing in French right before she pissed herself.'

Gregor skimmed the folded feature over the table and I scooped it onto my lap.

'What the hell made you move in?' It was a question that any friend might ask but I knew it was a ratchet; he was building up to attacking me in a less subtle way.

'Why not?'

'Listen, Hank, Brad is our diamond. Cases like BirdBoy are not unearthed twice in a lifetime. *Our data* needs to become the story. Laying around getting high and mooning over this little bird? That is not going to happen. You need to capitalise.' He pinched the sky above her head meanly as if he meant her to stand up.

'It was the scarf that saved her hair.'

'That must have been some fucking blow.'

'He gives her whatever she asks for.'

'Who does?'

I pointed out Lucien at the edge of the stage. 'He's paid to take care of her out of town.'

'Ho ho! This girl knows she's onto the real thing with Henry Sinclair MD.'

'I am not her dealer. You should hear her sing sometime.'

I had waited for three good reviews in a row before telling him about her signing with E&I. I wasn't worried about how much he knew. I knew enough psychopharm to be sure that DA agonists were the same in the desert or the lab, some a little dirtier at receptor sites but still motor stimulants with more or less tedious side effects, all very well documented. The stand-ins were preclinical, under the FDA radar and a damn sight cheaper and easier to sign off than cocaine. He jerked to the edge of his seat.

'Holy shit!' Gregor flicked my cufflink, a concave mother-of-pearl square. 'Look at you!'

I held a smirk, I realise now, too steadily in place.

'You fucking love her as much as these idiots do.'

Behind my mask, images shuffled: the slow but definite denting of the departmental truck, a bloated packet of sausages found in my cutlery drawer, me, *Zoot* in hand, exiting the subway two stairs at a time, knocking on her door in Bed-Stuy, half-shaved at 6 a.m., to show her a sentence, her answering in only a headscarf, her hair a tangled pile in a silky tube. When someone falls for you, it's hard not to take it to heart; hard to hold off. To tell him outright that he was wrong would complicate things. Gregor didn't understand sacrifice.

Her need to unburden too quickly had been her undoing. Jumping from the Perlman stage she had whispered, 'My whole life is in that song' and I whispered back, 'If you open up the poet in me he will kill you.' She laughed and I could

80

see that she thought she knew about people and their weak spots. Nothing is wasted. I have made a note for the book that *to throw off love takes one large gust of courage but the strength you gain thereafter is more than payment; knowing you have done the right thing is, after all, a definition of relief.* I looked at Gregor, at the crowd of fans on the page, everyone enchanted at her stepping out, and I realised that I hated Gregor as much as I hated Frank.

The wine appeared black when it came in a thick conical carafe, and my gin and tonic tumbler was overfilled.

'Ice in last, usually a mistake,' I said to the straight-faced waitress.

'Thank you,' she said.

Gregor worked hard on a look that said he was disappointed with my lack of focus.

'You need to see the fans to understand,' I said, trying to drink from the level of the glass.

'And that's all you are? A fan . . . '

'Her songs have you recognise things about yourself that you didn't know were there. And before you start, that's not me, that's *The Croak*.'

Gregor made a chute out of his hand to release peanuts piecemeal into his mouth.

'So what's our next step? Do you think Frank'd lend Jimp to us if we asked?'

'I'm trying to explain something to you.'

'I get it! She shows her wounds, she laughs at herself and this totally turns them on. Turns you on! She burns and throws up a smokescreen. Everyone privately activates absence and pain. No one is exempt! Every fucker's private candle flame suddenly becomes one huge constellation of desire, permanent and bright and open and connected and electric.'

Gregor always tried to doom the things that he wasn't in charge of.

'Believe me,' he smirked, 'theirs is not an innocent longing, my friend. What you see there is courted, fostered, incubated so that they swallow her whole and believe in her.'

'She packages "what could be",' I said.

'Yeah, a walking wow moment.' He took large gulps of wine. 'And Jesus wants me for a laser beam.'

I was about to remind him that every newspaper in the country was at pains to explain the phenomenon of 'Astrid' but I stopped myself. Gregor had no idea how tragically happy she was to be a version of herself, that she has many other selves that she could put on for you and they would fit just as well, and sometimes they meshed with one another, bits of who she was scalloping over other curves until you saw a self as intricate as lace. You needed an eye for that. You needed to know what to do with it.

Gregor lit up a cigar and sucked on it, pulling the magazine out of my lap, placing the photo back before him to graze Astrid's chest with the side of his finger. Greg leered as if those spandexed titties were pressing tiny Braille affirmations into the meat of his finger. Good thing she'd never meet him: I imagined him buying her a drink, pulling it away from her as she reached for it, his mouth in an open grin. She would grind the rim into his face. It would be terrible. He pounded the last of the wine.

'OK, so you got overexcited. I won't leave you alone again. ReThink is our priority now. If ReOrient isn't working, ReThink sinks too. Use Frank's tracker, get the results, get Jimp on side with the promise of a paper! You'll never need to see Frank's face again.'

I don't tell him about what has happened at Frank's.

'*I* do the experiments but *we* get out of his hair,' I said. 'Meanwhile, *you* get to be second author despite going round being interviewed on Minerva about your book.'

82

'ReOrient is going to be huge for both of us if you can just do the groundwork. Help me, Hank, you're good at this.'

'You are one lucky bastard.'

'Who knew I'd be on the Letterman where Sting cried?'

'Right. That's not luck.'

He poured another glass of wine, stopping just before the lip of the glass.

'Tell me something, Hank. Why weren't you at Black Rock?'

'Because you were coming back.'

'Nothing to do with Sandy?'

He shunned my answer, sneering.

'I hear there was some pushing over at Frank's . . .'

There was a wincing memory of me saying 'I was sitting there,' then Jimp bequeathing me his chair with his pale courteous palm.

'I want a meeting with your publisher,' I said, and I meant it.

'Ha! Stick with science. You haven't failed yet.'

'It's a scientific book.'

'Plan B for when Psychiatry realises you can't do math?'

'It's the one I told you about.'

'Frank says "Stats maketh the man."'

'Frank hates me because I refuse to devote my life to him. You should be flattered that I want to write a book about your subjects. All originality is faulty emulation. Remember?'

'OK. What's your elevator pitch?'

Gregor is truly a bastard. I was in no way ready to pitch to Gregor and I knew that pitching is about being eternally ready. I pretended.

'*How Cocaine Can Break Your Brain* is a treatise on the nature of regret filtered through the evidence from coke addicts and Regreteers.'

Jimp had laughed too when he found it but of course that was a power play.

'A case study?' His face was lazy from laughing when he pulled the supplement back onto the table.

'No, it's ontological tourism with fictional elements.'

'Jesus fuck. Do not say that to marketing. Marketing will have an aneurism if they hear that. Where's the science?'

'I'm working on a very strong hunch from being in the clinic that regret is addictive.'

'It's my clinic!'

'But *my* Regreteers. Who, by the way, love the LILACS banners.'

'I hope so, they cost thirty grand. Listen, Hank, it's *Lessons in Life after Cosmetic Surgery* that gets a guy on the NYT bestseller list. It's the backing by Minerva. This will never get a publisher. Or you will get a bullshit publisher who loves the idea but has no money and no idea how to market it. Who's your audience?'

'People.'

'People don't read, only women, and they have to be alone in tears, or reading to children. Could this be a kids' book?'

'Fuck you, Greg.'

'You think you know my patients in just a few months? These idiots are stealthy. Regret is their lure. They are never going to be satisfied, that's why this industry can never fail. Botox is, right now, inducing mass autism in the public till we don't know what means yes and what means no. As soon as ReThink goes beyond pilot I'm outta there. When will you stop dicking around and write the grants?'

Now I could finally lift the glass without spilling it, I took a large swallow of the gin and tonic.

'So what do I tell Frank. Hi Frank, we're setting up a nice clinic, we're calling it the National Facility for the Regulation of Regret. Tagline: Check in when regret goes wrong!'

'Right!' he cried, 'When regret becomes the thing you're searching for, the only reward that really satisfies you.'

When I look back at this, it is probably the squeeze that Gregor put on me here that crystallised the NFRR. When interviewed later, I'd admit that the idea had always been there but not yet quite fully imagined until this very point.

Gregor gave a barking laugh.

'Say Hank, before you open the facility? If Scarface here needs me to give her the best tits in New York State, send her over. She has the perfect rack for what I'm doing right now.' And he whistled and made a slicing motion. I watched his gaze sink into the picture of Astrid as if trying to get a taste of her, licking her into shape, getting up inside a version he thought he could handle. This would always be a problem; other people wanting her made me want her ten times more – she would kill you if she knew what she was worth. Gregor pointed at the wild-eyed heads of the crowd.

'Snap out of it. She's damaged goods, Hank.'

I couldn't tell if the frustration was part of his drunkenness.

'Everybody's little magnesium bird. Already on fire. Don't look directly at her. She's going to burn bright and quick and she'll melt your hands if you hold onto her. She can't belong to anyone.'

I suddenly felt intensely irritated that I had told Gregor so much.

'She wants me to go to Greece with her. The label's paying. They think she needs a rest.'

'But of course you can't. Frank will never let you go.'

'A summer in Greece would really help with the book.'

There was a long silence constituting a fine-grained assessment of our future together. It may have been the jumpy shadows from those thin candles that made the conversation turn.

'Forget the book!' he warned. Then, soon afterwards, 'I hope this isn't going to become something unmanageable.'

I joined my hands on the table.

'She has told Catherine she's never touring again.'

'Are you kidding me? There'll be a comeback video, rehab, phoenix from the flames.'

'For Christ's sake, Greg! She still smells like burning!'

'Stick with me. Stick to ReOrient. She'll only make a mess of you.'

He blew smoke directly into my face as if I still liked him enough to take anything.

'Or better still, use *her* for the book. Everything is recyclable. I'm serious, Hank, she's in every paper in the country.'

Gregor glittered behind the dull yellow of the candle and my heart, of its own accord, got in step with a steady wisdom.

'Trust me,' smiled Gregor. 'With Astrid in the frame, my publisher would bite off your hand.'

PLYDO

You were going to need a medical and a urine and a blood test before your management would let you start at Ray's. The doctor asked you the usuals and you replied in an adult way. Because drugs, you said, could be meditative couldn't they, but in opposing ways, relaxation and focus are opposites, aren't they, but get both and that's the jackpot, isn't it. Did she know anything like that? She cocked her head and rummaged in her sack but she had seen through you, and, double-bluffing, she gave you a book instead of benzos. She smelled clean and sinless as she took your blood.

'Catherine said you could use this.'

'Yeah,' you said, snatching up the neat little volume. It was Kierkegaard on anxiety: one could not predict disappointment. You would cut off her head for six Valium. Putting the book between your teeth you hooked your fingers over to fake paws. 'Can I eat this?' you asked. She narrowed her eyes, smiling. 'Say to yourself: reading about anxiety burns the same fuel as having the emotion, but at a more economical rate.'

'Woof,' you said and she closed up her bag with your fluids safely inside.

You did not feel adult about her leaving.

The Hôtel Costes was yours for as long as you wanted, Catherine said.

'Try the steak,' she said. You'd eat but these waitresses insisted on staring at you as a punishment.

'Does Henry know I'm here?'

'Yes.'

You had no need on earth to ask the next question.

'Has he called?'

'No.'

Today's waitresses were pink, orange and lime, and their smooth hair was pure liquid sheen. Your palms had not been dry since leaving the hospital.

'Paris is yours! Eat the steak!' Catherine said in sharpening tones because if you refused to rehabilitate with Hypno Ray, the label would have to drop you, sales or no sales. You did not touch the steak but you suffered Catherine's chirpy brutality until she left. The waitresses didn't talk to each other and you could not endure it. They left customers waiting to the last minute because they were certain that their tasks were beneath them. You couldn't sit and watch while they were becoming surer of their convictions! The space between the courtyard and the sky was way too open: you needed all the fetters they could lay on you. What if you could never do doubtless ever again? The espresso had taken you only as far as neutral so that the look that passed between orange and lime made you stand up. You edged by tables, past the conical flasks of vinegar and sweaty olives; their holes were hearts gone, pink-rimmed and violently absent. You could fuck the sliced olives in their little holes if you wanted. Not you. You didn't want to. What really scared you was not knowing what you didn't want. You patted yourself down for a pen to make a note of this for Henry and this plunged you into the steep impossibility that now surrounded him. The circuit of corridors around the square of courtyard cobbles was soothing and dark and you escaped the carefree tinkle of dining strangers, keeping to the walls. Face front, frisking the walls behind you with your fingertips, you felt intimidated by oversized tassels that tipped up soft against your shoulders. Under your fingers the flaws in the silk wallpaper became coded messages about your failures. Sensing atrocity from every direction you felt that something in you beckoned it. The inescapable was coming. You darted up the velvet stairs, because this slideshow was only ever on play or pause. Fumbling to get into the slot with the card, you held your breath to block out a severed limb then, just when you felt you would never get into the room, you were accosted by a well-worn gaping anus which prompted the flipping open of a sawn skull as the door swung back to thump the bed.

You must have slept then but you didn't feel any benefits. You had dreamed of an underwater village from a childhood day trip to Utah, the drowned roofs invisible until the reservoir ran dry, and within a second of waking you were certain that your brain chemicals no longer managed hope on their own. An addict unscrews the bottom of experience and doesn't care that time gets stuffed anywhere, that when time comes back it is super-pissed at having been stowed. Time used to be a joke, a breeze; now you have to be still, the eye of it in you while you pretend you're not looking. Without Henry, inertia keens at a single pitch of melancholy that will master you all day long.

The phone in the room rang with a foreign low tone. You refused the metro so there would be a car sent. There was a smooth, slim lozenge of chocolate under each pillow and you'd eaten all four before they came up to fetch you. The day's alarm begins to sound at the first thing you shouldn't do.

Forty seconds in a cab with Catherine and you realized you should have walked. She chatted at the window: Paris is yours as long as you keep up with the meetings at Ray's.

The flashing ribbon of Paris became a taunt. So instead you read: *anxiety is freedom's actuality as the possibility of possibility*, keeping your panic asleep in your belly, and you arrived at the turreted clinic overlooking a haughty stretch of the Seine, a view that helped you discover a hidden fund of fury for Catherine.

'It's in a fucking hospital?' You were more angry than ashamed.

Was this how divas happened? A hurtling ascension?

'Oh, dramarama! It was a prison,' she was scolding you, 'then a syphilis clinic. Ray's really made it his own and Hancock's worked so hard.'

The Directeur pénitentiare's office, the glowing heart of Ray's kingdom, was a glass and copper cage at the start of a hallway on the first floor and above it arched an asymmetrical word, a mosaic of bottle-green glass: PLYDO. Catherine held your face toward it and whispered, 'Hancock broke that glass himself.'

'Plydo?' you ask.

She held your shoulders.

'You're going to like Ray a lot.'

Ray. You had laughed with Henry at newspaper shots of Ray walking the beach steps in Malibu with his 350-pound bodyguard Hancock, wearing a heavy floor-length cassock and an LA Lakers cap. The line went, *A step too far for Hypno Ray?* The piece had questioned his abstinence, his sanity, his controversial but successful rehab program, his patriotism and his relationship with Hancock in five pat sentences. Henry encouraged you to go along with everything the paper was insinuating, and you did, happily.

But here in person, standing under his own gimpy welcome, Hypno Ray was smiling at you with his tongue out and barely an arm's length away you were unable to deal with how much he looked like an old lady. His thick coarse hair was tragically black and under it the features were chaotic: the lined cheeks had given up and his pocked nose was a melted lump. Gums that were a grayish-plum color swelled above immigrant teeth with a woody tobacco veneer. Ray was exactly the same as the tabloids made him out after his affair with the Czech teenager. A stinking cockney terrier ready to pinion and savage. A dog, tense and ready on its hind legs. In a cassock.

To avoid his dress, you stared back at the mosaic. He mistook this look for admiration and he patted his knees as if to beckon a pet. You moved toward him, lips between clenched teeth, vowing as he put his arm around you that you would never: ask for your water to be warmed; pretend to drink tequila rather than refuse it; be caught combing your hair in the women's washroom; or paint your own cowboy boots white.

Once released, you heard Catherine laughing with Ray pretending she wasn't shit-scared about whether you'd make it. This was still classed as a visit, so you called Lucien that night from the Costes, where you threatened him because he refused to come and then you set off a fire alarm. It was your own fault that you had to move into Ray's.

The first morning was spent listening through a door to amateur gospel joy. After a weak-ass knock, Hancock opened the door and you entered for the final burst of chorus from a circle of famous zombies singing new words to a classic tune. Ray weaved his way to you.

'Seize the Disease is our very own anthem!'

'OK,' you said.

'Carpe Disease-us!'

'Right!' you said.

'Plydo,' he said, like this explained everything. 'Please Leave Your Disease Outside? Come on in. We have key rings.'

Without warning you began to cry.

'Fobs?' he said apologetically, putting his face close to yours.

You blew your nose.

'Plydo is the way we greet each other around here, Sissy. I'm gonna call you Sissy. OK? Astrid's a harsh name. Sinead used to be Cynthia and every one of the healed know my name ain't Ray.'

You recognized Sinead immediately from Zeitghost, her wide red mouth and dark glasses, hair smooth, black and bluntly cut, a shiny acorn cup. She had spectacularly broken her back falling 'drunk' from a plinth in Trafalgar Square.

Ray said, 'Openness is oneness. An anagram!'

'No. It isn't,' came from the blacked-out windows of Sinead's eyes.

Ray continued, 'Cleaners and Sereners, she needs no introduction. Sissy, I'm so glad we found you in time.'

You are welcomed by a flurry of 'Plydos' in a circle of clapping losers, who you finally see have faces that are well-known enough to flip up instant bios for almost all of them. Ray nodded to Hancock and an a capella 'Dwell Time' started up. Oh, you can't do this, you cannot bear this.

'A welcome! Am I right?' Ray clapped on the offbeat then pulled you to his chest. You went to kneel to escape but he placed a large hand between your shoulder blades that flattened your tits against his encassocked belly, his knotted rope-belt at your sternum.

'The disease is coming out of you now. Can you feel it?' Holding you back in front of him he touched your heart, and that touch was dangerously close to your fleshy rounded non-hearts. Crouching a little, he pressed your face to his chest, where he placed a hand over your ear and you felt your lips pout mechanically. You were aware of the weight gain in a matter of days and the pressure on your face squeezed out a good deal of self-pity. You cried against his cassock.

The meetings were full of the needy dying to unburden. With all your life force (which turned out to be 'blowtorch' when clean) you wished that none of these fuckers knew you, that *Dwell Time* had bombed or that you really had burned to death at Black Rock. Scraping your lunch plate, you slid in the stinking truth: you were only interested in freaks who had done worse than you had. Girl-Band and Mexico had kept their distance, a prelude to natural selection. You'd passed Debrief, they told you: 'It's Baskets first, then you can progress to Self-Class if you break through.'

'Break through? We're only allowed to ask the questions that are passed round in a basket. Who made Sinead fucking captain?'

Mexico knew that since stopping the PCP, Sinead wrote bawdy songs for Koonsberg's seventy-five-year-old muse to make working with Ray bearable. The teenage boy she lived with on Île Saint-Louis had serial high-profile one-night stands which Sinead pretended she sanctioned.

The basket of questions was lowered into the circle, swinging from a hook in the ceiling controlled by a winch, powered by Hancock's huge arm at his sentry station beside the door. No one seemed to care that Hypno Ray wore a cassock to meetings. You were just to absorb this. You were reminded by Leadership that swearing was a symptom of remaining disease.

Trying to look stern, Ray asked today's first question.

'What underlies your reliance on Henry?'

'His huge hammer?' You looked round the circle for comrades; Mexico laughed, securing her place. Hancock wound up the basket. Sinead scratched vigorously into her notes. You left a gap then said, 'And he scores A1 cocaine?'

'Plydo!' Ray made the fingers of his left hand into an O, the nails clicking together like pistachio shells, and he held the tips of these fingers to the tips of the fingers of his opposite hand: Time Out with a P. Sinead's accent was as thick as it ever was in her days on Zeitghost.

'We've figured that Henry's a real sweet guy.'

'You have no idea what he's about.'

'But you do.'

Ray reached out and touched your knee and you thought your ears would bleed. You looked round at all the faces similar in one hateful way; they had unlimited time to fill, and in that second you felt the promised ennui of living without direction, a permanent leveling, all the weight of staying straight with both feet firmly, so firmly, on the ground. All the past had to do was tap you on the shoulder and you would turn around and recognize that everything had happened in just the way it said it did.

In the canteen, your appetite was ramping up.

'Break through what exactly?' you whispered urgently to Mexico at lunch, with too much potato in your mouth.

'You'll see,' she said. She was rolling a slim, her potato untouched. 'At Ray's things can go both ways.'

Afternoon Baskets were Sinead's turf. You couldn't see behind the black glasses but you could tell by the smug twist of her mouth that she thought she'd seen a lack of stamina in you.

'*How* does Henry get you to better yourself?'

'He's doing this for all addicts, not just me.'

'Trust me. I know what men like Henry are like.'

'There aren't any men like Henry.'

'And these signs, you read them as love.'

'Henry's not just a yes man.'

'You like to be treated like you're missing the point?'

You stared at her to show you didn't care what she thought because she was just another junkie waiting to die. Someone should tell her that she looked like a dimwit in a shrunken wig. You drew a circle at her with your finger.

'Are you trying out this look before your tour?'

She gripped one wheel. 'Henry makes things difficult for you so he can gain control.'

'He wants me to be better.'

'At taking drugs?'

'He doesn't want that.'

'Is that why he provides them whenever he needs to take control?'

'Plydo, Sinead,' Ray said. 'You don't know that.'

'He's not my pimp,' you added.

'Did he turn on you when the Handyman gave you a joint?'

Her questions were more important to her than any answer you could provide.

'These are published facts. There are obsessive behaviors associated with rejection in love. When I'm injured, I blame. I love big. I blame big.'

Sinead put down her pen. 'My God. He has really done a number.'

'He's a scientist, for fuck's sake. You could all use what he's got.'

'Save me from Henry's help. Plydo.'

The second the buzzer sounded people were scrambling to leave. Ray looked at his watch. 'OK, tomorrow it's Triggers. Remember how Box Set messed things up for Sissy.'

'I never said that,' you said, drowned out by scraping chairs, overdone exhalations, groans. Ray raised the volume,

'Bring photos, rap sheets, diaries, anything that points to getting here.'

They focused on you with their wide, warm beam of dead, consensual patience. You hated yourself for looking for complicity in these strangers. How could they bear this?

'Say it,' said Ray. 'It can't harm you.'

You did not Plydo but it felt like you were losing an important point in an important match.

You weren't allowed to join Baskets the next day. At breakfast Mexico and Girl-Band let you in on some info. 'She tests you right up to Self-Class. She can't stand women who can't rely on themselves.'

Sinead began before you had found a seat.

'Ray and I are very interested in your certainty about your relationship.'

'What made you tell a stranger such a painful secret?' said Ray, bringing an unwanted gust of early-morning compassion.

'I told you in Debrief, I knew immediately that I could trust him.'

'You *assigned him the role* of trustee.'

'I feel as sure today as I did at the Eliot Perlman.'

'Leadership worry that what you see as care, may not be.'

'Leadership has never kissed Henry.'

'And if they had?'

'Then they'd know.'

'You said the kissing stopped in Antiparos.'

'Until he discovered the truth about Petra and the dwarf.'

She scribbled furiously and shook her head, and you saw it. Once you knew it was jealousy, you could go to town.

'The kisses were it, most definitely. Head of the class. Like a black joy, a dead black joy. A throbbing need never to change. It's random but it's orchestrated.'

Mexico nodded, humming her appreciation.

'Pressure then stillness and fleeting and sucking, you know it right? Hard biting and suffocating and I guess kind of fathering? That's why he didn't need to fuck me, the kisses were it for him.'

Sinead looked up briefly at Ray. You smiled. *Anxiety may be compared with dizziness. He whose eye happens to look down the yawning abyss becomes dizzy.* 'Shall I go on?' you asked.

'Yes,' said Mexico in her molasses voice, lighting a cigarette.

'They were the kind of kisses that had signatures. All the stuff he intends gets packed into 3D. I can carry it with me. I can choose one by feel.'

You don't say here how you wish you had never, ever kissed him, instead, you blow one to Ray and he becomes suddenly coy.

'I suppose it's knowing you've met your match,' you tell them.

'A yes to death,' said Girl-Band.

'Two souls meeting?' offered Ray.

'Two assholes meeting,' you said.

'You just don't understand the trouble you're in,' said Sinead.

Mexico pointed out that evening that maybe complaining about the success of a relationship was not the right thing to do to someone like Sinead. You pointed out that if you were brutal you could say that breaking her back and the obvious appetite rebound meant she really filled the seat of her wheelchair, and while you didn't make the music business, it was hard to see her next video being a hit. Mexico drew her breath through her teeth and you felt a teenage pride. In truth, you had constructed Henry from very measly pickings. Had you straddled the missile of your prediction? Had you fired yourself into a dangerous future from the balcony at the Perlman?

Trigger prep, it turned out, was also excruciating.

'Yes, the party was definitely an issue,' you repeat robotically.

'A party you were both imagining?'

'A party that was happening, every night, without us.'

'And for this reason he was abusing you?'

'Why do you keep saying that?'

'OK, he'd lost interest in you.'

'God! He was happy to stay by the campsite. Believe me, after Black Rock? I was not on that island to make friends.'

'Maybe Henry's hearing was better than yours.'

No one liked helpful Ray.

'Oh, he would have told her,' said Sinead.

Your teeth clenched. 'There was a beat, OK? It bothered him more than I could understand. Henry wants people to connect with him.'

'On his terms.'

'I didn't give a fuck where the music was coming from!'

'Paranoid,' whispered Sinead, scratching a note.

'Tell us. How old's your boyfriend?' I asked her.

'See what I mean?' she said to Ray.

'You know this happens,' he said.

'God, Ray! You are such a pussy! Why are you so fucking scared of her?'

'Do I hear harshness?' Ray cupped his ear.

Flurries of 'Plydos' were offered to blot up this anger and wring it out elsewhere. You would never make another month of this.

'I guess I'm just unclear on how a party alone could make a grown man so hostile.'

. 'Make it clear.' Ray turned to you and cajoled, 'How would you describe it to your mum?'

'Loud.'

'Why?'

'She's dead.'

You weren't going to let on what the party had meant to him, that it was a goad prompting thoughts of what he should be achieving. As the sounds began to pattern the night, you flowered into an emblem of his failures and you watched Henry assessing those disappointments with every gulp of ouzo. Distantly, the party continued, while beside the fire, a persistent threat blinking orange then black, there played on his face some culpability for his dissatisfaction, the flickering shades of what you could have won.

Three weeks in, Nudes finally got a mention in the Daily.

'You can only paint nudes when life says you're ready to face it without the disease.'

'When you've passed Self-Class?'

'It's in the book. There's a purple fob.'

'We go on a field trip but don't be fooled. It's a test. And no one passes it.'

That afternoon, Sinead's silence encouraged everyone else's until she made her move.

'Relevant by accident, was that Henry's term?'

'Ray. We've been here . . . '

'Not your fight,' Sinead said to Ray with an arm out across his throat.

'He never said that I wasn't sufficient. He liked people to recognize me. '

'Have you considered that this whole story is a cage you use to keep the truth away from you?'

'Ray? Say something!' You were standing now. 'Do not forget, I attacked *him first*.'

'When you excuse him he controls you.'

'You *need* Nudes,' whispered Ray solemnly.

Your hands were in your hair.

'Ray! You don't, you cannot just *decide* to be a painter!'

'I did!' said Ray. He grabbed hold of your hands. 'When the press and Jeannie were poisoning me, I hit back – I hit back with seriously heavy-duty acrylic paint.' Ray held out both your arms in a makeshift crucifixion. 'Self-Class is only the start!'

'She's not even close to ready,' said Sinead, blackly confident.

'I'll look after her,' said Ray.

'I don't want you on my fucking team!' you cried out.

'Plydo,' he whispered.

You don't know why.

You felt sorry for his teeth and his gums and you said it.

'Plydo.'

DILPA

What catches the eye is this: the ferryman seems to be standing beside his boat in the middle of the sea. There must be a sandbank under him. Shaded by a triangle of brick-coloured canvas draped from mast to aft, he reaches into his sturdy hull and scoops florid handfuls of baby squid then, one by one, stuns his catch with a terse blow, his serious hand aware and uncaring: he makes death efficient and automatic as prayer.

I know there are deep waters between me and the ferryman because I have tested them on my swim. Standing in the still, mineral-green sea, the island of Dilpa behind him seems impossibly far away. From the sandbank now chugs *Petroula*, the boat they share for errands. It's warranted, staring at a boat returning to shore, no matter who is mastering it.

There had been no one on the beach when I tried swimming this morning. When bathers appeared, I had to leave the bay for the spit, where I slipped through the turtle cordons to a shallow pool where I might try new things. Unlike her, my time here is being spent wisely and I am able to distance myself from our continued awkwardness.

I'm increasingly comfortable in shorts, the blisters are drying up and I feel ready to deal with the mute insistence of the nudists. I stare at Dilpa beyond and wonder at how she can care so very little for the party. She doesn't want the problem-solving that goes into finding it, she is not prepared to exploit the natural interest these people have in her. Imagining her torpor motivates me. I glance at the murdering ferryman as another eight legs swing limp and I picture her pulling fast through the water, the faux suede silvered with a layer of minuscule bubbles, leather strands becoming mirrored as they drag through the currents. Dilpa can only be half a mile away but it is difficult to judge with the sea so hidden and translucent; the green merely signals what is beneath us and I dream down to an emerald cavern at the island's root. The party may as well be there. *Petroula*'s serious and ancient driver gives her his careful, almost grave, attention – she, full of trust, surges through the water with her broad, bright paint stripes.

From the cafeteria, the white-haired woman shouts 'Gigi', it's unmistakeable, and in front of me he turns and I look at my papers because what goes on between them is none of my business. I glimpse his wave towards the boat while I keep my own gaze towards the scrub-filled island, tousled with stunted trees. The distant bleached grass parts at random to make way for white and grey-green marbled eruptions and I wait.

Gigi shouts out to the ferryman before he trots back down to greet the boat, and I stiffen, unable to grasp any meaning (though I have been practising from the book I keep above a cistern). The ferryman volleys a sharp, sure answer that makes Gigi laugh. I feel Gigi about twenty yards away, the skin of my back is sensitive to his approach: a sign that between us there is something shared, unseen and unexplained that is waiting to be discovered. From his gestures, he seems concerned with the angle of the boat's return and this dalliance gives me plenty of time to observe him while also assessing the distance between our shore and Dilpa's. It's almost too obvious that the party is there. I would hate him if it were that easy.

With guidance from Gigi, the bright little boat noses easily into the sand. I am a tourist, I want to see the local catch and so I have every reason to be looking into the boat. Gigi comes close beside me and sees me peering for evidence behind the greying pyramid of their parts. I am merely interested in the catch: look at it, pegged to a thin red rope with sky-blue Hellenic clips, clumped fresh blooms of octopus bobbing in a clear plastic box of water. *Petroula* is balanced with rubbish bags at one end; a party glass has escaped. I feel vindicated and want to ask, 'Did you name this boat for Petra?' If he answers no, I may switch to 'Is there a party?' A bottle has leaked somewhere and I pick up a trace of ouzo. The old man says something cutting, cruel even, and Gigi nods sagely while I suffer the glare of the sun, not really knowing what is intended by their words. Without a pattern or signal that I can detect, the ferryman will swap in and out with Gigi all day, and I will find myself more and more preoccupied with the boat's comings and goings. I wait for Gigi to put on his cheesecloth shirt, which he does on the terrace to the café before he disappears inside. I am arrested by a strong desire to know exactly what prompts him to dress and undress.

I make sure I wait for a good fifteen more minutes before I enter the cool of the cafeteria. There is only one way in for the campers, which passes his chair, so it's impossible to ignore the instant blast of clean basilic heat; the perfect top note to the biscuitish smell of the sand. He sits on a stool reading a newspaper, knees wide apart, his near-black feet balanced on their balls on the silver rail, the heels tilting behind. Under the stool squats a painted petrol canister, nibbled at the unpainted rim by rust but billowing with healthy herbs. His habit is to rub the plump basil leaves between his fingers while he reads the paper. I have noticed moist green spots on the drachma notes he gives as change. Up close, I see he has salt crystals roosting in his eyebrows but whenever his eyes meet mine, I look elsewhere because no one knows better than I do that your dwell time betrays you. I scrape a chair and he flicks me a look but by then I have lost courage and am feeling crushed by too many actions untaken. Convincing myself that I have never seen him nude, I stare into his face. The weight of the gaze bothers him: he looks up again, puzzled but good-tempered. When I have counted my change, I leave.

Behind the café, I sit in the toilet cubicle and I try again at the bits of Greek that she has helped me pronounce. The crass, ready-made conversations at the back of the ferry book make me want to hurl it into the sea, but it is all we have. That she would love to help further prevents me from asking her; it would, after all, take us backwards. Suddenly from behind the peeling door I hear him and I am startled by a questioning word that sounds like 'crebosa?' and I hope to God he didn't hear me practising but I realise the shout is only a warning to make sure there's no one there before he begins the sluicing of the troughs. Today he also bowls water under the doors of the empty cubicles and the waves this creates kiss between my feet. I stay still until I hear nothing.

When I get back to the café the woman is there. At her command, Gigi scalps the stalks of oregano that wander up the wall from the cans around the terrace of the cafeteria. He seems only to accept advice from this stick-thin woman who has such dark skin (from behind my sunglasses she looks varnished). She knows as much about the rituals and timings of the camp as Gigi does. I try to gather clues to suggest that she is his sister, and after several false starts and lots of read-ing of my papers with extended arms, I have come up only with listable physical differences. She isn't horrific so much as she is physically acceptable by chance or by fashion. I still have a strong disbelief that this particular man would make do with this particular stick insect who wears a transparent flour sack over a crocheted bikini and always has bare feet.

He, by contrast, clothed or nude, is acceptable entirely by design; his form affords universal admiration. His body is athletic, there is no shame in noting that. Her face with its large nose and deep-set eyes has a slight overhang to the brow, and this makes her face eagleish in type. Her hair is kept too short to tell whether it holds a wave, but it has none of the luxury of the man's long spiral curls, that would resist pressure from a forefinger and thumb, that are shined and perfumed above a shallow, flat forehead beneath which sit a wide nose, full, matt, mauve lips and thick, coarse lashes. The colour of his eyes will take some more observation and thought. She calls his name, 'Gigi'; I want to reach up and catch it, bring it down to my chest for close inspection so that it never reaches him.

I choose my lunch to match what the workers select and in the queue end up behind one of the Swedes, who introduces me with absolutely no warning to the Handyman. As I hold out my hand, it is taken with raised eyebrows and I am sure he begins to smooth over my knuckles with his thumb but stops. Whatever the intention, I feel an equalling occur. Perhaps because of this, Frank's face seeps through and I wonder: when will the shame evaporate? When will the need to repeat those scenes with Frank lose its strength? Can't poison be processed? The cramp of injustice never diminishes in the slightest despite leaving Frank's lab behind. The pain rests in the childish excitement I felt about impressing Frank. How I felt the BirdBoy was mine. I didn't realise Frank had got to the top by hoarding others' fear and talent, by manipulating those whose attributes he coveted. My eyes follow the quote on the hard verso of my notebook. *The price we pay is forgoing the deep satisfaction of taking our own revenge, in person, upon those that have wronged us.*

*

'Frank? Can I come in?'

'Why yes. Hank.'

He mouthed it around the gratuitous length of a new cigar. A good mood? Nobody needed that much tobacco. Maybe it was because Frank was afraid of being seen as liberal that he yoked his staff to a hardcore timetable that always included weekends and holidays, employing a number of women who still lived with their parents. I always wavered, wondering whether it would benefit me to act more English or more American.

'I hope this doesn't sound pushy . . . ' I began.

Frank leaned back into the same position in which he had bragged to me about the condom sales in China, dividends harvested because of an excellent stockbroker who couldn't put a step wrong since bio shares peaked.

'That sounds pushy.'

'I think since Brad was referred through me, I should write up the paper.'

'That would be very wise. A *Nature* paper would get the Ivy Leaguers hungry and would certainly help your grant applications. Of course, a co-author on any of our papers is no less a privilege.'

'I mean, I want to write it up.' *Say first author, you fucking pussy.*

'Be my guest.'

'If I do . . . ' Frank relaxed further into the Chinese position, and this was sucking my need out into the open and letting it pool on his desk. 'Will you take a look at it?'

The smile melted through Frank's jaw and dripped down his fat neck. Dripped and drenched his fat fucking yellow chest because he knew that I had not dared ask what I had come to ask. They would never be able to call him a liar. I screwed up my eyes remembering the little squeaks of delight that the physical effort pushed out of me as I ran up to his room, teeth clenched, picking over the words I might use to describe BirdBoy for him.

The dwarf and the Swedes amble up and while I sweat with shame and blink at the Handyman, I also watch their easy interactions. Their familiarity is tiresome. What do they see in each other? How can they not sense what else is on offer amongst the dreck? Petra gets forever in the middle of things. And what has she done so right to get into his affections? I look around me briefly and am certain they would love to hear about BirdBoy, a boundless tale. I hear them say *Em Tee Vee* though she's not with me.

'Hey!' shout the Swedes.

Gigi looks directly at me. One of the Swedes gets hold of Gigi's biceps and points at me.

'Workout?'

I begin to sweat immediately. While they laugh, there is a split-second exposure of the roof of Gigi's mouth, the teeth protruding to a very small degree.

They want help carrying the lamb down to the boat. It's heavy: the Swedes take the front, I have the back end on my own.

'There's a party?' I say to anyone. They look back smiling but they don't answer.

'Dilpa?' I wink. 'Is that it?'

They stop, they turn impatiently.

'What is Dilpa?' a Swede asks. I drop the sticky side of meat in the sand and even Gigi curses. It never occurred to me that the name Astrid gave for the island was wrong. 'They had a house here,' I say to them, knocking off the sand as they lump it into the boat. 'Her grandmother, up over there.' But they are ignoring me because without her beside me I am of no interest to them. The gritty lamb peeps over the side while I rinse my hands in the sea and they jump into *Petroula*, one after the other, after dislodging her dainty prow from the sand.

Alone I can look for signs. If she stays in the tent for long enough, with the boat gone, I can stalk the showers, then perhaps move down to the beach later to get an orientation where the sounds are clearer, the music almost recognisable. I decide to walk through the back of the camp to get to the spit. How long could it take an otherwise physically excellent young man to learn to swim? On my way, I cup my hands to peer into the campsite office, a baked ramshackle hut but the backdrop of our first meeting with Gigi, and I scan through the window expressly for signs of a shared life between Petra and him. The map on the wall of the Cyclades and a cartoon advertisement of a glass-bottomed boat ride are faded, almost invisible, bleached by ruthless August suns. A mug on the counter says HYDRA, each letter containing a photo of island life. The worktop is covered with a wood-effect vinyl. Anything make-do is strangely exotic after being in the US for med school and now an intercalated psych program. I keep my face close to the window, trying to suppress the pain of losing out to that system.

The conference had been set up specifically to showcase the data we had got from BirdBoy, a fanfare for publication, but Frank had used it to give me a royal shaming in front of some of the biggest names in the business. He pulled me up on the most insane things: a definition or a turn of phrase that was used in every journal I had read on the subject but of which he was publicly doubting the accuracy. When I defined what I meant then Frank would circle again, pretending it was his duty to defend the standards of those present: 'I know what you are trying to say, but I think this particular audience will need a little more than a stock definition.'

It took a lot to get me to walk by Frank's office after that. Selma, a forty-year-old Korean postdoc, stared up at me from her microscope. She devoted weekends to calibrating the equipment Frank used and was secure in the knowledge that nothing worked without her. I knocked at Frank's door and was told to enter. Seconds later, Selma was there in her safety glasses and mask and gloves.

'Professor Leary, I need help with the molar concentrations.'

'Call Jim?' Frank suggested, and she nodded once but stayed where she was.

'And I need someone to flush through this tubing.'

Frank turned to me and I smiled and, under Selma's accusatory glare, kept on chirpily unravelling as I can do in silences, explaining that what Gregor and I were doing now was a kind of a rewiring of cognition through the eyes, that the pilots had shown that ReThink led to patients from rehab initiating fewer bouts of drug-taking.

'Perhaps you should move over there,' said Frank.

'I have to finish the control subjects for Brad.'

'There's already enough for a Brief Communication to *Nature*. You still have a lot to learn about science, Dr Sinclair. We're not students. We're in it for the long haul.'

Selma stood there with her fine-bore tubing, her pitiless eyes in the goggles despite dividends finally being paid to her. I gestured for her to step back and I closed the door in Selma's face, turning to Frank.

'Actually, Frank, you are being unfair to me.'

'Unfair to you. Oh really? He opened a drawer and pulled out a sheaf of paper. *How Cocaine Can Break Your Brain*? Quite the title. You have been writing this on *my time*?'

'Gregor's printer is bad.'

With Frank, I used it so infrequently that I thought honesty would get me out of jail. I wished now that I hadn't closed the door.

'You want glory. The quick buck. Hard work isn't in you.'

'I need a few weeks off.'

'Take forever,' said Frank. 'Take all the time you need.'

Gregor nailed it: If you chase two rabbits you'll catch neither. Distancing myself from Frank meant I saw clearly again and could concentrate on the book. The need for vengeance grows like yeast. Of course the book! I listened to Greg: If you are looking to get saved by something outside of yourself you are heading to hell.

I step back from the camp office window and remind myself I mustn't waste my time here. The entrance to the camp is just a diversion from a dust track leading off the path into town. The way in is elevated with a view down to the village centre and the harbour. Dilpa is romantically lit by dusk and I look for movement that might accompany whatever is going on out there. The island is giving us too much time with each other. She is my only chance of finding the party.

I slope down through the camp to the spit and slip under the cordon and have the water up to my neck as quickly as I can. There must be a way of convincing the body that it will float. There has to be another way of starting to swim. The laws of nature didn't change in order for planes to fly. Look at life before Fosbury, for God's sake. A grown man cannot learn to swim the same way as a baby can. Practice pushing away from the sand. OK, all fine, now pull up the legs, no bottom, reel, shout. I get my breath back. How can it be so tiring? How do the likes of she and Gigi make it over to Dilpa so quickly? She, of course, likes that I can't swim, she thinks it very English.

I dry off then take the short walk back and sit close to the volleyball, making a proper seat by digging down a half a yard and using that sand to form a backrest. I squeeze my haunches back into the hole and rest my back and neck against the heaped sand, ready to watch this game in comfort. *Petroula* arrives back with the early evening catch for the camp dinner menu. Unlike lunch, dinner is one set meal for all and always delicious.

The boat has come in very close to my beach pit and I see the ferryman is on the shore to help Gigi, throwing the octopus, two at a time. I do not at all expect the ferryman to throw a pointy-headed squid hard at me so that it thwumps into my gut. It is eye-white grey, it is still very much alive and it flick-flacks down from my abs to the hollow at my groin. I thrust my crotch up and I hear a *pfsst* as it drenches my shorts in greasy deep purple ink. Gigi stares at my crotch and smiles like I have passed a test, then retreats up the beach backwards, as if filmed on rewind, because of a loud exclamation of frustration from the white-haired woman in the kitchen. The ferryman sees all of this but acts as if nothing is wrong and gets on with his nets. I twist hectically, like a mongoose under attack, to dump the thing with its lurching head and shove its searching tentacles into the sand with my crotch. *These are my only shorts!* but these people don't understand shorts. I packed light and encouraged her to do the same.

The squirming thing is cast off and caked in hot dry sand, so I stand as if I have had enough of the beach or as if I have an appointment to keep but all I wish is to run away from that fucking monster of a thing. Walking doesn't dry off the shorts even though I take a circuitous and lonely route back to the tent, coming at it from the wasteland and emerging scraped and, now look, bloodied, from behind the bamboo. When I get to the tent she is still sleeping and I know what she will be like when she wakes up, it has been hot since I left eight hours ago. I call this phase The Recession.

I put my hand in the zip of the tent and know that whatever I grab will be a scarf. I use the Henry Ford to try to soak up the ink which is cloying now, thick like melted lipstick. The silk drags stickily through it and is almost useless and now ruined. I ball the scarf and put it into my pocket feeling renewed. I see a dark patch beside the tent, not yet dry, and wonder if it is her piss. She is stirring and I report through the nylon.

'If I were you I'd stay in the tent. It's hell out here.'

She must not see my shorts. She appears naked wearing *Noix et Baies,* bandana style. There's a giant silken pine cone dominating her forehead and she yawns. The volleyballers can be heard at play.

'How can I sleep when there's a rice pudding at stake?'

She wraps herself in yards of some other cloth and we set off back to the beach. I overtake her to get to our spot from yesterday.

'Jesus Christ,' she protests, pulling down her glasses, 'Hooey! That jellyfish take a big black piss on Buddy G's drawers? It's a sign. Jesus wants you nude. Phew, you shudda dumped them knickerbockers in the early bright.'

'Knickerbockers are not in there.'

She is laughing and touches my head playfully but I move it sharply and her hand dangles.

'You want me to go get you a drink?'

She plays with my hair.

'You miss the *Zoot*, baby?' she says. I tilt my head and her hand drops naturally because this is the beginning of a phase that needs careful recording. I mustn't blow it.

'Go find out what there is to eat,' I say, reclaiming my sand hole.

Ten minutes later, Gigi beckons. I look round to check she is not returning then I put my hand to my chest to ask, 'Me?' He nods and so of course I pull myself out of the hole and have to crawl a little before jumping up and running over, the only one in beachwear. I get ready to watch him being his best. This is just the beginning, I think, bouncing in the sand, which is very difficult. It all feels so deserved. The game starts and after a couple of great efforts there is a tragic shot from one of our men. I rest my hands on my shins and Gigi walks over to tighten the net but I watch as he bypasses the pole to sit down next to my hole, which is now filled with her. I am angry for a couple of points and miss easy shots. For the entire game I can smell the ink on my shorts, which is turning from metallic tang to protein rot. I hear him saying *Em Tee Vee*. He is trying to explain something to her but she is not catching his drift. I start over to them but he notices and he motions me to stay with the dwarf, does a digging motion, makes a winning smile and so I have to go back to play, only to have him resume whatever project he has started with his pen on her upper arm. I try to keep on with the game, it's important I am seen as a viable option for future games, but how can I concentrate when he has her in his hands? The game is endless and unbearably hot. I'm sure I chip my tooth clashing heads with the dwarf; he jumps up under my chin, the little bastard. I lose every point that I have a chance of winning. When I get back over to them, he is finishing his project and reveals a large Gaudi-esque prawn in biro on her arm. He asks her with an intonation for her assessment and she replies something passably Greek and he is extremely happy, in fact he cannot contain himself. I am almost steaming with sweat while he sprints backwards up the hot sand to deal with café customers.

'What do you think, Hank?' she says and squeezes the meat of her arm to display the full intricacy, the hard work that's gone into it.

Igor in the animal house had puffy beige flesh with a greasy sheen below a colorless cap of shaved hair. You knew Igor recognized you because he gave you the fixed smile you'd give to someone with a maimed face. Henry slipped around the desk to the cupboards behind the reception. Without turning from his station Igor said, 'Those compounds are not for use, Dr Sinclair. Not without FDA approval.'

'I need some Eppendorfs, that's all.'

'If you flush those compounds down the sink you'll need to use some solvent.'

You continued to smile at Igor from your chair.

'He won't put them down the sink,' you said and you uncrossed your legs while behind Igor's back Henry plucked the tiny colored cones from a tube rack.

'You want an autograph?' you offered brightly, and Henry's face flashed approval for showing initiative. Panicking, Igor stuttered out a gloved left hand and you grabbed a Sharpie from the desk and wrote *Igor* with a star over the *I*.

You would tell Ray that you were OK before the Eppendorfs, but that was not true at all – you were however instantly charmed by their dinkiness and Fashion Week colors. Who wouldn't love tapering thimbles with connected stoppers in matching pastel plastic? In miniature? Henry held them to the light to see how much each contained (he took peach first, but there was mint, silver, lemon, lilac), then knocked the contents of each inch-long body into the stand-in bullets. The final one (lilac), he made a show of emptying into a bin for soiled animal bedding then he rummaged in the chest freezer against the wall. There was the squeak of a Styrofoam lid and dry ice plumed out. Henry carefully snap-locked a chip of solid CO_2 into the Eppendorf. He took you by the hand then and you felt instantly sharper, more outlined, with feelings more sure and fine, perfect conditions for memory-making. You've had to discuss this since at Sinead's request because memories that stuck in you deepest have involved risk, as if your mind gets ready to catch best when there's menace, when someone's lying, when there's no one to look after you.

'This. You will like.' He pulled you along by your hand.

Weighted by a dry ice chip, the toy-sized missile was launched point first down the corridor, where it landed at the join of the wall and floor. Suspense was anathema to you after growing up with your mother but right now it was an elixir, delicious and preserving, and so you could deal with, enjoy even, the stretching to breaking point that made you squeal when the CO_2 popped off the teeny lid of the Eppendorf. You kissed him then, and whatever he has claimed, there was a need in him that had your name on it. You kept your chest close to his to say, 'Come with me,' but he laughed in your face so you laughed too.

'Igor was a sweet guy,' you said out front.

'You've met him precisely once.'

You still clung to chances for Henry to see you as a good person.

'But I signed his latex glove. That's pretty intimate.'

'Igor's legs never leave each other from knee to crotch. *That's* intimate.'

*

Maybe you were OK until the Eppendorfs. Perhaps it was when you left for Nashville that the connection was lost. Sinead said you were self-harming in Nashville. Was she right? Sinead said this was because you were afraid of success.

The Tennessee heat got Catherine antsy about the kink in her hair and about time-wasting. 'Don't, Stop' was causing you huge problems when you tried to lay it down and Catherine insisted hourly that it was up to you alone to keep people believing in *Dwell Time*. You wanted Henry but a week of silence told you straight: Buddy G was not falling for love letters in Jive.

Catherine became compassionate in front of the doctor.

'Call him if it means you can work properly,' she said sagely while the doctor handed you some won't-touch-the-sides prescription. So you called him daily from a plastic-hooded payphone on a metal pole outside the studio and he finally answered on the roasting Sunday evening. The curved hood of the booth enclosed you; when he answered, relief flooded you at adrenal speed.

'I've been trying you everywhere,' you said.

'Not the lab. Never the lab.'

'How's my old pal Sandy?'

'Gregor's coming back. You are not high priority.'

'OK!' you submitted, laughing. You could take a joke.

You turned at the sound of a door pushed too far back on its hinges. Lucien emerged into the heat, launched a butt into the dust, made a face like a mental patient then motioned for you to come back inside. You turned back to the phone, hunched your shoulders around the receiver and whispered into your cupped hands, 'Are you missing me?' Your forehead hit the plastic hood hard while Lucien dry-humped you fast from behind. The receiver smashed into the plastic hood and you dropped the phone and scrambled to get it back while your face stuck to the hood and Lucien was grunting and laughing and the phone swung on its wire and crashed about the pole. You got to your knees, juggling the bucking receiver you grasped the phone mid-swing and you cried out, 'Henry! Are you there?' Lucien was still cackling and truly you hated him with your eyes but you started laughing real hard and couldn't stop to explain to Henry that you were only laughing because you knew being in the dirt and begging to be loved was so very terrible. You never heard him hang up.

Back from Nashville the apartment felt strange, you were a little skinnier than before, your knuckles were shinier, and you had a graze. If you were going to start accusing Henry of anything, you needed to be in really great shape. Boxer fit. Ballet fit. Today your foot was bruised and your first two fingers when together made a raft of yellow and you were shocked to think how nimble you had been before you met him.

'You look ill,' Henry said as you entered the living room. He didn't congratulate you on the news of the tour. Instead he sat you down.

'Do we have to do this now?' you asked but he was already leafing through the gig reviews in *The Croak*. You wanted to tell him that you could feel he was going to leave you but he was frozen stiff in the jet trails of your interruption. After a pause he began again.

'"Don't, Stop" is an initially erratic track . . . '

'That just means they think we're high.'

'I'll do it when you're less paranoid.'

He clapped together the pages of the magazine and you hugged your knees. You just wanted to be something Henry couldn't wash his hands of.

'Are they right? Are you relevant by accident?'

'No. I am not,' you said.

'You need a stand-in.'

Straining to detect tenderness in this prescription, you knew he was right, there was melancholy that whispered after opium that would be drowned out by whatever was in the metal bullet he drew out of the blue plastic overshoe. You felt obliged to admit 'Lucien already helped out,' and you thumbed toward the bathroom and smiled. Henry hurled the bullets hard from above his head into the trash can, where they clanked loud. Your pussy swelled instantly, whispering *he's jealous*. Henry must never, ever know the healing power of his attention so you grabbed a bullet out of the trash, opened it, tipped the contents onto your tongue, and despite what you had already taken you swallowed it. Henry would say the feeling is *purely associative*, but you felt instantly braver. Sinead knew it was from slim pickings that you cultivated Henry's actions into those of a jealous man, but neither of them knew that this manufactured jealousy was the only thing that got rid of your need for him for a while. There was a quick phone call to the lab and off he went leaving you high as a Georgia pine. You would survive.

Twenty-four hours later you had not come down when he turned up with the next season. Despite you telling her differently, Sinead insisted on calling *The Sopranos* a 'Band-Aid' box set. Sinead didn't know of course that in season two, after the harrowing sequence at The Bing, things changed for the worse. At a loss, your hands scuttled for comfort to the slim book that Henry kept on the arm of his chair and you pretended to read. When the episode finished you had asked Henry never to watch an episode without you. When would Henry realize all you wanted was you and him alone forever? After another trip to Nashville, at the door to your building you stopped to take his hand.

'Do I need to tour? What will you do? What if I die on tour?'

He smiled. 'Lucien not quite the savior you thought he was?'

There it was: a glimpse that Henry couldn't let go of you as easily as he thought, and, emboldened, you suggest he accompany you on tour.

Immediately you knew you'd goofed.

The next afternoon, he bustled around the apartment, while you stayed cross-legged with your shoulders up near your ears, pushing yourself up on the couch, trying to disentangle yourself from this wretchedness that he so easily snared you with.

'Why do you have to go out now?'

'Someone has to do Sandy.'

The last of Lucien's morning delivery was almost out of you, the remaining goodness falling away, glancing off jutting ledges, ready to spark a slender fuse to fury. You locked your arms tight, forcing one of your hands into the slitty guts of the couch and you pulled back sharply because something nicked the skin between your thumb and index finger and from the insides of the sofa, you plucked an unmarked CD.

'What's this?' you asked, holding it up high above your head.

'Yours if you want it,' he said, 'You can take it on tour.'

'You made this for me?' You hold it now by its edges.

When Sinead offered her opinion about the CD, you laughed in her face.

Looking back to it, Henry's smile had said *take it or leave it* and you had to decide: which did you want less, uncertainty or the truth? The hole circled Henry as culprit while a fine line of blood traced the webbing between your thumb and finger. You chose to smile back because with Henry, you would let things balance when they didn't and he continued getting ready with exaggerated enthusiasm for any aspect of his life that didn't involve you.

The tour bus was as big as a building. At the moment of the bus's ignition you felt you were about to lose everything and you dropped the CD stifling a scream. Henry looked at his watch then checked his phone. The time to beg was not now, but no chance to beg felt like being dead. Taking away begging as an option really was a bespoke cruelty of Henry's.

You could have scuffed the CD under the wheel of the tour bus but you picked it up and placed it back at your breast-bone, finger hooked through its hole, knuckle where your heart beat. 'Hold on,' he said into the phone and whispered to you, 'Remember, leave the pink until Burning Man.' He held out an overshoe filled with stand-ins, a blue synthetic rose flowering up through the anus of his clenched fist, but the phone was back at his ear. The air brakes on the tour bus hissed in predatory threat and you felt orphaned as he pushed you gently toward the bus with his fingertips until there was enough space between you for you to throw the CD at him close range. Instead, you dazzled him with sunlight reflected from the disc in your hand while he talked. You whispered close to him, 'See you at Burning Man,' and he gave you a brief uncomplicated kiss holding the bag of stand-ins up above you like the Liberty torch. You suddenly felt like such a dork in blue neon suede stilettos and a crop top before noon and once you'd ducked onto the bus, you felt naked in the halterneck in the cold AC beside Lucien, who was offering you a slack sideways hand. You watched Henry talking into the phone and he pirouetted on his heel. You forced Lucien back out with the bag of bullets. Henry immediately saw the pink one was missing and did the fine smile. Lucien slunk back on just as the tour bus doors closed with effort, one door struggling like scissor through gristle to get rid of the space between Henry and you.

The bus moved heavily onto the road, wheels peeling doggedly off the tarmac, and you saw Henry laughing freely, free of the friction of faking concern. Tracking him through the window, seeing his sky-blue shirt tight across his back and his mauve tie whipping up to caress his shoulder; the color of the tie matched the sideways eruptions of buddleia that sprang from cracks in the parking lot and bounced now between you and him. *This is not a joke* you wanted to shout and you knelt on the back seats until he disappeared and you became nothing more than the reflection of your eyes, marveling dully at the super-speed of their own small jerks, tears spilling at the flashing hedges and wires, returning desperately to their twins in the glass.

Catherine was driving to the first gig with her husband so Lucien offered you a fat beige line from his tray table. You grabbed the bag of blue corn chips from him when you saw the green warning triangle. 'Olestra still legal? Man, you'll shit yourself by Buffalo if you eat those. Don't forget, I was their brand girl.' You point out the small capitals on the pack: MAY CAUSE ANAL SEEPAGE. He gave you another line. Whatever it was rolled your heartbreak in a rug.

The first song on the CD was in French and you pressed your pussy down into the seat but its aptness had instantly fucked with your high. It gave you a seriously seductive insight into what he thought of you – you had no idea Henry's French was this good. You had to remove the headphones. Lucien crunched his blue chips extra loud while breathing hard through his nose. With his own earphones on, he stared at you, softly disengaged. The killer move by Henry was that he had left no clue to artists. No titles to songs. As though a title would stop the goodness from these songs from getting into your bloodstream as quick. The AC made the blue-yellow heat outside suspicious. You held your throat and smiled a little through the tinted window at how coy he had turned out to be.

Without a playlist there was absolutely no preparation for how deep this plunged you into his motives. Lucien gestured to some beers. You asked for another line saying, 'Henry says that shame is the emotion that encourages us to do our best but guess what? A kid isn't built for shame.' He slid the cup of the headphones from ear to cheek, then he slid it back again. As each track began you felt like you were digging emeralds out of horseshit saying things to Lucien urgently like, 'The only content worth dealing with is timeless and tragic.' You listened to more: there was a concerted peace in the luxury of pulling apart and putting together the coded messages which could shock at first but would then heal as the meaning clarified. Truthfully, the only artist of the twelve tracks you had instantly recognized was a lesbian from Ohio. It was further into blues than you had comfortably gone before but Henry knew your tastes better than you did and people like Lucien would not understand that thrill. How much time had he thought about you? In a bliss of possibility, you leaned back into your seat – these layered imaginings were the closest thing you had to prayer. Because of these songs, you were satisfied to call off the search for what was so wrong between you and it made you pine for Henry. You fell asleep hovering in a future with him.

The rest of the band was at a movie when you arrived in Buffalo. You didn't want Catherine to lecture about drugs so you said you were upset about Henry. She argued with her husband Max, a short man with the cowardly hunch of a hyena, while you scurried up to your hotel room so you could slowly untangle the uncertain interpretations from the certain and so you wouldn't have to speak to anyone until after the set. Catherine, Lucien and Max kissed you on both cheeks once offstage because you, sweating into your pale pink lederhosen, had been everything to all of them. Up on stage is the one place you don't feel like you are lying. 'Whatever star means I'm ready for it!' you said to Catherine. Pretending to be someone else is the only time you don't feel a fraud.

'Stop that!' she said. She hated Janis Joplin. Max chuckled while hanging awkwardly at the rim of your group hug. His face was close to yours and you apologized. Ray would ask you in Paris, 'Did you ever think to ask yourself what you should feel so sorry for?'

Next day, as soon as the bus set off for Boston you put in your headphones. Every lyric's lesson sat waiting in the Discman. After only 48 hours without stand-ins, you had noticed a surge of cruel energy that was an early signal that sleeping could become a problem. Daytime pot left you wired and paranoid. You started to write thoughts on track choices, soon realizing that writing was great at showing what you didn't mean. You chose titles and ranked them, deciding what a title was responsible for, its duty.

1 You Maybe Ma Baby
2 Cheroot Girl (Beware the)
3 Crazy Lover

Into Massachusetts, it hit you: the religious track was clearly about never being able to be together despite the right connections. 'He doesn't know it,' you mouthed loudly to Lucien. 'He's a seeker!' The fantasy of your connection intensified and thrummed just beyond your reach.

In a backwater lunch-stop with a town pump and a tobacconist, you actually bought cheroots. 'Cheroot Girl' had now become your favorite track. 'Straight Out of Nowhere' lyrics were still achingly ambiguous but showed that he had gauged you with a surprising sensitivity, making you pine for him at a level you could never have foreseen. Such strong wants caused problems and ten gigs in fifteen nights meant that you were running into not enough food territory. Somewhere around Chicago, writing responses to the tracks had to stop and Catherine warned Lucien to cut back on both weed and blow but they didn't understand that one track placed after another was not random, the tracks spoke to each other! You blamed those two for ruining all the unspoken good that Henry had done by placing the tracks in this order. How dare you tether things that should free-float? When Henry pulled the phone off your wall, when he turned up bleeding with his possessions in a single black garbage sack, you need never have been afraid. He would appear at Black Rock and this was his way of getting you ready for it. You began sleeping with the pink under your pillow.

The switch back to blow made being with people unbearable; Lucien and Catherine and their nonstop whispering. Anticipating all the shit there was to eat on the next day of the tour made you anxious, Catherine knew that. Somewhere in the Midwest, you turned your back on solids altogether. You longed to show your track notes to Henry instead of hitting college towns but also swore that you would never ask Henry how he chose each one. Faced only with saltine crackers and canned chicken noodle soup you threatened to strangle a waitress who claimed you had spat at her, forcing Catherine to explain that this was what happened when your salt appetite went up. Lucien thought a weed/acid combo might be medicinal and for a day or two you were able to dig into fry mountains and waffle slabs, eating every scrap without enjoying a mouthful. In your room in Oregon, you got in the bath, drank gin fast on an empty stomach then puked. Cath called the doctor but your bloods were OK. Saltine crackers and Kleenex would now do fine if it meant you'd look good when you hit Black Rock and because there wasn't long left, Lucien managed to smuggle you a couple of Berkeley microdots just in time for the Fillmore. You were high as an iguana in the toilet as the bus entered the Bay area.

You had stopped at a gas station because you told the driver you'd fucking *had enough* of trying to shit while swaying. In the gas station bathroom, you went into a cubicle and locked the door but there was no actual toilet, only cleaning products and a low sink, then the mop fell on you and bottles rolled. You figured the only choice you had was to piss in the janitor's sneaker and you stopped when the liquid bulged at the mouth of the shoe. When the driver broke you out he accused you of acting like a jerk while you squatted among the detergents. A couple of hours after, Lucien was on stage at the Fillmore, messing with your skirt so you punched him. Who knew you'd pulled your skirt through your panties? They say the gig was the best yet. Sinead said your ambition was commensurate with how desperate you were to be loved.

Catherine chose your Black Rock outfit with you in a consignment store in the Haight called Pedro's with items arranged on hangers by color; it was a spandex aquamarine jumpsuit with a zipper for your final gig. The label was faded though the spandex seemed in good shape. When you asked the store girl what size it was and she said, 'You need to be confident, that's all,' Catherine caught you by the shoulders, pretending your threat to headbutt the assistant was a joke.

Before getting on stage at Black Rock, you could hear the vast desert night filling up with sound. There were a couple of times that night that you imagined his voice. You stared at the pink and played out in your mind seeing Henry front and center. You knew that for Henry to be there, you had to know he was going to be there and imagined clearing the stage in one electrified leap to get to him where, in your arms, he could finally experience the true value of his surrender to you. With him in your jaws you could drag your grisly property across the flat desert and into the dark ravines above which the mountains rang, solidly pretending not to know each other.

DONUT

The woman in the flour sack finally appears through the beaded curtain, her shoulders only as wide as twelve or thirteen of those fronds. She cocks her head and stares at your scarf instead of your face and this makes you put your hand to it. You chose *Corail* for today, right? Does she know about Black Rock?

Flour Sack's dark scalp makes the white hair pale pink, and to escape that, you peer into the hot lunch dishes warming in the bains-marie. She cannot stop you from being friendly and you smile at the bubbling food.

'You know when choosing actually hurts?' you say to her, via the lunches. Gigi runs in, gives an enthusiastic 'Yassas', bounces on the spot behind the counter, which you can see Flour Sack does not enjoy. You could never love a man with buck teeth.

'I'm just looking,' you say to him.

'Just looking,' you say to her.

He stops pogoing, then waits in silence as if she will give him instruction, but they shout at him from the beach and he sets off fast back over the sand. Flour Sack mutters something to the sweating hot lunches, rearranges the spoons that you have touched. There's a pause that pulls a loud *gah!* out of you and you waggle your hands over each of the options.

'What's the sauce on this one?' you say to her, looking up but she has disappeared. After a long time, you shout 'hello there!' like some lame pirate then you hear bare feet on the concrete terrace. From separate entrances, they both flop in at once and are annoyed to see each other.

'The sauce on this one?' You point then apologize. They whisper. He shrugs.

'Goats' flesh,' she says with contempt.

You need to let her know that it is her attitude that is going to force you to make the wrong choice.

'Any flesh in this one?' You sound sunny and you choose by pointing though you haven't yet made the decision.

Handyman carries the plate on a tray to the cash register and you fully expect him to realize that this is not what you really want, that if he cared anything at all about you he would choose for you. Instead, handing you your lunch, he takes the money, puts it in the register, grins at you and sprints back to the game. Really and truly, you have no choice. Jesus Christ. You feel like Hypno Ray, whose myth says that while on tour in Japan in the 80s he had roadies warm his bottled water so it didn't hurt his teeth.

Flour Sack is about to leave and you shout, 'I don't want *this*!'

It sounds so bad that you begin to explain, knowing your explanations will make her hate you even more.

'I wanted it *in theory*, if you know what I mean.'

'GIGI!' She shouts it loud and you grit your teeth because of how furious and foreign she sounds. You look out of the arch nervously because if Henry thinks you are bugging the staff he will kill you. Gigi comes in and you choose the goats' flesh this time, much too quickly, and when he has put it on the plate you say 'Stop!' and tell him in whispers that the woman is angry and is rushing you but he doesn't understand your message. 'Vegetarian!' you say.

'What theory?' she says to Gigi, appearing like a hazelnut specter. His smile endures as he takes it from you and he slides it back into the steel tray and he is already trotting out over the sand when you discover that this is not what you want to happen either and you run to the arch and shout 'Sorry!' to Gigi, then 'Sorry!' to Henry, who doesn't hear you because he is clapping wildly for the finest serve of the match.

This failure sets the afternoon on a treacherous course, and you go back out to the beach with the feeling that the noon sun is definitely much more upsetting than its 11.30 self.

'So what's for lunch?' He is angry teacher: you are student willfully flunking tests. You want to warn him that his beloved Helman wrote that his regrets are all failures of kindness. The light is more demanding, harsher and much more of an attack than when you left. You lose your verve and switch points to ReThink. You sit on the sand next to him and he brushes stray sand onto your towel from his. You are prepared to pretend one last time that he hasn't been ignoring you.

'OK, so there are stuffed peppers and tomatoes with rice – you know, the rice already mixed with onions, garlic and parsley I think, maybe dill. I tried to get in and smell it but stick lady shut me down. I told her I'm just smelling it and she goes "Don't smelling it", like a fucking executioner.'

'Maybe she doesn't like her boyfriend drawing on other women's bodies.'

'Oh my God, that is not her partner!'

'Of course it is,' says Henry with a premium brutality that shocks you, and, looking back, you probably segued to the food for your own sake.

'Maybe there's peppermint in the rice or spearmint in there, not sure of the difference here, anyhoo it's oven-baked cause I saw her take it out and it's crunchy on top – one edge slightly burned – and it comes with feta cheese and Greek yogurt. Don't have to mention there's the Greek salad – tomatoes, cucumbers, peppers, onions, feta cheese, with lots of beautiful green extra virgin olive oil and the gas-can oregano. And then *on its own* there's feta cheese sprinkled with olive oil and oregano. A slab. And then there's the Ya-Ya special, you know, my granny's green peas with carrots and potatoes, cooked in the amazing tomato sauce with onions and shitloads of dill, also with feta. I ate pounds of it as a kid.'

'My God!'

'What?'

'You!'

'Me what?'

'Unbelievable.'

'And the eggplant that's baked so when you press it with a fork it melts in with the roasted garlic, so good with lots of chopped parsley and olive oil. On these small plates out front they have fried zucchini served with tzatziki, you know, with grated cucumber, garlic, olive oil, vinegar and lots of dill, then there's the breakfast crowd leftovers, warm bread with fresh butter and wildflower honey but also the Greek pie: the crunchy Greek cheese pie . . . '

'My God, the hunger!'

'You asked me what there was and I'm telling you.'

'And you didn't see it?'

'See what?'

'The donut.'

You try to get a match between what is going on and what you think is happening. You ReThink. When happenings start to layer, the video begins in your head and you won't be able shut it down.

'Should I go back?' You worry about how wrong his choice of lunch is going to be and what will happen then.

'OK, you go over there!' And you push his chest with both hands. 'I didn't check out the cabinet on the left.' Maybe you're shouting.

'The enemy . . . '

'Don't Henry . . . ' you plead.

' . . . of love . . . '

'I said *shut up!*'

' . . . is anxiety.'

He leaves and back under the shelter, the paranoia shears off you in sheets: he'll be telling the staff about how he calls it The Recession, referring to you as if he's presenting you to a colleague, which makes you want to puke hot goat in his face. The Blaming caught fire as soon as he connected you to it. Of course he cares about you, he came here with you, didn't he? Wanted you to get away from all of that. The video was a mistake. No one's fault. Quiet under your sheet, just above yourself, you do not notice his return but after a minute he says through the flap:

'Is this blessed ignorance or unbearable suffering?'

It is hard for you not to talk. You are shocked that this is not the bottom after all and your mood takes a further dive to thicker, darker waters and you gird your teeth against each other wishing they'd shatter. Your mother was a crammer, a stuffer, a tamper and a silencer. The thought of carbohydrates traumatizes you and he knows you feel as phobic of starch as you do of vomit. Food and mood can be sliced clean through with a sharp white line. You sit up. If you had even the smallest idea of how he felt, you would push off him like a swimming pool wall.

'Damn!' he says, hovering.

'What?'

'I forgot your donut.'

*

A guy pulled a dog's jaws too far apart on your lot and your mother knocked him out with a stone-hard cabbage, even though it was her dog that had woken him up and her bed that he had leaped from. Was this the mother that cares and protects? There were always men in the house. What did she need a cabbage for?

He doesn't notice you have lifted the flap. What he really cares about right now is how well these guys play volleyball. You look at the Greeks for anchorage but are grossed out by their nudity and by the very idea that the prize of a dumb rice pudding means so much to them. Henry turns back to his paper, reading aloud for your benefit: '"The brain in no way anticipates the possibilities of its own damages." If you let these wants come back full force you are going to get hurt. I can help you.'

Henry, the sight of him, makes you fucking starving. Handyman should try looking somewhere else for five seconds. You go back under the shelter. You are sincerely and absolutely not high anymore and it is like holding up the sky with your hands. What the fuck is rice pudding anyway?

You look at the blondes among the Greeks. You have to believe in what you imagine because you've come this far. One of the Austrians is sitting out and playing a scuffed orange guitar and because of the sound of strings, you get flooded with rebound chemicals so strong and full of glory that it is all you can do to stop yourself from running over and snatching it out of his hands, telling strangers en route about the high points of the tour, even being in the fire, what came to you were snatches about the divinity of counterpoint. Hope can take you over.

He's holding back because he wants you to be the person he knows you can be.

Remembering you are a lens for him, you touch his shoulder, this time with the tips of the fingers of one hand.

'I think I have a new song.'

He taps the page with his pen. 'Activation of areas involved in cocaine addiction may help explain the obsessive behaviors associated with rejection in love.'

'Is it the shrimp?'

'Hey, an idea! Why don't you eat it?'

Is he angry because the shrimp still hasn't come off your arm? You don't like it when the questions pile up. You see one through the other. None of them are themselves. After you signed a T-shirt for the cabin crew, didn't he put his arm round you on a plane? In public? This change since arriving, is it you or him? He is making you pay for something but you don't know what. Henry doesn't want to talk about why chords shouldn't form the basis of modern pop anymore, or get into why more songwriters can't experiment with harmonic features. Whenever you feel desperate enough to explain what you were trying to do in the video, he doesn't say anything and silence from Henry makes you question whatever you are trying to convince him of. Oh he will say that he never saw you as fitting blah blah but it would definitely be a lie. You'll frustrate him with your truth and he'll say you should stay off the blow or get back on it; at least then you'll have the stamina to build a proper argument. Otherwise this is lazy rhetoric and that if there's one thing he hates it's brainwashing by the weak-willed. When the fire's puttering out at dawn and you address it with Full Focus, you know, you know without question that it's not him that brings you down. It's you.

You stretch your arms above your head and the sand is already hot.

'You can make us famous with BirdBoy.'

He wags his pen impatiently above his notebook.

'So you think that's the end of your singing career?'

'I showed you the money, Buddy G. I'm done.'

'I am only interested in people with real ambition to further their careers.'

'*You* are only interested in people you can impress.'

'It's impossible to trust an artist who says their intentions are otherwise.'

You feel a strong swell of your own power. He wards you off.

'Oh! I should have recognized what this was with the description of the food,' he says. 'The Recession continues. Goodbye reason!'

He makes to get up. He cares all right and this tiny push your way is all it takes to show you that your power need not be his weakness. You can still come out of this with what Ma called bones of copper. Invisibly, you get giant. You are a whale with a thousand teeth. You are a thick arrow on a strong bow and now you know he senses it.

So you ask Henry if he can tell how great you feel.

He tells you that staying clean is the hard part.

You say it's hot standing here without the sheet and that you're going to get a drink and can he hustle and decide what he wants.

You want Henry's eyes on your ass, not yours Handyman.

Henry says so that's why you didn't wash it off.

You say you're going to get a drink.

He says if you mean a beer say a beer.

You shout over your shoulder that this sand is hotter than you think. Everyone loves a running man. To the woman inside the café you say, 'Was it always this light in here?'

You look at the ceiling fan.

You leave the café, go back to the beach and give him his drink.

He says please could you stop yawning.

You say you're not hungry if that's what he's getting at.

He says let's see how long that lasts.

There's a faint flashing in your vision and you feel like singing opera. Must you be conscious of everything? How can you be addicted to regret when regret works *against* your strong desires to do something?

Drink your drink, he says. I'm going for my swim.

You don't say *you can't swim* but you do chuck a spear of anger at Handyman as Henry trails through the white reaches of the sea foam out of the tiny bay and further round the coast toward the spit. You are surprised to see your beer bottle already empty in your hand when you suddenly notice he hasn't taken the notebook: after all, he only wears the shorts to carry this. You wait and wait for him to turn back for it but he rounds the bay onto the spit.

It's a leather-bound book the color of claret with a mint-green ribbon. You know you are doing something you shouldn't. Nothing good will come of this. You turn the first page trying to blink away the flashing in your vision but the words rise up in a recognizable hum. The handwriting seems to be eager to tell you a tale you don't want to know about him. Not the words but the writing itself. Not the writing, the voice. A warning that you connect with him turning up at your apartment when you bathed his foot with a kitchen towel and relieved him of the garbage sack. Inside, a picture of himself in Africa, the glass frame clumsily wrapped in shirts.

'This all you own?'

'I'll go back when Jimp's not there.'

'You as a baby?' A picture of little Henry and you stared greedily, as if you have more chance of knowing him from the picture than from the man. 'How old?' you asked.

'Two, in Nigeria. Born there.'

The picture showed Henry crouching with a straight back, a sullen little snot in long grass, two sets of black legs, one thin, one fat, standing sentry on either side.

'You're a fake! You're no more British than I am.'

He tried to ignore the victory. There was a blank space around the faded sepia picture, at the bottom was some writing bleached also to a light brown: *Henry, ahead from the beginning.* The handwriting is the same here in the book. You close it. You look over to the spit and into the sky, where a lost cloud looks worried about where it might find more like itself.

He won't be gone for long. At first you leaf through thinking, what kind of a man brings a copy of *Love as Temporary Brain Damage* to a beach volleyball game? but you get into the rest quickly and read some notes in diagram form. You are convinced that it's OK: taking notes on love as a concept is not just appropriate but really very him. Very you. You continue, you are not mentioned but you find yourself answering questions from the book. You do assert yourself, you don't abase yourself. *Who* loves in weakness? From other notes, you see that whatever he is working on means more to him because it's a springboard away from Frank and from Gregor. You read *Woman mutilated, insufficient unto herself* knowing it's at a conceptual level that he deals with this.

You scan the horizon then flick back a few pages, start at the more conventionally set-out notes and buck against your bestial desire to steal the whole fucking thing, devour it like a jackal up in the scrubland. You spot what seem like little reviews by Henry, observations from gigs he's been at, what crowds think of you and even without the comedown, you feel your heart double in size, there are reviews you have never seen, and then you see what looks like a verse or a song. They aren't your lyrics. You make a mental note of the initials HM. There is a quote that has a page to itself: *Her reality changes as quickly and absolutely as is necessary to reinforce her motive and can represent the opposite of what was just a second ago a certainty.* The accuracy makes it a medicine. He is fascinated by you.

Then there are what look like headings (Black Rock/ LONGING FOR LONGING: An Addiction to Regret?) or chapter titles crossed out but you don't have the nerve or the time, more observations then numbers and tallies for pages. Strongly underlined is IGNORE TIL DAY 7 and EMOTIONS UNRELIABLE IN THIS PHASE. Silly doctor, you smile. There's a page headed MYOPIA FOR FUTURE CONSEQUENCES but these opinions, barbed by being both intimate and distant, are not Henry's – you have seen both FL and GP in the margins. A song then, or at least something versed, you read only two lines because you don't dare look at who you might have found: the Henry with half a beard cuz you called him over; Henry in the first days of the *Zoot*; Henry choosing the ciphers of the CD he made just for you and a profound triangulation goes on way below you. Or is it above?

When you look up again, the speck of his paleness is blurring the horizon. Perhaps it's the shock that dared you to remove the song page. With the sheet in your bikini, you smooth your finger down the ribbon against the last clean page of the notebook and you place the whole thing back in its indent in the sand.

Soon he is standing above your towel, placing the shadow of his head over yours. You stay still while he drips into your face. You want him to confirm that there is some good in what you have discovered.

'Go to the cafeteria. Confront the new object of your desire.'

The swim must have gone badly.

'What object? I have no desire.'

He stands with his legs spread over you and shakes his hair, saying 'Your donut awaits.'

You scud your leg into the beach beside your towel, raising a fan of sand that sticks to his wet back. He joins his hands in fake kung fu prayer and bows:

'Ah so! IMPENDING DOOM OF WOMANLY LOVE!'

You feel lightheaded. He crouches closer to you.

'You are already invested in your trajectory. Don't fight it.'

He rubs his hair vigorously and lays himself down on the larger towel to dry.

'What did I take in Black Rock?' you ask him without fear.

He closes his eyes and you feel his smugness, his unbreakable self-belief and trust that he can say anything he likes. He still cannot swim, you think to yourself.

'You will always be a slave to your urges,' he says. 'Know how I know?'

He smooths his towel. Your eyes are stinging.

'You put sandwiches too far into your mouth before biting.'

'And you are a matte black fucking helicopter about to crash.'

He raises himself onto his elbows to warn you:

'Love does not always have to be about mortal danger.'

'I do not love you.'

'Just donuts,' he says, laying back down.

You watch yourself as you spit in his hair. You should only really ever stamp on an insect or a snake and spitting has no place outside of a sidewalk fight but something turns you and you kick him back to the ground at the shoulder with one boot, then make to crush his groin with the other but connect with his bony white hip as he turns to protect himself, a hint of gray appearing on the skin immediately. You are deaf from the detonation in your chest and no you weren't physically provoked yet you feel the bright astonishment of the attacked.

The deafness subsides and there's the echo of the boom in your chest and the boom powers the walk you take over the sand. Turns out that when violence is inevitable then you finally feel alive. Danger alone fuels your flight from need. A burst of guard chemicals makes you invincible and stops the sand from burning your feet. Inside, your heart is asking your belly *is this pride? why did we do that? are you scared? I still can't see*, your chest says, *but I know it's fucking serious*, and whether it is good or bad, it quivers ready to warn other important parts of you.

When you finally get back to the café, it is so blissfully cool inside. Comedowns know a chance of euphoria when they see one; an opportunist, the sky floats on its own again. Henry stands, legs apart, watching them, so you haven't hurt him so terribly. After a violent altercation during which you did not die you want to revisit what has happened. In the wavy aftershock you wait for color to return, the power of assessment has left you for a second, like when they told you the results of the test, way too late, and you fainted right after noticing the inside of your shirtsleeves were grubby as hell. I've been sick for weeks, you said to the nurse as you fell. Henry's the only one you told.

Out there, they are still playing volleyball and you look on through the arch, your mouth crammed full of donut. You try to swallow.

'Getting high before a show is not cool.'

'So go tell Catherine.'

Lucien pauses then asks, 'You want a repeat of The Fillmore?'

On stage in San Francisco, you had punched Lucien because he was trying to grab your ass with both hands. Who knew that your grasshopper-green ice skater skirt was all the way tucked through your underwear when it felt like the hem was right where it should have been? What the hell were you supposed to think was going on?

The possibility that Henry was out there tonight must be kept open and you looked out from your hiding place into the crowd and you heard Lucien approach but keep his distance. Funny how hope can easily light up hate. Hate to you feels a lot like disappointment. Please don't start telling me that there is nowhere to smoke in the desert, Lucien you skinny stand-up slug.

Catherine as always was panicking. She has an idea you can't cope with open spaces so of course she is no help. The crowd is chanting your name loud and then you feel it as a stab or a bite: the announcement of his absence. And in a need to tip this pain straight out of your hands, you turn to the crowd to blame them because if *they* listen to you, Henry must turn away; it is the physics of how you fit in. Only now can you see, math messes with what you want to believe in so you will blame the crowd for as long as you can. You hear him say Blame minus truth really burns, but it does not mean he is there. You can't bear to look at the crowd after that and when you turn from the truth, it floats wherever your eyes go, an afterimage, white against the red floor of the wilderness, the blue-smudged distance. You can't shake it. You should not have picked *The Sopranos*. You should never have left him alone because it gave him all the space he needed to forget you and you can think of nothing but the relish of freedom that his pirouette displayed. The bus hadn't even left the parking lot.

You are forced now to know that you gave Henry your rights because *you didn't want them*. Therefore, if Henry doesn't see you seeing this, you don't see this. If he is not here to interpret for you then you are over, fallen, filming the floor. But when exactly did you go? You search the faces, your gaze travels across rows upon rows shouting 'Astrid' then it pulls back from the eerie space of distance to the edge of the crowd where the heads and faces become froth. You have waited and Henry has not come: he is not here and you will have to keep your stupid bucket-of-mud heart swinging for this last night of the tour and to do this you fasten your hand tight around the pink, you bring it into your chest and you unscrew it.

'Catherine won't be happy,' said Lucien, standing beside you like a traffic cop.

'They are here for me.'

This crowd is not going to disappear. Let the singing turn to tongues, you think. You want this longing out of your hands but where to put it? You swallow all of the pink in front of Lucien, dinking the upended mouth of the container back and forth against the fine edges of your teeth, rattling it at the end making an *ahhh* noise, curling your tongue into a tube while it sizzles at the back near your throat where nothing ever touches. Man! It burned but you swallow it up good, and when it's gone, it's depressingly good to know that all decision went down with it and knowing that is all you need to keep going. You outright hope it is doing damage, says your face. Lucien shakes his lizard head.

There is no deciding now and that is how it is. Soon enough, there will be no more easy choices at all and that is a phantom tragedy that escapes these two eyes and breathes only into the future. You take Lucien's offering for balance, do both lines: that should give the pink force and scope. Only one song in, go figure, you feel the edges of how you are to be changed, separate.

Now knowing no
and *that* is
Feelings, meet Thoughts.
Feelings in the gut
its head. I
her way. I
that sound like
impersonate a singer.

longer recognizes me
how it is.
Thoughts punches
then stomps on
watch her go
can make noises
words. She can
Let's see her.

From beside the stage, Sluggo twizzles his finger at the floor and her body does what it is told and she is facing them again. Is it the law to face the audience when she has a microphone? Listen to that. Their noise is the music for her. The faces are the faces of people she doesn't know who are saying the same words that she is going to. Fake it, everyone, don't hesitate. If they all fake it it's true. She enters into it, why not? You know, so the shapes are the same for all of them. So they all get it. *That* must be what is meant by safety – faces that she hasn't seen before and yet are saying the same things as she is. She thinks *they don't like me* but when it's just the words without their roots making a mess into her, it means she can rip right through this and go even faster and smoother. Wow, she is sweating and the sweat is soaking her jumpsuit around the crotch and they point at it; maybe because the color down there is not the same as up above. The color bleeds, royal to mid- to sky blue, lightening toward her knees and if you want to take a look at her face right now it says relief, that's better. She stops singing because they can't believe it and when she crouches she pulls the elastic into a point and a cupful of air bounces against her mound as she lets go. She's right on the edge of the stage and she pulls her elasticated crotch further into a squat blue glitter cone and when she lets go this time it spatters first then puffs back: the elastic shivers back to her cunt. Do it again, just to watch it happen. A guitarist twangs, it feels the right thing. They shout what could be warnings but just as correctly they could be hopes and wishes. She looks back out at them as much as to say *did you see that?* Dance for them! Dance again! That's what they want. The sun is going down on these people, the elastic can't stop it and these people who are a lot more people, more people than she can see, are telling her to come here. Over here! they say. No one tells her not to go. She can leave the stage. Lucien says no! But she knows her body can say she is going. She walks out into them, on top of them, and she stands on their hands and their heads, and faces if their heads are back. *Behold!* they say with their necks, throats like snake bellies join to make a path, her steps are working like they do when she walks up the wall and she moves forward and she don't go down. She escapes above them, her heels are solid cupped in palms and she peels the jumpsuit from her body. She is bare to the waist and she leans forward because what they have been trying to tell her is that this must be the sea because she has to be

at the prow of their boat. *Don't confuse her* some of them say
with their arms. Put her to the floor and let her run through
a trench of them in the dust and they do this and they part
and she sees (she gets it, she's got it!) that without them she
can sprint fast and clean in bare feet and she imagines the
arms of that jumpsuit fill up with air and hinge stiff behind
her. The sea is red and she is down with it. This heat makes
her stay down there and the heads and shoulders are the
roiling boil and she suddenly is the stone in their soup. She
clings to calves. Heavy. Get her up. Her blue sleeves dangle,
her chest is bare, she is no longer moving forward very fast.
She's not cooler up here above them. Her legs are apart and
they have her tight round the ankles and she stands making
a firm triangle of noise. The noise never flares up past her
knees. It shoots toward the mountains from her crotch like a
pussy-laser. Is that where she left him? No one is telling her
what to do and she needs nothing. She looks down to see how
some of them have only grown so far. That is so neat. Lucien
is here with them, shouting, waving what he wants her to
do and she can hear him above the words that are coming
up from the crowd she is walking on but she turns on him
because what there is to care about is not here in Black Rock
and the names that remain choke under these feet and the
inescapable dust. She steps on some faces that say they are
laughing and faces that say they are upset and faces that say
they are surprised. A shoulder disappears as she steps on it
(Feel Jesus) and she drops down and a man with a face that
says I'm sick catches her and pushes her back on top of heads
with his hand hooked under her crotch, his thumb in her ass
but for the elastic. He fully wipes his hand on her leg and she
thinks whoever this is happening to should be mad but without
despair or encouragement she becomes free to go and go. It's
obvious with any processes, coming, going, and she sees hope

or despair but she doesn't know what to do with them and so it doesn't matter. She has never been free before and that makes this the place: it could not be anywhere else and she could not be with anyone else. You guys! You guys make the floor come under her feet and you walk with her and you touch her and you pull down her outfit and she steps out of it and you lift her again and she sees a three-story head between her and the mountains and below it black ribs and far through them the terracotta mountain gone gray. Two hands hold and squeeze her tits and there are whispers that there are fires. You have arrived. You part to show her. One fire is dead orange. Flat. The kind of orange forever. Nothing holding her. She doesn't laugh but she could do that if someone reminded her of how that is different from singing and talking. You shout to her over a low glowing mound. It is obvious that she must get to them. Her face gets touched and two hands hold her neck and her feet leave the floor. This is what she does. She hangs. In your hands. About her, all this freedom. A face rubs round the scarf and breathes through it into her hair, an animal's face comes through. It's breaking hers and it won't be mended. Animal faces are easy she tells everyone who can hear and see her and she walks in through the orange and it's all suddenly fall and give up and she suddenly falls and gives up. Flames finally tell her again what it was she wanted. Flames are good at telling her what she wants. That's easy! She can do that. She's not even in and you stop her. Someone comes through and pulls her up and out horribly. In a tin man's funnel hat she sees that silk burns quick in the desert.

And now I wish my heart was still in it because I'm on fire and the smell of my hair dashes from mountain to mountain. Don't fucking pull me out. People pat my head with planky hands. I get it as they pull me out. But I can't smoke! That's me. I'm not to own. Cold or Hot – we won't do either. Regret and relief are once again the names of paint colors.

My scarf stays in and burns for me.
   My hair crisps away to red dust and I watch it clapped off in a stranger's hands.
   People scream but they don't know what's happening.
   'It's a hairpiece!'
   I feel my
   crotch is hot
   and still wet
   when I'm out
   of the fucking
   words.
   I said words,
   I meant fire.

DESPOTIKO

I'm glad she's finally done something unforgivable. As I've told her before, non-fiction also needs a narrative, which is exactly why I need to document <u>everything</u> from here on in.

I look through my notebook boldly now. Openly! This is permission to devote myself to caring about this. It's open wide for me to write *SPITTING: LAST STRAW,* but my arrow goes through the page because this pen isn't mine, it's far too sharp for how I write. And now see what's happened? The pages are loose and her spit has soaked through the ink and in the scuffle that YOU have pretended not to see, some pages are actually coming free of the spine.

I want to catch YOUR eye and YOUR eye is on HER suede-covered arse, HER skinny legs grinding booted heels to get HER up the beach. If there were any chance to tell YOU what I plan to do, I would. YOU don't shake everyone's hand like YOU did mine.

Copying text will slow breathing:

Eye movements are described as ballistic because once an eye movement is initiated it cannot be stopped until it reaches its destination. This means that there must be some conception of what is outside the centre of the gaze before a movement of the eye is initiated.

Which means YOU have watched arses and their movement before and that is why YOU are an expert. I look at YOU but of course YOU are still tailing HER. Well, eyes right mate, because that deceptively scrawny leg just powered a vicious attack. This is what YOU'll be getting into. The pages jag at a slant from the spine of the book before coming free. I want to show YOU what your little mascot is capable of.

First I must find a less vicious pen. I am not the attacker, I am the attacked. I breathe deeply, circling and boxing in more evidence:

In eye-tracking experiments, attentional capture may be an endogenous process, in which participants actively control how they allocate attention in order to achieve a goal (Ruz, 2002) or may be exogenous, whereby participants allocate their attention to stimuli unintentionally.

YOU want me to believe that YOU are completely unaware that SHE stamped on ME and spat in MY face. I am going to let YOU know in no uncertain terms that this humility YOU see in HER is a fucking ruse. SHE uses it to create a greater distance between what <u>PEOPLE</u> expect and what SHE really is. SHE is not the one you need at the party. SHE gave herself to me 100%. You know what that's worth?

I realise that drawing an arrow is not the right symbol here but it will hold place for now and I will explain later.

(ARROW) *Consequences are what shape future behaviours. They need to be planned carefully – let her know once she is calm. This is response disinhibition at its very best (e.g. sample for Gregor). Talk about: the movement, dance and violence / certainty and violence, movement extremity / action speed as predictor of impulsivity? Extreme violence special case?*

I can use this; this out of everything can really be leaned on / really be banked for the book. Ballast for the book. An explosion makes you keep your distance, is what I have been waiting for. Inevitable with her history. Impossible to say whether it was brought about.

Can decisions be over-made? Must decisions be binary?

CLASSIC DAY 4 – <u>Title?</u> When I say to her that 'Impulsivity is the tendency to act prematurely without foresight' (Jimp to find ref), THIS is what I mean. Talk to Greg about the possibility of a glutamatergic kickback from the contrasting high dose before abstinence. Now you and others will understand exactly what Day 4 looks like from a professional's angle.

I know the island is called Despotiko and I found that out without any help from her. Whatever that island was called I can get to it on my own.

I am pretending to write now but, if you fools don't want to make enemies, you need to keep that volleyball on the court. Don't expect me to pass the ball back to you and don't you dare look at me as if it's my duty. I wonder if it's YOU or the dwarf who's drawn a face on it – stoned-looking eyes, a sharp angle for the nose, a spliff drawn as if held by gap in teeth. Looks simple but hard to draw so was probably YOU. Closer and there are elements that are more than reminiscent of the prawn.

(ARROW) *What would you draw on me? Geometric/heraldic? Not Celtic.*

Here is their ball again. Now it's on purpose. I won't look at it. I am not uncrossing my legs. Keep chattering chimps. Yes, leave it there all day. OK don't come for it. I'm not moving. YOU are doing an impression of the dwarf, his return gone wrong, on your knees crossing your eyes and despite the new dull pain in my hip, I find this funny and charming because I imagine it is for my benefit. Aha, YOU are a coward, you've sent the dwarf for the ball. Well run, run faster little legs! I am a writer not some ballboy and this is what I do, I write.

(ARROW) *NB: The reasons I hate the dwarf have nothing to do with his height (need to explain?) or lack of hair. (Prove it?)*

(ARROW) *There is no way in this world that YOU should be friends with someone like him. NB: rip out before travelling? Frank's warning.*

Revenge quote (Find ref) as excellent way of saying, HE WILL PAY and it will be MY WAY.

YOU do a celebratory twirl. My hand hurts so I shake it out. Do YOU think I'm waving? I freeze. I am not moving until a mark from her boot comes up fully (there will certainly be a mark). Oh look! More spit strings from my hair. Charming. How much was there? I don't try to remove it because I want YOU to see it. Is that the kind of party you're looking for?

(ARROW) *RIGHTEOUSNESS/Leonine/a white heat. Acad/pub needs to know that this book is going to be THE book on the subject. I love it b/c it's high concept; no one is immune. The drug angle is just a portal to all human compulsion (do in market-speak – don't ask G).*

(ARROW) *PREP FOR INTERVIEW (poss to field questions like they've already been asked). Why at first it didn't seem possible (talk about why?) I always need permission, it's a weakness (expect laughter here probably?) How only now can I hold all of the project's angles, its intangibility its confusion its ludic skeleton, its satellites with open flat hands. This shit **needs** writing about and only now can I get to a distance where I can really see what's going on. The writer must stop trying to be understood. (Swearing? Greg swear on Letterman? Check.) For interview: She insisted on telling me her secret and I went with my instincts, I didn't stop her. I banked the information – invested it. Oh yeah, I learned a few tricks from Frank (exp laughter).*

Gregor is a fucking dog but he's a dog who knows where the bones are buried. He's entrenched. I am spirited in a way he can never be but now I must make the most of him.

Fragility is Underestimated. Chapter title? SHE is going to pay for this. This is direct evidence to suggest A high dose, the last one I gave her before the abstinence produced the most distinctive effects Day 4. Even in the face of no overt increase in impulsivity Days 2 and 3. Read thru notes before discuss with Gregor. GET IT RIGHT. Alt. To proof?

If she has cooled down at all, even if she's able to recalibrate, the decisions will be catastrophic at this point. (Where has she gone/for how long?)

(ARROW) *Title: A British History of Putzing.*

(ARROW) *WHY TELL ME IT'S CALLED DILPA WHEN ITS NAME IS DESPOTIKO? THEY AREN'T EVEN CLOSE. IT'S AN INSULT TO CONSIDER THAT THEY BEGIN WITH THE SAME LETTER.*

TEST FOR BLAMING / RETRIBUTIVE TOURETTE'S (think Tower of Hanoi/attribution test spliced for computer)

I put my notebook up as shield and switch to a pencil which will have to do. NOVOTITS is a new nudist, scars still fresh, grey sandcastles stood sentry on the chest like the ones that didn't touch down on the tarmac, the ones that you, Greg, have shipped to Costa Rica. Did you tell Minerva *that?*

GREG: ON TITS (ARROW): *Give Gregor context, THINK 'ghost-pale as jellyfish and rough with gooseflesh'.*

NT has legs that are perfectly shaped and I see that aesthetically, the difference in rack makes sense. Those are the kind of legs that Astrid might aspire to because hers are altogether too skinny in the inner thigh.

(ARROW) *Write down food discussion word for word. Do as rap? History with Olestra abuse.*

Journo piece to coincide with launch: WEIGHT FLUCTUATION and dopaminergic agonists

or

Why I forced Jimp to ditch Frank and come with me to the ICEM convention, Vegas 1995.

An Imperial Palace waitress cannot afford to register how irritating her customers are. Imperial Palace is where I first learned about tits that weren't your own. I marvelled askance at the skin protesting, stretched, tan-tinged-blue, the waitress in her satin dress with lace edging – she earned her money that night, filling plastic cups of beer for me and Jimp before I knew what a fucking traitor he was.

Gregor's actions rather than his words have what I call a profound grammar that keep me attentive even if I don't instantly know the meaning of those actions. Like the brain knows I'm being threatened. The stabbing and puckering, the grazing and scraping, the smoke in my face. I have thought about our last meeting a lot. I have never told Astrid what Gregor said to me about her rack. On the plane here, when the scandal was all over the news, she argued with me about fake tits. I made Gregor out to be a good guy. I agreed with some of what she had to say and I made an effort to drag her from the spiralling perspective she can get on these things when she feels threatened. I made the mistake of straightening up in my seat.

'I guess I just don't know Gregor like you do,' she said and she pulled up my shirtsleeve to lay her bare cheek on my upper arm saying, 'You think that's it?'

I think that a man shouldn't run across a city half-shaved. I think a man should be careful what he does with a Lexicon of Jive. I had some good times to thank the *Zoot* for but nothing lasts forever. I don't boast about it but I think a private education provides strategies to stop this kind of thing from happening. I've changed since coming to the US. I don't think these people are fully aware of what my schooling to date has furnished me with and I told her that straight.

'I think maybe this is the kind of talk that Frank didn't like, sugar.'

I wanted my arm but now she had it clamped behind her.

'Frank and Gregor are very jealous men,' I said.

She liked this answer a lot, much more than I intended. I could see she thought that Antiparos was our new beginning, would clear the air, like sex did in other people's relationships.

Gigi belly-flops into the sand with a brief glimpse to ME.

(ARROW) *Idea RUGBY: LESSONS Major diffs NFL and Rugby, metaphor for why can't work with Frank? Essay? Elegance/parsimony (IMAGINE LIFE WITH FRANK LESS HUMILIATION / LESS STRENGTH) People better. Other stuff.*

She should never have ordained me her absolver. I wonder when the blaming will kick in. What form it will take?

(Hypotheses about form it will take – definition of Tourette's – apply)

The ball lands on HER towel this time and MY leg is now touching it. I pull it towards me and balance it on my palm. They are waiting to see what I will do and I can make them wait. Gigi stands with his fingers interlaced on top of HIS head, then as if HE never cared less, HE trots up the beach to greet Petra outside the cafeteria, nude, both arms around HER neck. While I stare at them, the dwarf snatches the ball from ME.

SELF-CLASS

The last days at Ray's were the hardest. Sinead was pushing for evidence that Henry could support your future career. The graph paper, in your bra since Greece, had pressed into a soft cup. You barely needed to let your eyes rest on the over-leaning handwriting that belonged exactly and only to Henry.

There were heads in hands, some of the circle were held in a blank trance by the basket's lazy ellipsis. Sinead had asked for this.

'*Regret, they say, is what Astrid does best. She lets us know that we are to be destroyed for our own sake and we have paid and signed to say that was OK. No insurance; we, her audience, partake in a willing jeremiad. By the end of the set we want to die simply: the audience is connected by that which none of them could possibly know. The enchantment is in her unflinching way of telling how it was love that we let shred us, and that's exactly what we wanted.*'

'You sure that's Henry?' said Hancock.

'I think I know Henry's voice,' you said.

'Are you finished?' said Sinead.

'Keep going,' said Mexico.

'*And when everyone's longing to know more about themselves, their uniqueness, she finishes on "Comedown": The first chord is a steel bolt that rips a hole into our silo and we speed from our confines stranded together, a long way from where we started.*'

'If that is Henry' – Sinead held up an eyebrow – 'you should also recognize this.'

Ray took the paper from her outstretched hand and looked to you, scared shitless.

'Who let her into my things?'

You kicked over a chair.

'Just read it, Ray,' she ordered him.

'She insisted on telling me her secret and I went with my instincts, I didn't stop her. I banked the information – invested it.'

'Don't you see?' Sinead was not asking a question.

You got the sense that if Sinead could stand up, she would. Snatching the paper back from Ray, irritated he was not doing it justice, she continued: *'For this information I was expected to be in her debt but I will not be stepped on, trapped underfoot like a hectic dollar bill on a windy day.* This, people, is also Henry.'

'Maybe you have what I have?' Mexico offered.

'HIV?' you said, but jokes sent Sinead into military drill.

'Priority Failing: demanding to know that she's not made the wrong choice at all times. Approval is everything to her. This is what got each of you into your mess. You do not trust yourselves. You choose to squander your trust. You misspend your lives on things that aren't worth it. You have to pay with self-respect. There is no easy way out.'

She thrust another piece of graph paper at Ray; he replaced his reading glasses. You kicked under the basket and the colored cards rained into their laps. One slotted into Ray's backcombed bangs. You ran out, swinging the basket violently toward Sinead.

The door beyond Ray's office was locked and you dropped to your knees. Ray, kneeling behind you, whispered into the back of your hair, 'Trust me, Self-Class is going to help you. Like it helped me.'

'Get Lucien!'

'Plydo. And breathe.'

'Tell that skinny bastard he owes me and I have not forgotten how much and if he can just get his dick out of his boss for a few fucking seconds . . . Tell him!'

'We need some tea. Come with me.'

The Disease Room was a corner suite with yards and yards of flawed green glass giving a close-up on a turret as soon as you stepped through the door and the river once you entered further into the space. Ray walked you reverently around his early pieces, through to the works that everyone knew since the *Finally, Nudes* retrospective.

Henry had sprayed coffee down his nose when Ray admitted on TV that he didn't feel embarrassed to be compared to Warhol. You would sit among the weekend's wads of newspapers and music magazines; on the wall, the gray space alarmed by its lack of telephone. There would be sides of reefers, opium, or pancakes and salsa while Henry poked into others' sore reviews. Your eyes would squeeze tight with silent, stoned laughter and once you knew you could make Henry laugh at the captions you invented, you lampooned the chumps who found their way into the supplements, while Henry did impressions of them, assassinating them with their own language. The pooled effort was what you cherished; you would not have been delighted alone. Now, without Henry, you felt diminished, raw, sickened.

Ray had steadily surrounded himself with idiots until Sinead's crippling and his own charge of unlawful sex – timely coincidences – had saved both their careers. The clinic was seen by the label as the safest and most cost-effective place for both of them and the effect on Ray's art had been unimaginable. Ray's uncritical artworks had really gotten to viewers, disturbing them along so many dimensions that they had felt *something*, and Ray's childish enthusiasm translated that awkwardness and distaste by some perverse alchemy into appreciation. Somehow. *Finally, Nudes* had opened in New York and had more visitors in its first six weeks than Staten Island in summer.

Looking at the paintings with Ray induced a toxic sweat as you remembered the review of *Finally, Nudes* that Henry had read to you, a week after the opening: *When not turning his spackle-enhanced acrylics to foreshortened views of building-site vehicles, or watch faces, Hypno Ray's paintings can be touchingly personal. The exhibition highlight, 'Jeannie's a Cunt,' shows a middle-aged man in his undershirt, his heart glowing a palatinate purple. A menacing female nude – Jeannie – prowls in the background, while Ray rests his head on his arm against a Babel-esque tower plastered with hammers and sickles, mourning, one supposes, his lack of knowledge of Eastern European languages with which to woo. Bringing home the private tragedy of a public relationship's demise, and the ugly bickering that results when disentangling one life from another, Ray presumably didn't want to 'bring the viewer down' and so he has given Jeannie clown shoes and a rainbow tie.*

Even your untrained eye could pick up competence issues from *Jeannie's a Cunt.*

Objects and bodies seemed to float in midair and dubiously placed shadows loomed from uninhabited corners. Your longing for Henry pushed your need to be high to a scintillating peak, iced with a new fear: you had given yourself to Henry and had returned changed.

'You know, your downfall was also mine,' said Ray.

'Too deep, too quick?' you said.

'Music was never my métier.' He thrust a paintbrush into your hand, encouraging you to caress it. Ray wasn't ashamed to brag about his evolution as an artist to a woman who had just broken down.

'This art couldn't have existed without the pipe.'

You would regurgitate this line for Henry, vomit it *from right here* if you had to, and despite evidence, even in the chill of misgivings, you would keep Henry in your future if only for that purpose. That what connected you was rotten was irrelevant. Let the future reverse decay! To play out life with him, standing on corpses together, was the only way an addict could hope. Rafts of cardboard can keep you above the ooze of the swamp. If that floor gives out, lasso your future and pull yourself towards it. Use Henry to lasso Henry.

'I was still diseased when I did this,' Ray whispered, heaving out a couple more canvases. A figure rotated into view with a Pierrot skullcap and pompom buttons that glowed as if he had whitewashed over them.

'What do you call it?'

'*Undressing the Clown.*'

Ray reminded you that pieces from the retrospective were as collectible as Pollock as of last year. He used the phrase *raw talent* a number of times to underline there really was no other way of describing it. You didn't mention training or discipline. Henry hated the damage done by celebrating mediocrity. If he was expert in anything it was this: Henry knew all about being mired in envy for those he claimed he would hate to be. This had to be a test to see if you could resist telling him.

Then a magnificent canvas, the nude Pamela Curtain, commissioned for *Finally, Nudes*. She lounged on a couch with her head in his clothed lap, a brush held under his nose by his lips. You heard yourself ask if he'd done many nudes before this one.

'Not til I was clean and serene. This is what happens if you start too soon.' He dragged a heavy box of thinners aside to get to a safe. On the canvas he pulled out was a figure that looked like a barrel tied to four sticks. You gazed at it together.

'The nude does not like the disease. The disease can't cling to the nude. The nude humbles us for good reason.'

You had to ease your conscience and so you asked Ray for details of how he knew he could paint.

'At school, everyone used to say, "Draw me a horse, Bernard, or a digger. Draw us a lighthouse, Bernie, do me a horse". Every dinnertime! Me, I love painting anything with movement – the horses, the water, it's all movement really. But you know what I'd love to do? I'd love to paint in miniature. I could see me holding one of these paintbrushes with one hair and wearing one of these magnifying glasses. I'd love that. Oh yeah, I'd love to do that. Give me a brush with one hair on it!'

You must remember the order of the sentences for Henry, the exact wording. Ray takes this attention for rapture and cups your face.

'You'll be there yourself one day. I know it seems impossible now. Sinead sometimes needs reminding about indirect methods.' His hands are still at your cheeks. 'Sinead doesn't quite get the abandon of people like you and me. The passion.'

You incline your head out of his hands and ask, 'Shall we go back?'

Among other revelations that night, you discovered through Girl-Band that Ray had taken to dressing in a cassock after the Czech debacle and that no woman who had cried in Triggers had ever made it through to Nudes. Your sleep was fitful and the Box Set featured heavily. You dreamed of Tony in his skirt. You had been Henry's facilitator, his accomplice. Tony stayed with you the whole next day.

*

In Triggers the basket contained cards with a word or phrase to describe what you would rather not talk about. You chose a few of your own and the group placed in their cards with what they believed were your triggers because, to quote Ray, 'After a lifetime of narcs, we are not always aware of where it hurts most.'

You wrote down your biggies – BOX SET, *ZOOT*, ANTI-PAROS – and placed them in the basket. You purposefully did not write CD, but after the sessions you couldn't let some other chump put BOX SET in for you. Sinead put in her hand and drew a card and read out *MTV* through certain, smiling teeth. Ray read out *BURNING MAN*. Behind you, you heard the whisper, 'No one wants *that* choice.'

Sinead pressed play and you appeared like an aquamarine ant on the platform they'd built for you. Then they zoomed in on the jumpsuit looking fine. You were dancing little staccato steps that were neither goofy nor cool but you faced the back of the stage for a very long time when you should have been singing, and you tried to work out whether you could have died never knowing that you did that. On-screen, you are dangerously close to the edge of the makeshift stage when Lucien reaches out to you, your knees are out to the side. Then you pull at the crotch of the suit as if you don't believe the audience is really there. You stood to ask Ray if you could stop but Sinead asked you to sit down. They are rapt. You are moving backwards on screen with fast, sharp kicks.

'What is this, *A Clockwork* fucking *Orange*?'

Then your head is back and relief spreads across your face as you watch yourself piss through spandex then walk out on top of the sea of fans, becoming immediately pliant, a soggy-crotched star undulating over the surface of the crowd.

In the silence that followed, the need to joke was exquisite.

'Hey – I did that! To myself! Henry wasn't there.'

'Henry didn't turn up when you dearly expected him to.' Ray had his fucking arm around you again.

'Has he called you since you've been here?' Sinead asked.

'Catherine has told him not to.'

'You are expert at hiding his attraction.'

'Has anyone ever given you a commentary of a volleyball game in Jive?' You took two steps toward her. 'I'm asking you, have you ever played a really good game with anyone?'

'Games are an excuse for manipulation. I know that for some people, that's fun.'

Between your throat and your teeth you made promises about what you would do to her.

The next day, Sinead decided that the group had not yet discovered the 'core specifics' of what finding the party meant to Henry. The circle was so sick of you and she knew it. Without Ray there, things heated up too quickly.

'He *wasn't* joking about my humiliation! It was day four of a comedown. Standard degradation of decision-making.'

'Henry is excused yet again, and in his own words!'

'Gigi had speakers in a plastic bag for Christ's sake. Henry felt he was close!'

'And when you found the party?'

'Then things changed.'

You jutted your chin at her and clicked out your two front teeth to freak out the circle.

Addicts outside is a circus you don't want to see. Sinead called out directions as if you were blind and you pointedly ignored her. The walls in this area of old Paris looked brand new yet ancient: low-rise, pink beige. Le Marais wrapped around you, reminding you in its medieval way that the outside world with its disorder and its cruelty was intoxicating. At one point Ray, seeing your excitement to be on the field trip, asked you to push Sinead because his cassock was catching in the wheel of her chair. You refused, sticking instead by Mexico, who was showing out in a midnight-blue ballet skirt with a thick orange belt, brick-colored tights and yellow leather clogs bought in Saint-Germain. Together, you walked the mile or so from Ray's to the Musée de la Chasse et de la Nature, on backstreets in scarves and glasses. Mexico linked your arm. 'You sing like a fucking queen,' she said to the air. 'Fuck Henry, it's all about you.' For the first time in months you felt a spark of chance in your chest which pinched right out when you arrived at the venue and you saw just how much Henry would adore a Museum of the Hunt.

The door handles were ridged golden antlers that everyone wanted to hold onto with both hands so you squeezed into the museum slowly, like junkie paste. Once in, you huddled jittering in the hallway. Sinead wheeled through you, then you peeled off to follow Mexico to the toilet. The symbols on the toilet door were cut from aluminum: the woman wore a wire skirt and held a gold-colored spear made of strands of wire lashed together with tiny wire loops. The man figure held a wire bow and arrow. Mexico pawed them in admiration before opening the door saying, 'No matter how long I'm clean, the smell of a public bathroom will always loosen up my ass.'

As you entered the main gallery, Ray clapped for everyone's attention. 'OK, listen up! Hancock has fixed us a studio in the tapisserie.'

'Back home we say deli,' Mexico whispered. I sniggered.

In there was a wall-sized rug showing an antler embedded in the shaggy throat of some other poor bastard; opposite hung a huge flag in blues, reds and yellows from another time which covered a large plate glass window. Easels were set up around the room. Hancock had worked hard.

'Why are we here again?' you asked him.

'Nobody ready for Nudes,' he said.

'Animals are the next best thing,' Sinead corrected.

Ray unveiled a canvas, announcing, 'My first *Donkey*, 1968.' There's a silence.

'Are you addicted to regret?' you shouted.

Sinead wheeled closer to you while Ray answered.

'When I was fifteen, I did a woman eating a hot dog. I think that's when I knew . . . '

You put your hand around your throat and made your eyes bulge for Mexico.

'For this first lesson I just want you to ask yourself, what's *my* hot dog?'

Sinead tried to wheel through the two of you but Mexico sidestepped and the chair rolled snugly between two plinths.

'Hancock, the curtain!' The flag was pulled away.

'We are here to witness our bestial selves,' you said to Mexico.

Behind the plate glass was a pack of bloodhounds, loping in and out of angles of sunlight. The hounds' fluid pelts, black, biscuit and white, slunk against the sandy rose of the stone walls.

'Hounds?' You were unimpressed.

'Come on! Where can you get real live animals to paint?' Ray asked.

'Are you the hunters or the hunted?' Sinead said, all fired up from escaping the plinths.

Ray carried on. 'We have this place all day. If you can't get inspired, there's some guns upstairs.'

Girl-Band showed you that she had already started to sketch a massive crossbow aimed at Ray while Ray slowly walked around, hands behind his back. You impersonated him in plain sight of Sinead then, amped by each transgression, you snuck with Mexico out to the nineteenth-century room.

'What if we meet the disease?' you shriek with mock fear in Mexico's face. Sinead wheeled right behind you, jucking her footrest into Mexico's heel and making an angry oily line on the yellow leather of one of her clogs.

'You wheeled right into my heel,' said Mexico.

'I'm in a wheelchair.'

'How about I step on your fingers?'

When you walked away, Sinead wheeled with you saying, 'Ray hasn't hired these dogs for nothing.' With a couple of strong turns she was in front of you both. Ignoring her, Mexico examined the painting behind Sinead's head: an executed boar, teeth bared, with ferns underfoot. Mexico sidestepped Sinead to where a stag impaled a horse and you backed to the wall, creating room for Sinead to wheel off. You high-fived and did your best English accent while pointing out what mattered.

'You see, what you think you're seeing is based on thousands of rapid eye fixations of small visual areas that build up via an elaborate eye-brain recursive loop which then builds an internal model of a cohesive image or scene.'

Mexico laughed so loud that Ray swished in. 'Some guns before you start?'

'Out of my cold dead hand.' Mexico grabbed a paintbrush from his belt and ran away. You caught up with her outside and you laughed through your cigarette smoke. Hancock, guarding the door, warned you, 'That will shorten your life by a quarter of a day.'

You guffawed 'I fucking hope so,' the cigarette wagging in your lips, but the bravado waned some as you watched the dogs in the yard. You envied their purpose; their job was either circling or hogging a triangle of sunlight.

Back in the tapisserie, Mexico stood defiantly, her hip thrust to the wall. Sinead was soon beside her. You whispered to Mexico 'She's gonna blow!' but she heard you and turned.

'Can I remind you that you were crying over a man not half a day ago?'

You looked down to see Sinead's feet lolling to the left. Showing off to Mexico, you said to Sinead, 'And you are married to a teenager because you are shit-scared of punching above your weight.'

You were about to turn and leave when she slammed her footrests into your shins. You fell forward and had to use your palm to paddle back her forehead before she bit you in the stomach. You grabbed her hair tight in your other hand and she cried out, 'Admit that you want to get hurt!' Your hand was a muzzle that she forced her words through. She pressed her tongue between your thumb and forefinger to say, 'Learn a new language. Stop looking to him for something you have only imagined!'

You shook and shook the heavy bag of her head to make her shut up but she wouldn't so you jabbed her smartly in the face and her nose bled instantly. You wound your fist further into the hair as if her neck no longer worked while she grit her teeth against the flow of blood.

'Punch me again,' she said. 'You do not have to sacrifice yourself.'

You tried to push her backward but you were not heavy enough to counter the weight. Ray, late among you, started in on you like a wrestler so you flung his cassock over his head. Girl-Band got your arms on lockdown behind and you already had Sinead's spit and blood all over your palms. You had her hair through every one of your fingers.

'If you leave here, it'll be three days before you're back at Henry's door begging him to want you.'

'Try two,' you said, close to her face.

'He has never wanted you. Can't you see that?'

'You were not there,' you said gleefully.

Ray, finally freed from his hood, was on his knees, talking to your thighs in turn.

'Think, Sissy. Is this what you want? To never ever make it to Nudes!'

'The label will drop you,' Girl Band said, head tucked down behind your back.

'Who bought her Silverlake?' you screamed.

'Sissy, please! Don't.' Ray pushed his face into your pussy in supplication. You wriggled out then managed a snap kick that didn't connect but that scared everyone enough to let you go.

Your way blocked by Hancock, you ran down a hallway through a heavy curtain and out into the courtyard and through the riot of barking dogs to hammer the plate glass with your fists. You breathed a rectangle of steam onto the windows and wrote *Henry. Fuck. Me.* Then, you lifted up your blouse and flipped your underwires to press your bare tits against the plate glass, imagining the effect of their flat alien eyes ogling these clowns. Mexico doubled over in the gallery while the dogs jumped and scrabbled your side, their claws threatening to score the glass as they stood up on their hind legs, their front paws finding then losing purchase on your shoulders and torso. The thick partition shook as the dogs launched themselves against it while you tried to smear your tits around but they stuck to the glass and dragged. You stepped back, grabbed one tit in each hand and jiggled them like crazy for the dogs then bent to let them to be licked but the dogs weren't into it. Hancock, all uppity-faced, was calling security over his shoulder but Ray stayed totally still with his head cocked. Your tits still bare, you shouted as loud as you could:

'You brainwashed assholes! You can't keep me here! You can't make me believe in you!' They couldn't hear a word.

You back-heeled the window and, angry that it didn't smash, made your escape, accidentally kneeing a dog in the jaw whose teeth clattered when its muzzle bounced off the glass. From the quad, you made it down a hallway and, pausing in the lobby, you tore the tiny female warrior from the bathroom door with your bare hands and barged through the antler doors, baying out into the street. Oh, the power that comes from running to nowhere! A shoe under each arm, there came from you a tube of pure sound and you flew frantic, the balls of your feet barely sticking to the cobbles, strong and fast and you yelped for all fours, wished that the clothes would peel from you and you'd be shaggy with fur let loose, dying to get at the throats of all real lovers, even the dead ones and reaching evaporating speeds your fur is dust, your blood escapes thinning to midsummer rain, becoming spray, someone else's sidewalk steam.

HE WANTS ME

From his gestures, I can't immediately grasp what Gigi is after, and in panic I gather up the loose pages as if he must know that I am writing about him. He has no idea what's just happened, does he?

Nevertheless, Gigi is shouting with his hands to his own throat, the dwarf is poised between us but I am certain Gigi's shouting at me. He's fraught, he's shouting *Em Tee Vee*, but yes, it's clear, he wants me. I get up; the loose pages flip off into the sea where they could be ruined.

I walk as directed to the cafeteria, I don't run, and when I get closer I am disturbed to see Gigi's tongue thrust down to his chin. He seems to be strangling himself. I am terrified that he is aping a swimming move of mine; I choked horribly on the seawater earlier, but no, not that, he continues to beckon. I don't hurry: I wave at him casually but increase my speed when I hear the dwarf's furry little legs scissoring up a path behind me. Gigi, still nude, crosses to me, gesturing at my genitals, and I am dumbstruck by this proximity and freeze where I stand in the cafeteria until he begins to frantically unbutton my shorts and it feels right that I place my hands on his bare shoulders. Anyone would have done the same. The dwarf looks on at me puzzled, then we all look at Astrid out cold beside the counter, panther-pink icing on her lips.

My shorts are stiff with black ink and are tough to remove with just my feet and my hands on his shoulders. I endure standing naked as he rolls them up then gently works the shorts under her neck. Choking on a fucking doughnut is not going to get her out of this. I notice his cock is grazing her thigh as he clears her airways. As to my own, it is because of the excitement, the shock, I had never been this close to him and anyway it is subsiding. I don't kneel down, I don't want my balls lolling on her chest, we haven't had sex for days but this will certainly not make me give in. After an expert swipe around her throat, he pushes further and she gags as he retrieves a clump of doughnut, pincered between the back of one finger and the front of another. Her flickering eyes find my cock. Even semi-conscious she is coy. See what happens if punishment isn't contingent, immediate? I kick myself because I should have dealt with this directly, on the beach, as it happened. This is Basic Learning Theory.

She struggles to her elbows, the dwarf slaps Gigi's back and they collapse into each other. I grab my shorts back and put them on. He lifts her like a child and she says my name weakly, trailing a hand, her arms lolling back, her tits straining at their fake suede triangular confines. I am forced to follow them like a eunuch back to the tent.

He lays her carefully on the raffia mat reserved for our lonely desperate slow-motion evenings. Feeling her forehead then her glands, he waggles her windpipe till she coughs for him. I need to tell him that this is pure bullshit, invented so that I won't stay cross at her.

Before he leaves, he opens a watertight cylinder around his neck and produces an artfully crafted joint with what look like fish scales; the paper twist flattens then curves up into a tail. I try to take it from him: I don't want to have to fight him on this but, oh look, she is fully awake, demurely accepting it from his other hand, looking at me as if I were denying her an antidote to a snakebite.

I understand the spiral sign he makes above his head as the universal sign for Hermès headscarf and I am the one who has to scrabble in the tent for it then he wraps it around her face, to keep her hair back. She is staring at him now, her arms limp with gratitude. I kneel down beside her because he tells me to with his hand.

Both on our haunches, Gigi gestures, spooning from the bowl of his hand.

'Tonight? I. You. Eat.'

'Me?' I said.

'Yes,' he said.

She fraily points at all three of us. 'He means we all eat together.'

'Yes,' he said.

When he's gone, she crawls into the scarf nest and has the nerve to ask whether I am happy now.

'You've probably damaged my pelvis,' I inform her. 'Don't even try to turn this around.'

I have to get away from her.

From a sun-bleached chair on the terrace, I watch Petra at her duties and wonder yet again what Gigi sees in her. From any angle, Petra is unlovely. Despite having striking individual features, combined they became ghoulish; the nose too sharp, the eyes too deeply set. Petra with her white hair, sun-white not snow-white, has light grey eyes. Her arms and hands are thin and bony and every rib in her chest can be seen. Her skin is the colour of a burnished hazelnut. I feel spiteful when I consider their relationship. Had Gigi followed her blindly from childhood? Because there was a boisterous ease to their movement suggesting they had developed together, but closer in it became confusing: she gave him orders like a sister, tracked him like a mother but berated him like a lover. Today, she wore a fine mesh shift dress instead of the see-through flour sack. The same minuscule crocheted bikini was in evidence beneath it. She always went barefoot. Twice I had seen her stash a Chesterfield in an ashtray on one table while she smoked another.

I do not notice Gigi arrive but she does, and after tutting at his approach she begins to address me.

'I am disgusting. He is the owner, I am the slave.' I have never heard her speak English before. She comes one table closer and I can see her teeth, grey also from chewing something black, compounding the fascination: a table closer still I see it has left a thin black line at the wet/dry junction of her lips. I try not to stare. The sweet background smell is of liquorice.

'So the idiot is back!' she snorts and takes steps backwards, her hands out ready at her sides. He corners her expertly, taking her firmly by the back of the neck, forcing her to notice what jobs he had already done and what else needs doing. This ends with a wrestling disagreement, her trying to free herself from a headlock, bleating for help. I feel it's for my benefit that he presses her face dangerously close to the ashtray. She resists laughing and my breath stays high in my chest until she releases herself and steps back, snapping her heel up only millimetres before his face. The Swede enters and laughs at them. Petra goes outside to empty ashtrays, cigarette in hand.

I nod toward her, saying to the Swede, 'I am jealous.'

Inside the café, the fan above us turns out of balance. He smiles briefly, I know he speaks English.

'I am jealous of her cigarette,' I say.

His focus is on the guitar.

'So you're a musician.' Too upbeat.

'Austria is famous,' he says, inexplicably.

'Astrid is the singer, the musician.' I sound as if I am talking about a child that isn't doing so well.

'You work for her?' he asks.

'God, no. I'm a doctor. We've been sent here for her to "rest".' I make a gesture of insanity which Petra now catches. There is already a cigarette in the ashtray beside the Swede with wet grey lip marks around the end. The crushed body of it has tiny pencil-drawn tufts like clumps of marsh grass on a miniature map. She sees my longing. 'If he leaves my cigarettes alone, there will not be confusion.'

'One cigarette is never enough,' I say.

I consider going into detail about her problem, but the trace of a sneer on her lips as she exhales puts me off. I don't know the woman after all. I have a compulsion to mention the evening's dinner arrangements but stop myself.

The Swede's brother turns up, his butterscotch face creased and his eyes swollen from a hot tent. His fine blond hair is alive and curious with static. I dare the title of the book to Petra and I see them turn, the dozy satellites of their heads show they are very interested in the psychiatric stuff, touchingly unaware that this information is not really for them.

'Well isn't this cosy?' she says, suddenly there, scarved up to her limit.

'Hey, Em Tee Vee. Why can't he smoke?'

'He hates smokers.' She lights up, throws the lighter to me. 'Don't you?' She blows her smoke towards the Swedes and smiles as if she never stamped on me. I see that they giggle at anything she says. She leans over to me and I refuse to attend to her and address them.

'I gave up because I *know* how regret works.'

'Have you ever given up?' she says lightly to Petra, who is still wiping surfaces.

'Yes.' She stubs out her second cigarette. 'Right now.' She widens her smile and I note there is no colour change from the purplish-brown of Astrid's lips to the skin of her face. The black line is the only contrast. She lights another Chesterfield.

'Henry says that we are all addicted to regret, all of us motivated by the lovely sharpness of kicking ourselves. I gave up once when I had pneumonia. Only knew because I couldn't play my sax.'

'You play sax?' the blondes say together.

'And trumpet!'

'In Austria, he also!'

'Buddy G, hear this! Between these Jacks they play the spark-jiver, the slush-pump and the gob stick.'

They titter away at her despite having no knowledge of the references. It doesn't seem to bother any of them.

'Where do you work in America?' Petra asks, sitting down.

'With Gregor Pinkus? Eye movements? ReThink and ReOrient are our patents.' I can see that she is the only one serious enough to get me and it is probably for this reason that Astrid rudely tries to tattoo my arm.

'They try to use their voodoo on me,' she whispers to Petra. I continue my chat with Petra but Astrid insists on interrupting. 'For Gigi,' she says, handing a harlequinned cigarette to Petra. 'For when he gets back.'

I look at my nails.

'Has he gone far?' I say to the Swedes.

'Later' could mean anything to her of course, and trying to choose an outfit in a tent is impossible. When she arrives, I escape to the toilets where I think I hear the squeak of the squeegee. I return to choose another shirt but Astrid is now asking my opinion on scarves that 'go', for tonight. She has absolutely forgotten this morning but I have not.

'Shall we get a drink at the taverna up the track?'

'You mean the one where no one goes?'

'We could go into town?'

'I don't care.'

She can't cope with lack of enthusiasm.

'I'm going Mermaids then, if we're going out. Are we? Because I don't want to waste it.'

It's because I don't answer her immediately that she sparks up the joint he gave her. She holds a lot of smoke in that little wedge of chest.

'You're going to smoke all of that after three days without any?'

'Do you want some?'

'No. You've only yourself to blame for spoiling this.'

'With this? Ha!' She laughs after letting out the smoke.

'This is rehab.'

It is almost 10.30 when I find my way back to the café. Petra is filling up bottles of oil, wiping the outsides with her chamois rag. She smiles when I arrive.

'Oh my God. You are beautiful. Like a king,' she booms. The shirt is the wrong choice of course because clothes should never be chosen with the gut. When I return in an alternative that no one comments on, Astrid is annoyingly stoned, wearing swimming goggles left in the restaurant, watching Petra and the dwarf as they begin a game of backgammon. I simply cannot imagine that anyone can possibly take this dwarf seriously. They cannot have seen me and I overhear:

'Has he talked to you about his book yet? No? Oh, he will do.'

I stay out of sight but I can tell from the movement of her arms that the weed has made her truthful.

'I'm no longer one of the people he wants to impress . . . ' she is saying. Arms splayed on the tabletop, her chest is almost part of their game. 'But you own this place! Wait till he hears that!' she laughs outrageously.

'Well, my father does,' the dwarf says, quietly indulging her. Embarrassed, he fingers the counters hunkered at the point of the board's triangles. Not one of them cares that she nearly killed me this morning. In a trice, I'm spotted by her and she totters over to me, her hair piled up in the towering scarf with mermaids slopping around it.

'You hear this?'

I whisper fiercely, 'Don't mention the party.'

'God! Lighten up. Come on over.'

'I'll sit with the Swedes,' I say.

'Austrians,' she corrects. 'What's wrong with sitting with me?'

'Is this for attention?' I said, waving towards the goggles.

'Hey!' She holds my shoulders. 'He said he'd be back later and he will.'

I'd hoped the heels would put her off but on the uphill walk to the taverna she smokes the rest of the joint. Walking ahead of her in the pitch dark, I say that there should be a psychology of dwarves.

'He's amazing at backgammon,' she tells me.

The moment the taverna comes into sight she jumps on my back and whispers into my ear:

'Thank you for saving me.'

'I didn't.'

'He used your shorts to open my airways.' I wriggle her off my back but she holds me in front of her then puts a finger between my waistband and my belly. I remove it and she says conspiratorially, 'You know, I see you when we swim to the island.'

'See me what?' I can ignore the heartbeats as they stack.

'Looking at us.' She says it as if she understands that it is irresistible and she forgives me for it.

I walk the last steps up to *Kou-pepe* alone. The awning to the tiny clifftop bar was once navy blue but is now ruined cloudy-white with sun and salt. The view through the bar and out the window shows the shavings of moonlight across the lagoon and the darkening wild scrubland of the island beyond. I scan for light. I scan for anything. Anything to do with him.

'So the Swedes are Austrians!' she says idiotically. 'How does it finally feel to be in the gang?' She tries to nip my cheek.

'It always happens, once they know I'm a psychiatrist.'

'The big one plays saxophone! Buddy G take Jack for a slush-pumper?'

There is no chance of meaningful conversation when she is in this state. She has pounded the beer she brought with her and the ancient owner finally arrives at the table just as the first airs of the party reach up to us. He has a thick white moustache and no more than three teeth; his tongue, young, red and liquid, leaks between them as he greets us. She immediately asks him in Greek about the island. He holds up a cautionary finger and she translates for me once he turns to the bar. 'Despotiko has a jealous spirit, but bonds made there will last for ever.'

'What a pathetic story.'

'If we find the party, can we go home? Finish the Box Set?'

'Give your management what they want or they'll send you to Ray's.'

'I'm done with them.'

'Nonsense,' I tell her.

With her silliness, she has put me in a savage mood. The music seems close then infuriatingly distant on our downhill descent. She squawks at me to wait. Diehards are playing bocce under the camp floodlight, and a couple of swimmers can be heard slitting lengths of the lagoon. I look up at the overdone stars and she gets out the bottles from her boots and I fantasise about the conversation I will one day have with Greg about shaking her off. I see the moonlit scramblings of a goat, and listen to the thrums of the party while she cracks open a small bottle of ouzo. I must now pretend that I am not waiting for anything and that sitting here, beside a dirt track, with a jug of warm retsina, is 'enough'.

The music releases an urgent energy which leads us to grind off each other. Perhaps it is not rude to miss an appointment in Greece. She serially claims to know the songs and tries to distract me but I get up and walk to the cafeteria, equally and eerily empty of people. I have no choice but to return to the tent where she is waiting meekly for me outside. I try to sleep but am not drunk enough to ignore the heat.

I hear a shout and know it immediately as Gigi. I quickly scramble to put my shirt back on. I hear activity close by (someone pissing) and I think I hear the Dwarf's squeaky laugh. I finger the seams on my shirt. It is inside out. I stay very still.

'What's that?' she gasps.

'What?'

'Something ran up my leg.'

'I told you not to smoke the whole thing!'

'It's something big!' she squeals.

'We're in a tent. How big can it be?'

She hunches up rapidly, knees to chest, then grabs for me. It is impossible not to cry out when someone does that to you. I grab her arm to warn her.

'Where's the torch?'

'You had it.'

'These *fucking scarves*!'

'Where are you going?'

'To the beach.'

'What for?'

'I'm not sleeping here.'

'Don't be insane.'

'If you'd felt the thing that ran up my leg, Henry, you would be coming with me.'

'Good luck!' I call out. I am now angry.

Ebbing ouzo makes me cruel.

'Gimme a call when it touches you,' she hollers back.

It is as if a medium has puked silk in the hot tent. The removal of the clothes is hellish, each item bound to another by one of her scarves. I'm cursing the knots of clothes when she returns. We sulkily work to dump clothes on the grassless patches between the tents. I hear voices and announce 'I do not want to be out here,' choosing at random a velvet jumpsuit to accuse her with. 'I don't think I have ever seen you wear this, even at home.'

She thrusts a slack tower of vests and scarves at me, over-laid by something fringed and embroidered and capped with a pair of rollercoaster-steep sandals.

'Just right for camping,' I say and secure the pile with my chin, biting the sandal strap very hard. An unused CamelBak issues from the tent flap and hits me at the back of my knees. She is seething because we have found nothing that matches her description, no snakes nor scorpions. I can hear her scoop-ing into corners and whooshing her hand between the solid floor of the tent and the rectangles of foam that we sleep on. When her legs crawl backwards out of the mouth of the tent she stands. I bow, sarcastically.

'Well?' I wait for an apology.

She turns for the beach.

'Where are you going now?'

No way am I going to start packing things back into the tent. I bend to put on my trainers and have to force my foot past the tongue of the right one when an armoured millipede winds up and round my ankle and I scream and with all my might I kick it into the night. It clings tight and so when released it whips straight up into the air, landing back outside the tent, clattering onto the pages of a sun-brittle magazine, and I scream again and she screams at my side. We listen for the sound of its legs, tattering around the dry paper. I point to the magazine.

'Get it!' she insists.

I take one of her calf-length gaucho boots and, holding the sole, I pitch it but it misses and when it lands the leg of it flops to one side and as it does, Gigi appears from nowhere in a spotless white slash neck, hair in a ponytail, oxblood leather thong around his neck. The dwarf has been beckoned from the kitchens by the screams. Astrid points and clings to Gigi. The dwarf smashes the thing to death with a fire extinguisher.

FINALLY, NUDES

'Where have you been, Sissy?' Ray barred your entry to the Disease Room. He wanted payback for the bloodhounds.

'I think I killed a guy.' You slid your hand to the package in your pocket.

'Don't try to turn this around. What guy?'

'A pap.'

'You're shaking. Sit down.'

'That's what happens when you murder someone.'

'Sinead has gone through the roof.'

'You need to stand up to her once in a fucking while!'

He stared at your chest where the tahini had spattered your sweater.

'What the fuck's that?'

'Lunch. Will you hide me?'

'Sweetheart, this is France. If you had killed someone the coppers would be here already.'

The package from Lucien glowed in your ass pocket like you stole it from a video game. You looked over your shoulder through the door.

'She can't get up these steps, can she?'

'Let me see your face.' Ray held your face then examined your hands; turning them palm up he saw blood. Ray gave himself the right to embrace you.

'You see what a mess you get in when you do not follow your path?'

'I stepped out onto the path!'

'Admit it. You never fully Plydo'd.'

He pulled your head toward his midriff, and you showed him the graze on the heel of your palm by raising it in the air. 'Silly, silly girl, I told you not to run,' he moaned. Your head slid down the cassock and was quickly clamped into his cock, and you played dead until you felt a tumescence which you took as your signal to abuse his generosity. Your hand still in the air you said:

'Can I use your bathroom?'

You had run from the bloodhounds with the kind of sharpened purpose that usually came from uppers, but you couldn't stay spiked up there high on defiance and bloodhound fumes with nothing else under your feet. An about-face is always unthinkable at first but instead of admitting that, you tried calling Henry for the first time since you arrived in Paris. Sitting in the Costes courtyard before you tried him again, four citrus wipe-cleans appeared, taking to separate corners to stare at each other.

You moved to the bar where you still had a tab and used it to order a third of a bottle of Chablis, until someone snitched that you weren't to be served anything else. You asked for scissors from the barman and he asked a wipe-clean for permission before handing you a brand-new pair.

'Where am I, fucking Alcatraz?' you said, snapping the scissor-jaws on the way to the bathroom. Undressing, you elbowed your way around the cubicle in a fit of self-righteousness. The pages clung to your tit even when you removed your bra. There was one page you just couldn't ditch yet, but the rest were gorgeous to slice through with the stiff new blades and dropped piece by piece into the bowl, boxed fragments that you had chopped all sense out of. The swirl of the flush left most of them there. Booze drunk too quick begets pity. You'd blocked the gleaming turquoise toilet in its golden mirrored cubicle with Henry's high-quality paper. You finally felt how it could be to leave Henry and so had, in effect, made the move. This test complete, there was no need to make the effort yet.

You told yourself that there was only one end to this, and that there was no point in fighting it. Abstinence becomes impossible once reprieve is mentioned. In the maelstrom that gathered, you called Lucien, letting him know that screwing Catherine didn't mean he had to do everything she said. He arranged to meet you at the Café de Chambéry back in Le Marais, which meant walking off the spite of the carafe of wine made worse by lovers everywhere, those kissers who, the hateful bastards, were doing all of it without you. The booze, your first in so long, made you starving, and you quickened your step to the café, brightening; the very idea of Lucien made you romantic about bumping into your clinic fellows. You touched your scarf, no one would recognize you. The smell of spices sucked you into the district alleys, and you felt the swell of a long-suppressed appetite about to be satisfied. Is this the very best state there is?

You told Ray that if you hadn't been so fucking hungry you would never have kicked the guy so hard in the chest, that appetite had a lot to answer for, right? Ray, still sniffy-looking, nodded toward the bathroom.

'It's all yours, you know the rules.'

Before closing the bathroom door, you confessed, 'I called Henry.'

'Oh Sissy, you are kidding!'

'Lucien can get me a flight if you sign me off. Say I completed?'

'I will not fake a nude, even for you. There were witnesses to what happened with the dogs.'

Inside the john, there was a needlework sampler on the bathroom door that said *No Blunts No Blow*. There was also a cross-stitch reefer. A cross-stitch cross. Maybe the cassock was real. You remembered the scoop under your pussy and felt the need to jam your legs out straight. Running the faucet as loud as it would go, there was blood on your hands after all, you stayed in the bathroom long enough to give the impression that you were not concerned with what impression you made. You pulled the last song out of your bra and rolled the good stiff paper into a tube. The words along its length said *Who Knew Greek Stars* in blue, smudged now because of how the party, when you finally found it, had been spoiled.

You mourned the loss of being clean before the blow kicked in, and opened the door slowly because if you were high you wouldn't do that.

From nowhere came, 'OK. Let's do this together.'

You couldn't figure out where the voice was coming from and stooped a little when you saw in front of the excellent view of the Seine, propped on one elbow, a pale-bodied Ray lying with his cassock puddled around him. Something clarified too late: novelty and highness are not best bedfellows. 'I am your only chance to complete,' Ray said, cool as a windowpane. You have to stay intent on the puddingy slabs of his chest, choosing these over his sparse dyed pubic hair.

'To gaze,' he went on, 'is to think.'

Stick with the usual rhythms and you could get through this quickly. Ray was a message and the message was this: No

Fucking Way. How could you escape? Concentrate. Etiquette could save you. Routines were your friends, remember? He was taking you through Nudes and you had to focus on what a non-high reaction to this could be. Newsflash! Rocky panic breaches high waters. You are fully staring at his cock.

'Two gays,' you attempt, 'is not enough.'

'Warhol,' you offer, unbidden, remembering that if Ray doesn't get a joke he remains silent.

You have never painted a human body in your life, have always deferred to those who dare to know where to start. Faced with the task, you are about to spin out or have words drawn out of you that you are not prepared to give. It's happening. He was staring at your tits under your sweater thinking this was legal because he was the nude. Henry said that men need more dwell time but this freak was boring through your tits. A new stratagem was needed – go with this, accept it, why not relish the high? Live it double time. You looked around at the choice of paints but his nudity had transformed your perception.

'First visual fixation divided by number of fixations stroke amount of time spent on defined areas or dwell time,' you say, for absolutely nothing.

Were there grounds to complain when you were witnessing his ballsack splayed on the floor? At Burning Man you didn't die and you didn't stop breathing and you didn't fall through the hole in the world that you found. And there's the tilt you felt at Burning Man so you make your legs into a big triangle. Then, for some fucking reason, you channel Henry again: 'Erotic pictures depicting female nudes with direct gaze elicit a startle response in men as measured by magnitude of eye blinks.'

Ray stared expectantly while you reached for a brush saying, 'The face then becomes focus of attention and body receives less.' Were you able to pretend without speaking? Your face was speaking, the screaming eyes, your body was a traitor, maybe you were best at not being high with words. You were failing in the one thing you were left with, you were failing not to be high. Ray, now a lizard, said:

'I have a feeling my bollocks are going to be perfect.'

'To gaze is to think after all.' You could think of nothing else.

'So you're thinking about my balls?'

He sensed something that he thought was desire.

'I'm thinking how I can get them just right.' You were thinking about Czech ass bouncing against his puckered papery sack. 'And how one of them is twice the size of the other.'

'Really?' He wiped the back of his hand under his scrotum and looked at it. He swiveled back to your tits and you got the feeling that the tahini was a bonus for him.

You couldn't help yourself. 'Breasts receive a lot of visual attention irrespective of whether they are clothed in swimsuits or nude.' Why can't you stop? 'Your nipples are the most astonishing color,' you said. 'It's not the color, it's the contrast with the rest of you.' Then you said: 'Do you know that the areolae contain twice the amount of melanin that occurs in the skin of the surrounding breast?'

'You'd rather I was on the piano stool?' he asked seriously. 'Sitting on the stool maybe, you know, looking over my shoulder?'

'Sure. Let's go with that for a spell.' He creaked up, limbering to the stool. You painted frantically, idiotically, a picture emerging out of absolute necessity. Ray soon had a beak and the beginnings of a grass skirt. Good Lord, you were so thankful he couldn't see what you could see. When Ray got up to look you thought it possible that your face could fall off and you stepped out to hold him off with your stiff arms. 'What's the rush? Gimme all fours,' you directed meekly and he obliged as if he truly understood your needs as an artist.

'What about with my guitar?' He placed the guitar flat on the floor with the neck toward you, then squatted toward the strings, his bare ass bouncing a little on the bridge until something caught, forcing him to examine the nip. You put on a pair of rocket ship-shaped sunglasses lying in between the paint tubes, and felt more horrible at the change in light. You thought the answer to surviving this was to feel the body acting without thought. How much novelty could a high brain take? Could a person die from unpredictability? In your head, Henry was trying to make you say all of the things you had discussed about Ray's art, you must say these things out loud and admit your treachery. You chose a wide brush and began to create a dark green-black background to the painting, with your brain cells firing at microwave speed to gag you.

'You doing OK?' he said.

'Fine!' you said, and wondered if you would ever know what fine meant again and whether you had ever known. What is there apart from what we say we are? No philosophy, not now.

Holding a bicycle saddle in front of his genitals, he was putting on socks because you asked him to.

'A real difficulty with nudes is bringing out the personality,' he advised. You knew Lucien was waiting for an answer from you or from Ray and it was getting dark. You mixed more brown because on the canvas you were giving him a coconut bikini top.

'How do people do this for a living?' he said, rubbing his elbows. You continued the only way you could.

'Did you paint the little Czech girl?'

'Many many times,' he sighed.

You just meant to nod; it had started as a nod.

'Do you think pedophiles spend longer looking at the genitals or at the potential areas of breasts?' you said. 'Do pedophiles always have sexual preferences? Do you wonder if their eyes spend less time on areas with pubic hair or with breasts? What if you gave them a kid's head on an adult's body? Where would the eyes rest then?'

'You missing Henry?' he said with a smile and limped over to assess what you had done.

'You poor thing,' he said after a few seconds, as you daubed more brown on the coconuts. Had you finished? Good question. His advice was becoming tinnier. He looked at the glasses sliding down your face, and he must have thought it was the painting, the artistic rapture so you tried not to breathe the same air as him and your heart tripped out. It was your first panic attack since Tony punched the wall instead of Carmella.

HOW TO BEAT A DWARF

A dark heavy mass splats on the panel above us and the tent bows alarmingly. I sit up, blink once, twice. Still asleep beside me, she doesn't stir and so I have to dare my hand under whatever it is. I spread out my fingers and turn my hand, more ready to gauge it. A T-shirt of mine? He's found it at the beach and brought it back for me? But on contact, the lump writhes and pushes between my fingers and I begin a low growl of disgust that mounts as I stand too quickly, stretching the dome of the tent into an uncomfortable point that jams my neck towards my shoulder and lifts the base of the tent at each side, tipping piles of her clothes into her sleeping face.

Outside, I can hear him sniggering and I quickly rub a hand over my face, exercise my mouth, scratch around it, rake back and forth through my hair. I bend to open the zip and there he is, amused, pulsing ink out of the octopus's insides into the hard orange earth a yard from our entrance. The tent by this time is in full sun.

He has a lemon and a small rectangular oil canister on which he chops up the blueish point of it into raw rings and then wallops a spiny urchin with the butt of his knife handle, cracking it open mercilessly, offering me the orange innards which he has untethered from milky sinews with the point of the knife. When I refuse, he places it back in the casing and shucks it down. With it swallowed, he bangs his chest and tucks one elbow against his abdomen, pulling the clenched fist up towards his chest with a teenage smirk which I return involuntarily.

Astrid appears then in her panties and a tight vest top, and they greet each other in Greek. His arm with its clenched fist stays where it is and I want to slap it away.

'Today!' He points at the ground urgently. 'I eat you!' he explains. Why he thinks I will believe him after the betrayal of yesterday, I do not know. He taps the canister with the tip of his knife, then they exchange a signal and he scuttles his hand along the floor screaming high and terrified, like a child. Astrid laughs her little scarfed head off with him and I realise that I am bored of the search, the strain of waiting.

I leave the tent for a leisurely turn of the site, where I find myself still searching for clues. I scold myself but images of the party remain inflated, will not be pressed down. I take special note of the comings and goings of the camp to be accurate in the retelling for Greg.

When I return to the cafeteria, there he is at the till, cutting his endless curves with his thumbnail while he reads the paper. He is wearing the white flour sack today. I think of his hair and the back of his neck and I feel a weakness under the weight of possible opening lines. For the first time, I consider outright asking if he will take me to where the party is tonight. Instead, I sit and watch him raking over the potatoes and rice under the heat lamps, bursting then sinking skins on sauces with his wooden spoon. I can smell the salt-and-herb sweetness of this food, breathing in through my nose, these combined elements represent him perfectly, give me his full shape. I want now to be the moment that he notices me as distinctly different from the rest of these idiots and at the height of the wish, I snap the band on my shorts. That he doesn't look up brings all my stories to the fore at once, to tell him about my work, BirdBoy, how I was cheated by Frank. About how I am going to show those fuckers. But I've stared too long because he's looking impatiently right at me and I scurry off to the beach, remembering the millipede. I feel emotional because my sleep was broken.

I try to otherwise account for the ramp in disappointment as I trudge out to the cordon for my swim. My routine at the moment is wheeling around very fast with all limbs under the seawater while keeping my head as still as possible. This can be dangerous, as I discovered yesterday when I strayed into a deep part of the lagoon and had to run underwater until my toes scraped against sand again and I was forced to sit out to compose myself. I walk out to the end of the spit to see as far as I can onto the island.

In about half an hour, Gigi is up on his lookout rock and I shade my eyes to make sure she is also there. In the little time it has taken for me to exercise then edge around this curve of beach, they have been able to swim over to the island's shore. Gigi stands on a rock above Astrid and helps her out of the water; it's just the two of them today. I would never, ever get that tanned and it strikes me anew how similar their colours are.

Gigi's shorts are Hellenic blue and white but his almost black leg makes the thin white nylon stripe of his shorts disappear. Standing beside him, she holds up her wet hair so it doesn't drip and today he puts his hand gently on her bare waist. She doesn't move as he swings a limp yellow plastic bag which sets off her skin tone; it waves back and forth across her deep brown belly and thighs. She holds herself politely while he offers her something from the bag. I place my hands firmly on the rock behind me to keep me steady as I watch him point to his lips but she laughs him off, crashes through the shallows and dives, flashing the triangle of her bikini bottoms before she disappears, momentarily surfacing but staying there, knowing that under the water a fire can't start.

The high horseshoe of the rock around me is a natural screen from the beach and the higher ground of Antiparos. I move further into an alcove in the jutting rocks where I know no one can see me and I take off my shorts. My eyes are perfect at distance and he moves towards her into the shallows and I see they are talking. I'm the only thing they have in common.

Then, without warning, she hugs him. I see him turn into her neck and nuzzle her hair and instantly he's out of it again. Did he bite her hair? Apart again just as quickly, they both look off into the distance but at different angles and I lower my shoulders under the water to keep watch. He makes motions towards the campsite but before he goes he opens the white cylinder, his carry-case (which I know up close has transfers of anchors and a ship's wheel that have all but rubbed off through use). Whatever he hands her she puts in the plastic bag. They return to the sand to dry themselves then he drags the boat in heavy jerks through the wet sand back to the sea and vaults the boat's low side once it is moving and I watch her track *Petroula*'s steady line across to Antiparos. I feel her gaze acknowledge mine though it cannot meet it over these dozens of meters. She swims back in what is left of the mild wake of *Petroula* with the bag held above the water. I put my shorts back on.

When I arrive, she is lounging on her side on top of a table on the terrace saying to the Swedes, 'Songwriting is a job that you need to be completely in control of when you're asleep, and totally out of control of when you're awake.' Nuggets she usually saves for me and our evenings together. They always agree with her emphatically. I move inside and my heart sinks at the sound of dice. There are rote utterances and scripted set pieces that come up interminably in backgammon between Petra and the dwarf and today, this shunts me into a brutal mood because they are so tolerant of each other, so forgiving of these little repetitive tics, fostering each other's weaknesses.

Seeing her coming to watch, the dwarf offers her a game and I am glad of my papers which I brought for just such an occasion. Astrid beats the dwarf and celebrates exaggeratedly. Petra crows over this defeat and it becomes public enough for anyone to join in yet the dwarf looks up at me saying, 'Hey! Stare at your own girlfriend,' at which Astrid laughs like a primate. I can think of nothing to say that won't shock them.

'I am joking!' he cries with his hands up. 'Don't fight!'

Petra drapes herself around his neck. 'Fighting is our job.'

'You hold hands?' the dwarf says to me, Astrid by my side.

'We hold throats,' she says.

'We don't hold hands,' I assure them.

The dwarf ruffles Petra's hair then holds her chin. 'She clings to my back all the way from Brazil.'

'Because I feel sorry for you.' She grabs his chest hair and he presses back her fingers in play.

'Oh, Brazil!' says Astrid dreamily and I listen to their story in a dazed amazement. Petra hadn't been back to Brazil for fifteen years, she had Dutch parents and her 'thought tongue' is also Dutch. She learned Greek on a boat from the Caribbean to here owned by an Italian electrical goods magnate. That's where she met the dwarf, who came from Athens and whose name was Ernesti. He had been her skipper.

'And Gigi?' Astrid asks.

'My cousin,' said the dwarf. 'Georgios. Gigi is his baby name, neighbours in Athens. Our mothers are cousins.'

Petra kisses the dwarf after this; it's brief but tender and I, in a stunned rigor, stare as if I were involved in it.

I feel light-headed no doubt because I have tried too hard at the swimming. There will be no more time for swimming now. I stiffen with my pledge to find the party. I grab Astrid's hand as she passes. 'Why don't you go and put on the mushroom scarf, or better still the helter-skelter one, and we'll go for a walk.' I don't feel guilty for the enthusiasm this evokes. She returns wearing the scarf and has put on a diaphanous skirt over petite turquoise shorts. The brown triangle of buttock below the shorts presses against the light mesh and is mesmeric as she walks a rocky path in front of me and we are soon high up behind the beach. There's a field to our left tall with khaki meadow grass and I spy a gap in the drystone wall surrounding it. In the corner is a weather-turned olive tree and it is under this that we come together and, after, lie on our backs, relieved and sweating. She is naked now but for the short transparent skirt and decides to straddle me again to put a lid on what has happened. She drapes her gaudy bandeau over my eyes.

'You love this colour, I knew you did.'

She is still sitting on top of me, the sweat cooling in a breeze through the gap in the wall and she leans down to kiss me with her eyes closed. I put the back of my hand across my mouth and her lips unexpectedly meet my palm. Her eyes brim with betrayal.

'We need a shower,' I say, clapping my hands at her waist but she steals my sunglasses from me, puts them on. I see in the reflection that my hair is stuck awkwardly to my forehead. She catches me looking at myself and becomes brattish.

'Why do you care so much about what strangers think of you?'

I won't answer that. There is a bruise appearing at her neck where I have sucked too hard. She drags her feet and heads off through the grass to the gap in the wall.

'Hey peola,' I shout. 'Wanna go into town tonight? Down to the harbour?'

'You hate tourists.' Her voice is flat with hurt but cowards don't have the stomach to bear a grudge, so on the walk into town I know I can bring her round. I hold her arm as we enter the square where children whirl in white clothes and some of the older people from the camp are gathered. Relieved to give up, Astrid lets out squeals when she sees anyone she has ever seen nude from The Camping. I want to tell her they remind me of circus dogs. In ruffs. That guy should be walking on all fours, but she is so happy to greet the old slack-bodied nudists, they are eager to be identified and she appraises each one, her mouth open, her finger flicking in an upwards stripe from the genitals to the face. She hugs every one of them. As she flits, I look around to see if any of the small boats leaving the harbour have anyone we know on their decks. I try to look out past a clarinet-led band but she takes my arm and whispers, 'When we get home, I'll stay clean.'

'You've had a lovely day,' I remind her. 'Can't you be satisfied with that?'

When I recall it, it was Petra's voice that made me look up. I step back a few paces to see that the outcrop of rock above the street has been hollowed out to make a solid-looking grotto which holds the electric light like liquid gold. Jasmine flowers peep in heavy clusters above the opening, framing my first sighting of them. Like trick candles lighting themselves, the dwarf appears beside Petra, the Swedes pop in one and two, and there, ten seconds later, casually nipping the end from his cigarette with his thumb and two fingers, is Georgios. The froth of the minuscule flowers brushes over him gently then sways around his dark face and hair. 'Em Tee Vee!' He calls to her but he's waggling his finger between the two of us. 'Come. We are here!' he shouts, pointing to the floor with both hands. This is the only memory I own where everything is as I imagined it would be.

I make to move and she stops me, grabbing my hand, her face quizzical then crestfallen as if some tryst will be ruined by the company. I put my arm firmly around her waist and at this she concedes and I tighten my grip to ascend the steps with her two at a time.

The balcony is cosy but not cramped and leads through to a rock-floored restaurant. The terrace of the bar is roughly hewn and wondrously old. The stone of the steps and the balcony are still warm and, without asking, they are ordering drinks for us.

'See?' I say, 'They have decided for you,' and I hand her the stout glass of vermouth. The view over the harbour is modestly proportioned and is intricate and beautiful exactly because of its limits and I wonder what they have said to each other about me on our way up the stairs.

She gravitates toward the Swedes and Gigi because they have a joint, which makes it difficult for me to join them, so I look around for where to stand. By the bar I see polythene bags, speakers in plastic, which I have seen in the camp. I hover by the dwarf, who puts his hand on my shoulder yet continues talking to Petra. One of the Swedes does the dip in the knees to get a laugh. I narrow my eyes at the set piece and she doesn't laugh openly because she knows I am watching. If they could speak better English I would explain that in making that video, she tried to stitch us together in front of the whole world because she thought that I would not dare to challenge her. I will never get along with those who are too easily satisfied.

I want to use the speakers as a topic but am thwarted. I have barely exchanged two words with Georgios before we are seated for dinner. The table is circular, the best in the room, and overlooks at a distance the newborn lights of the opposite shore. I sit two seats away from her. I am not her keeper, nevertheless from her seat she looks at me beseechingly then puts out her tongue and smiles bravely and begins what I imagine will be incoherent small talk that will annoy those who want to tackle a particular subject of interest to them. A baby begins to grizzle at the table beside us and the parents, glancing nervously at our varied adult party, try to subdue their bickering in a language that isn't Greek or English.

Meanwhile, Petra has seated herself beside Astrid.

'So what does Georgios do off-season?' The vermouth is in her hand, hardly touched.

'He is a butcher,' said Petra.

We all turn to Gigi and he smiles disarmingly, asking in Greek what this is and when the dwarf tells him, Gigi's face drops and he slaps the back of his cousin's head. Everyone laughs but I hope he sees that I really don't. The translations continue to be frustratingly rough and clumsy; too short, they lead to nowhere. They simply don't give me the openings or segues to reveal what they could know about me.

Against strict instruction, the father of the baby is taking him out of the high chair and the baby, seated on the table in front of him, promptly knocks over an empty glass and the circle of their party tinkles with relieved laughter that peters out to brittle amusement. Gigi smiles over at the father, giving me a chance to linger over the junction between his skin and his dark brown dress shirt. His trousers are navy, slightly short, above his ankles and his hair is taken back with a string that I recognise again as a fastener from the bamboo huts. The waiter appears and from the way he eyes him, I sense that Georgios in his good clothes feels awkward and this stings me and I ache for him around the point of it. Astrid has taken on an anxious mask of paranoia. That's what happens if you pack a blowhole with weed, I want to mouth, but she won't grasp it. 'Why don't you look at someone else?' I say quietly, as Gigi is telling a story.

This, of course, sends her flying to the bathroom. Everyone but Georgios now has their menus open. The waiter is asking about drinks in Greek, gesturing with his face to the view, shrugging that to him this is everyday. When the waiter leaves, Ernesti explains to me that the waiter's family are friends of theirs and that he is a local harbour porter, and when he works days he takes them to La Luna at the end of his shift. I clench at the mention of La Luna, but as I lean to ask Ernesti what it is, Astrid returns, kicking the leg of the high chair, which jolts the already whining baby into a wail. She apologises, accusing everyone, 'There's no room in here!'

The baby's wailing is hard to ignore and Astrid is struggling particularly. She looks to me, saying out loud, 'How can anyone think?'

With everyone else having chosen, the waiter returns to her, where she is speed-reading the English translation, her lips moving, her face close to the menu. The baby's escalating whimpers are somehow amongst us and, squished back in the highchair by the mother, the square-mouthed little thing wails luxuriously and kicks and kicks with its heels at the footrest under its sturdy little ankle boots. Astrid looks up and begs Petra with her eyes to do something. Petra, pitying her, makes a strangling gesture towards the baby.

'Oh no!' Astrid says, horrified. 'It's not that!' She looks to me to reinforce the strength of her feeling while Petra asks the waiter for more time and he leaves with a brief smile and a bow. Astrid is weak with relief and flicks her eyes wildly around the four corners of the menu. Half a minute longer, right on cue, I lean over to her and she bats me away with her hand, saying, 'Tell them about Frank, why don't you. Tell them about BirdBoy.'

'BirdBoy?' says Petra.

'No big questions please.' She makes a flapping gesture and incredibly they find this very, very funny. She smiles at me hopefully, brave now with her comrades.

'You are the BirdBoy?' Ernesti asks me, egging her on. 'No!' she squawks, like a parrot; hilarity all round. When the laughter tails off, I nod at the waiter in the background, saying, 'She blames when she feels under threat.'

Just then, the baby flips a small plate of half-eaten olives and the pits hit the floor at speed: some shoot to the farthest reaches of the terrace and others come scuttling around the legs of our table. The father, on all fours, tries to pick up the closer ones and must dodge the waiter who approaches our table now with a tray of drinks. Independently of each other, Georgios and myself have ordered ouzo; Astrid has ordered a beer and a Coke and a coffee.

The baby is screaming now and the intensity increases, so the mother tries to remove its plank-stiff little form through the bend in the high chair. As she does, the whole chair lifts from the floor and she berates and begs the husband in their fierce, opaque language.

To Ernesti I say with a wink, 'Adults-only campsite. The future!' I raise my glass.

'I am with *you!*' Petra says to me, slapping the table and pointing at me.

'Look how angry the mother is because the father won't follow her instructions,' I say. Petra giggles.

Ernesti sees Astrid's soppy face and says to her, 'You like children?'

'Oh my God! I don't want kids!' Astrid pales, looking to the red-faced baby.

'Little late for that?' I mutter to my menu, widen my eyes.

'Excuse me?' says Petra.

'Lesson for you all. Stay away from TV repair guys.'

I knew she'd act as if it were the worst thing I'd ever said. For the record, the Greeks were bemused, had no idea what it meant. The waiter is still waiting for her order with his pad raised higher than his chest but now she stares at him with fat tears in her eyes, looking down at her menu ensuring that the tears spill. Petra looks at me and I make a subtle unstable sign with my hand just above the tabletop while the father walks up and down with the baby crying monotonically in his arms. There's an embarrassing lull.

'I'm sorry,' she says to everyone, instead of choosing.

'Fragile in this phase.' I nod towards the Swedes, who look on, stoned double dummies. Gigi chats with Ernesti while looking at me, and I note the way his hand flicks, a half-screw to the left in a non-verbal pause. The waiter clears his throat. It's now getting ridiculous.

'The words have not changed!' I lean over, the waiter looks on; I pretend to blow my brains out with my fingers.

'Would they do a simple grilled cheese, do you think?'

'I don't work here,' I say.

Worn down by the cries of the child, the father sits heavily on his chair, struggling now to maintain polite conversation with the rest of the table. After a shrill accusation, the baby is roughly snatched up by the mother, but the child has gripped the corner of the blue tablecloth and as the mother pulls away the stubborn little fist keeps hold of the cloth bringing down glasses and carafes, plates and cutlery yammering to the floor. The waiter's eyes close and he tilts back his head and he is once again on his knees.

'I've decided,' she says to him on the floor.

Hands full of olives, shards of glass, he gets up, he nods and he smiles. I consider telling Ernesti how addicts often panic like this but he's commiserating with the waiter. I tell the waiter he's missed some broken glass, to which he bows.

'There's a great paper,' I say to Petra, who as of tonight seems the most intelligent. 'Decision-making deficits linked to real-life social dysfunction in crack-cocaine-dependent individuals.' I've finished half a carafe of red. 'They become stuck, obsessed by what their choices *mean*.' The mother is now back since she can no better stop the baby's cries than the father. She stuffs the squat sack of its body back into the high chair and it protests with all its might, rocking the high chair on its spindly legs. The mother violently clamps the tray table with her hand to stop it. I chat to Petra in an attempt to ignore the scene and continue until the waiter announces:

'Cheese sandwiches and fried potatoes.'

'Do you have ketchup?' she asks. I cover my face and she pushes the plate of food she has ordered away from her. I whisper to Petra, 'Myopia for future consequences,' raising my glass to her.

'Ah, our food is also here!' Petra is relieved too; Astrid's behaviour is unbearable. The waiter swiftly places our food on the table. Tirokafteri, a great slate with a slab of oregano-covered feta, a plate of fresh calamari and four quadrants of lemon on navy blue plates, handsome on the red cloths and napkins. The baby stops crying at last which beckons a cheer and a joke that I don't understand between the tables. Astrid's tears have dried. Gigi toasts Em Tee Vee with his hand covering hers. All but Gigi include me with a movement of their glass afterwards.

'La Luna,' he says, his hand resting with hers.

DWELL TIME

When Sinead said you were only attracted to men who put you under threat, she had tugged the ripcord to the truth.

'Come on! Are you kidding me? Fuck you!'

You read her silence as a retreat and stared at her lifeless legs, whispering to Mexico, 'Like I said, she can hide but she can't run.'

'So you think that the mess you're in is Tony Soprano's fault?' she said.

'You think I'm lying?'

Back from Greece, some things had become impossible to ignore. If you talked during an episode, he would physically strain to hear exactly what Tony was saying. Henry didn't flaunt past lovers, there were no gumars, right? But Henry had been cold about you when he talked to Petra or the Austrians; you were never more than an outline to third parties. Did you protest? The party to Henry was a symbol of what both of you could achieve if you really tried hard. That's all. But you heard him forget your name on the island more than once and, convincing yourself it was deliberate, you felt *motherly* toward him. You were devastated to discover that the intensity you'd felt from him when he stared at you in the walled field was aimed at his own reflection in your sunglasses. Could he ever be listening to what you said while chewing that fast? Not speaking was to him merely waiting to speak again. Henry left you in no doubt that he had let go of things far more precious than you. You would never give in to Sinead and say that he wanted the party so much more than he could ever want you. Back home, Henry would always hold you responsible for withholding from him the freedoms Tony enjoyed. You had become an accomplice, and for that, he hated you.

If there was an order to what happened you were unaware of it. You had hoped that the Box Set was a durable mosaic of stories that, by way of their cruel insight, might help Henry explain away any unsavory parts of himself. Dwelling on its abhorrent aspects proved that you had nothing to do with a world like that. But viewing it together had allowed the violence and hatred of Tony's men to contaminate, not immunize, your union.

What would happen was this: the opening bars of the theme tune focused you on Henry's take on these finely scripted mobsters' behaviors. Was he jealous? What exactly was his type among the women around Tony? Would *he* look bored during a blow job? Immersion for you was not possible because surrounding you there had to be a thin sheath of your version of the episode to breathe in, just so you could survive it. You watched how Henry reacted. Before you knew it, you were pretending that you totally got what it meant to be a man in Tony's world, that is, by willfully misunderstanding (for the sake of your sanity) you had become an enabler of monsters, more than that, an advocate of hatred, a hatred that bent ludicrously back at you, like the round-the-corner gun in Campbell's *Believe it or Not!* How so? Wasn't this Box Set a gift for you both? A shared patronage of that world? Now you had to suffer the shame of becoming invisible once you'd sneaked Henry into it. Invisible people still bleed and die. You had to protect yourself and that had meant becoming visible in a new way.

You know now. *The Sopranos* had been the wrong backdrop. You should've chosen something less caustic, less intimate, shittier. The consistent pounding force of the stories bent you out of shape. Astonished that people could feel they were owed so much from life, you wanted it right along with them: primed but never receiving you were yoked to these dogs without getting any action. The end of an episode brought a flood of blame and lust and spite and cruelty after watching barrel-chested men raking through other lives like thick rolls of barbed wire. How should you displace the discomfort of comparing the motives of these men with Henry's? Without breathing in, there was the suffocating strain of trying to give form to the vapors that seeped from TV baddies, but being careful not to taste what exactly it was that they would be satisfied with, conquered by. To stay alive in that atmosphere meant becoming a cloud that they could walk through, or a clump of drizzle, a bank of miserable cloud to bounce the massive fuselage, the bellies of their jets against. You started to blame those women on-screen; witnessing the agony of someone who is unloved when they think they are loved produced a pain that had to be transformed, leaving no room for pity.

You couldn't tell Sinead that once in that world there was no way out, that you'd spend episodes braced, barely resisting the suck; the more you found it diminished you, the more you were left wanting. Sore as a lollipop, you craved the pull of the story's dirty mouth once it was over. Henry would click off the set in a funk, raw also from what was denied him within the territory of the sharply drawn plot lines. The shared fiction ripped you apart and got up between you, put mirrors behind the two of you to see life reflected and distorted through it.

Your lives became compressed in a stack of frozen images that were brutal with loveless sex: it seemed everyone but you was taking it up the ass while shutting the fuck up. To keep Henry next to you, to watch just one more, you offered popcorn Rorschach to let Henry discover what you so deeply felt about Tony's crimes. He didn't want to play. You wanted this: you were a colluder who had given Tony and Henry their platform.

Wasn't it lucky then that Sinead was there to help you understand exactly what Box Set was responsible for? 'Seems to me,' Sinead said with great confidence, 'you pinned the rosette on Henry before the competition ever began.'

Before even the first season ended you caught yourself in the lag of grief at the watchfulness being only one way and were devastated at his lack of concern about how the story might be affecting you. Trying hard to get into Tony's gang, Henry pulled away from you, sacrificed you, wanted you to disappear once an episode had finished. There was a jostling that went on as you watched because you both wanted to impress him. Privately, you began to wonder whether Tony might love you? When Tony wanted someone, to fuck them or to kill them, you felt hunted and completely defenseless and frantic for cover in your own apartment because now you were part of their territory and your thin soul lay taut, immobile and desperate to be discovered. Who should you turn to but Tony? Because Henry was nothing like Tony. Was he.

You feigned tiredness but it was honest-to-God heartbreak when Henry wouldn't watch just one more. Such sadness followed you into sleep and that sleep pushed you into dark corners with Tony who would always stay behind after hours but made you do the things that frightened you the most, testing out what he could get up to in a country where the borders weren't fixed and the laws had loosened; where he didn't have to care which cops to pay off; where modern reforms weren't able to endure. I don't give all women this chance, he'd say into your open mouth, ripping your stitches wide: stitches made from precise narrow strips of your own skin. After you dreamed of him, Tony always left a stain, a shadow.

Some dreams made Tony your therapist, arranging sessions for you on a canal boat that moved sluggishly as though through tar. He'd sit with his legs wide open as if he wasn't used to skirts of this length, and his Laurel-esque feet jutted toward you in a V and as he rearranged himself you could even hear the sticky squeak of his patent heels rubbing together. The sky and the water were oil dark and had an apocalyptic depth to them that threatened to overwhelm you. Tony sharpened his pencil shavings onto the tight skirt bridging his knees. You knew that Tony wasn't wearing underwear and the gap up his skirt tugged hard at your attention. He always looked you right in the eye and that began a melting invasion of wanting.

Those dreams with Tony found you up to your neck in rapid waters rolling with flailing limbs, arms and legs jarring, forcing unwanted connections to the thousands of other faceless women also in peril. You breathed shallow and tried to shrink away but at some level there was already copying, duplicating, cells replicating those they saw as winners. Before you could stop them, the autonomous cells left you, broke through the surface of the water and swarmed into an animated bear trap that, when you stepped back on land, chomped messily through your legs at the shins. You had crippled yourself for what? A nearness? Henry never gave you any information that you could actually use, all information ever on offer was vigorously thought through. You had discovered nothing more of what Henry's intentions were toward you since your first meeting.

One night, Tony took your hand in his and you pencil-jumped together, his bulk forcing you far deeper into the onyx canal than you could have managed alone, whispering in bubbles, he had you tight by the wrist. Why do you need to chalk up the falls you've had in red to truest love? Love needs to become for you a source of life and not of mortal danger. You should stop trying to mend yourself. There is no way a wound can heal where the two sides of it shear away from each other. You need to know that it's OK to be an open wound . . . you'd get free and break the surface. These lessons left you injured: you lived with your throat pressing against piano wire. What really can a Box Set do? How is it more than a dream? What had you expected?

You expected Henry to learn that desire without cherishing would eventually lead to everyone's downfall, from Pauly to Tony, but stories don't change everyone in the same way. A good story is a good story because it makes you its own, but it owned you both differently. You thought you had to adapt, widen, stretch your life to fit the stories if necessary. No one would expose you as an imposter in your own living room, not if you could observe them from the inside, toughen up that way, be more yourself in the armor than without. But even with the armor, you limped away from every single episode. In the day, you became vigilant for bleeding but still maintained that if you could endure the Box Set you were going to be stronger for it.

In theory, by watching treacherous relationships in peril, by watching people crossed then double-crossed, biding your time with them, grudgingly postponing revenge, you could hoard solutions to situations, thicken your skin, win him over. You had imagined that watching together would soften Henry up, let you put your stamp on the new molten reality, with him, unfixed, plastic, you might get your chance to impress upon Henry *I am not what you have decided I am.* Why not? You don't kick or scream like Carmella. You wouldn't turn a blind eye. You are rational and look unflinchingly to what you can patiently learn from their unfolding dramas. You understand the rules of that world *as it applies to those characters.* You can laugh along when it's warranted, ha ha, you are brave from over here. In your daily life you become better to other women, allow them their emotions but don't envy them. You will never be one of those desperate owners of men, scrabbling and scrapping for monopoly while the men remain uninterested in small-minded politics and sniff out the sex that you don't understand, the sex that hums in the marrow of the bones of the women these guys serially deign to fuck. Will you.

You scraped your fingers beside Ray's daybed for cigarettes and a lighter then blinked around the walls of the studio, focusing finally on the tip of the cigarette. The lighter wouldn't strike and you bit it then threw it at the wall where it left a mark. You used Ray's bathroom to check on your front teeth in the mirror. You clicked them out and stared into the dark tunnel that was left; it was in your throat that you did your mourning. Ray's toilet was old and didn't look strong enough to take the paper but you peeled down your panties and the final piece of paper was shoved to its death in the toilet bowl by the fuzz of your bush. The ink instantly darkened in the bowl and you saw *Greek* blooming deeper and deeper blue. You missed your mother exactly the amount that you wanted Henry. Eureka.

You heard Ray descending the wrought-iron stair to the Disease Room.

A cab beeped. Ray stood quickly, asking, 'So you've decided?'

'Yes.' You wafted the Nudes certificate at him in thanks and kindly took his hand.

'I'm going back to New York.'

'For what?'

'I have to see what happens to Tony Soprano.'

'You won't survive it,' Ray warned you.

You stood up, smoothing your hands over your jeans trying not to linger about your pockets. You put your bag over your shoulder. In the end, you would be grateful to Ray.

'Stay here,' he said.

'You ever had someone Jive-talk you undressed?'

'Not even my main man Hancock has done that.'

You embraced.

'Will you stay clean?'

'Like a marine, bro.' You dug in your bag. 'Take this.' You handed over the *Zoot*, scuffed and battered. 'Practice with Hancock. No more role-playing *Velvet Goldmine*.'

Ray huffed a laugh and watched you run down the stairs, out onto the Paris street where he blew you a kiss as you ducked into the cab.

LA LUNA

The Swede makes his hand into a hooked claw to show me that from above, La Luna is shaped like a crushed comma. There is a route to the islet that they are going to take up, over and behind The Camping, to meet a dirt track that absolutely no one would know was there unless they were shown. Whether the island was called Dilpa or Despotiko did not matter; the party was never there.

I keep close to the big Swede as we set off from the harbour, winding our way to join a meagre track that will put us on a course towards the middle of the island. Only after crossing a hostile field of stones and stumps does a more established path appear: foot-wide dust trails flow into it at intervals and strangers freely join our group from these. The Swede holds a kerosene lamp with a new wick, not yet lit. With his large left hand, heavy as a discus, he holds my right. Astrid, herself once again now we know where we are going, scampers close behind me chatting openly to the newcomers, welcoming them. Gigi follows her without any need to talk to anyone, carrying a long plastic bag of speakers slung around his shoulders like a giant's lopped limb, his back shining with sweat. In this loose group, we inch up and over the island with our common purpose.

The Swede stops before a chalky incline that rounds the hump to light the lamp. 'We'll need it soon enough,' I say, and

I am right. Astrid appears beside us glowing in the light of it. The burnt umber of her bandeau cuts across the deeper brown of her flat belly. Her legs hang from the small neat turquoise shorts beneath the sheer skirt, their skinniness conspiring to make the opening of her boot seem oversized. The sheen of her scarf appears above her forehead as a column of light.

After a shallow rise around the hillock, we tumble right through a gap over furry stones into a meadow where there is a medley of mixed grasses and tiny delicate blue flowers twisting closed as the sun sets. Astrid throws herself on her back in the middle, swiping her limbs up and down, rubbing her cheek and temple into the grasses, laying on her back breathing in their scent. Others do the same, though the scent could just as well be detected from up here. I try to evade them by heading for the rim of the meadow when the Swede bars our passing and holds up his lamp over her. Unprompted, they laugh at each other.

After the meadow comes a slope to a set of narrow inter-locking terraces and, with her energy replenished after the performance at the restaurant, she leaps between them, taking two steps up onto, and then several back down. Catnipped also by the new territory, she twirls and prances from one pitch to the next, giddily pirouetting in the middle of the velvety strips, balancing on one leg before teetering and purposefully falling from one natural stage to another. Her dance is a delight to those who don't know it advertises a certain smugness. Breathless beyond the terraced steps, she moves aside into the rough to let us pass, paddling her hands forwards through knee-high fronds, beckoning the blessings of this unexpected outcome. She shouts 'Hank!' behind me but I don't turn around. 'Hank,' she shouts, her mouth I imagine is open and fixed, her face undaunted – but I have surely now disappeared from her view.

We are truly going inland now. The familiar breath of the sea is behind us and the vegetation, relieved of the sea air, is plumper and giving off a warm herby moistness in the very last of the sun. A couple of slender trees come into view; hearing music, though distant still, I stop, Gigi overtakes me, leading the group towards two sentry trees where our queue slims to pass between ashen trunks reaching towards each other in an arch. Complacent in ritual, we pass through in ones or twos when again the crowd thickens as the ground slants forward and down. The track underfoot becomes less rugged, changing from half bricks to fist-sized stones then to grass, green and giving, utterly unlike the springy scrub at the beach.

At an unmarked checkpoint, the Swede stops and lifts up his lamp and the group pulls up too. Whatever binds us swags forward as we stop, then settles back around us, drawing the new faces to focus mutely on the wick in the shivering flame before he lowers the lamp and we continue. The smell of kerosene lingers. There is a term the Russians use for the draw that regret can have, a damnable sweetness that lures us back to doing what we no longer want to.

Standing at a promontory, we look to where the Swede points, down at La Luna. Nobody has mentioned its name on the journey. I see the smaller island below and splitting the tail of the comma is a deep-looking inlet. The Swede makes a rising water sign with a flat hand before his face, hoping to laugh at my reaction. As we descend towards the inlet in the dusk I veer off to circumscribe the length of gully on land but the Swede pulls me back. Apart from our path, the plain bordering this inlet is becoming mud: the Swede gloops his hand up and down, performing the lifting of his knees with his hands but I have already guessed it from the feel underfoot. Gigi passes close by, grasping hands naturally with Astrid, then stops to take off his dark brown dress shirt.

Others follow his lead. Gigi undresses fully then and shows us just how we are to cross the unexpectedly deep water, that is, nude while holding clothes and perishables aloft. He demonstrates first with the speakers and then with his clothes. In the growing dark, it is difficult for me to distinguish whether the land beyond the other side of the inlet is part of the smaller island or another new and different place. Astrid is already in after Gigi and though the water had been over her head at points, for a small woman she crosses deftly. Now in an exaggerated gesture she beckons to get me to pass over, crying out that I shouldn't worry because she is right there. Birds escape the frightful volume. Dusk has leached any colour out of the water and so its hidden movements and depth are difficult to gauge, and as soon as I step into it, the current tugs my steps out of line and sends me off balance. The Swede grabs at my arm just as my body seems to snap to, remembering the strength in my leg from previous challenges. Stretching my chin to keep it out of the water, I wade stiff but stay confident in the current until I come up against the slop of the silty bank. Using the rush roots between my toes and both hands to get out, exclamations escape me at sharp angles. 'Good job!' She encourages me and birds flee roosting in the reeds at the shrill praise. I want to shout *go ahead for God's sake* but I don't so she remains rooted in the fine sludge of the bank, clapping me as if I were a toddler, beaming as one who believes they personally have brought everyone to safety.

On the other side, the Swede lights the lamp of a man he greets as Dinos and Astrid passes through his lamplight, her shoulders glistening proud and easy, goggles at her forehead, she strides through tough grass that flashes white in the beam's sweep. Coming from somewhere is the familiar *tsk tsk* of a pop song but not the bass that will come later in the evening from Gigi's treasured speakers. Such bass can be felt in the gums from a good distance.

We reach the comma's outer edge and follow it round a narrow ribbon of sandless shore, then at a piercing whistle we switch left inland over to a copse of short stocky twisted trees, whose horizontal boughs twist back on themselves as if their growth in a certain direction has suddenly embarrassed them. Despite the trees' silhouettes, the relationship between them is distinctly present among their difference. More torches are lit now, showing carpeted avenues between the trees awash with blaring green, as though fine felt had flooded them, slopping up the base of their trunks as it ebbed. The bark, uniforms of fine sand. Finally through, we head towards low pale rocks in ambush beyond which there is something. Something – crowned with a puff of light from a source unknown, suggesting that what has been promised can no longer be contained. The light gradually becomes brighter than the light of the lamp, beckoning us through the low rocks to a rim like a caldera that looks down into a steep hollow. She stops suddenly at the caldera edge and the Swede sweeps his arm towards it, welcoming us. 'La Luna,' he says. I look back and forth for Gigi. The rocks on the incline from the rim to the hollow have been carved into steps that bottom out in sand. From behind she cries, 'Hank! Look! We're here! Oh my God, is this it?' Her pupils are huge despite the wash of light. 'We found it!' And she begins the descent, digging the sides of her boots into the hillside, then with steps quickened by momentum and following the long curve she trips down to sea level. I stand still at the ridge.

When I finally get down there, at the bottom of the staircase is a rocky cove that seems to have its arm around an almond tree five times the size of any other I have seen on Antiparos. The tree is hung with swaying strands of tiny silver lights; the effect achieved is that the tree seems only resting and could become animated any second. A wooden bar has been built around its thick trunk and under this people sit and stretch, roll joints. Between the curved rugged wall of the cove and the bar that encircles the tree a lean body or two can fit. From the tree, the bar reaches out in the direction of the seashore where a small, sacred scrap of beach lays like a paper cut-out. It is a promise that I have known yet not known was here, one that has captured a moon and grown around it. Out in the bay *Petroula* rocks, her engine chugging after her longer journey, in a sea now scattered with moonlight her single bulb winking as she waits to be unburdened of a couple of steep dishes of lamb, bottles of ouzo and retsina, and a mattress of still warm, uncut, spanakopita.

The cove is already hissing with a cymbal and the tight toot of a tinny-sounding pop song. The bar is being stocked by the ferryman; his checked tablecloths are draped over the end of it where bottles huddle with candles. There is a low table further out and on it a cardboard box of records. The bag of spare speakers hugs the base of the bar.

When I finally catch sight of him Gigi has changed into a yellow vest with two bright green stripes separated by a red band. Standing on the tree's waist-high wooden skirt, he picks between glasses with his bare feet to secure a speaker in the fork of its boughs. He fiddles behind the smaller speaker and the music disappears and there's the groan, I search for Astrid to qualify it. Gigi leaps up again to connect to the larger speaker and a boom of noise ricochets round the curve, followed by the nightly cheer. She is beside me now followed by the Swede who produces a joint and gives it straight to her. I protest 'Hey!' but no one can hear because of the music. Buoyed by the new volume, I put my hand up to help Gigi but he jumps down in a different direction. I scan around. Frappés are everywhere.

Up at the bar, I look at Gigi's glass and order my own ouzo and water. Astrid orders beer. Gigi puts his arm on her shoulder and since no one is offering I snatch the joint from her to take a drag. At the bar, her silhouette tessellates with the brown-to-black profiles of the Athenians. The music suddenly gets louder and jolts in a wave through the crowd when the ferryman gestures to me (me?) to help him unload the boat, forcing me with a shove to shuttle the heavier trays of food and canisters of water. First I graze my knuckles on the metal lip of *Petroula* then I pour meat juice from a stupid dish down my shirt as some dolt backs into me from the bar. Meanwhile, Gigi has Astrid by the back of the neck and is pointing her face to the visible history on show and, with greasy trays in my arms, I watch him touch the almond tree with her hand. Astrid is looking around and it must be for me but I am struggling with a stack of coffee cups and a bucket of bottles while Gigi is lifting her up by her waist to push a puppet on a swing hanging from the branches. Everyone is clapping as he lowers her. I put down plates to go and look at the puppet too: a wooden butcher with pupils in relief, a black moustache, a little leather apron, so much part of the tree, lead knife and all. I push him, he swings. Back against the bar Astrid is readying her lips to be fed a cigarette by Gigi, who places the dummy of his finger in her mouth instead of the filter. He does this twice before allowing her to take a drag. The ferryman signals for me to stop leaning on this part of the bar, and meanly mimics me staring at them while he fires up an ancient coffee machine that moves not an inch when he slams the handle of the portafilter into place with the hard heel of his strongest hand.

The Swede finally hands me a beer and I bend towards my stomach and flap the wet stain of the meat juice to dry my shirt. The Swede points to my neck, nods at Astrid and chomps his teeth together with a low vibrating seethe. His eyebrows raised, the Swede hoots wildly, nodding for a long time after, and I look away, even turn my back but the Swede stays put. Gigi continues to parade Astrid around the cove introducing her to ever more people and at his suggestion they beg her to sing, at which she pulls the goggles down over her eyes. Gigi lets go of her neck, she waves a tiny swatch of her skirt back and forth with one hand and is charming them.

The smell of charcoal scents the air now and it is Gigi's turn to chivvy me into helping the ferryman and so while I struggle with a warm tray of cheese pie and a clear bag of octopus, Astrid and Gigi serenade each other. I throw the octopus to the ground behind the bar where his rubbery little suckers press against the bag, determined as fists. When I finish my new round of chores, Astrid has also taken my stool and is sharing her joint this time with the Swede. I let her know subtly that I am sitting there and she slides off the stool smiling, padding barefoot over to Gigi who is building something on the sand by layering pallets and skewing each one above the other into a short helix; a twisted mini dais which he centres with a bar stool. Without a word, the ferryman pulls me back to the boat to help him with a trestle table. Picking it up, I trap my finger and promptly drop it. The ferryman shoos me away from him with both hands.

Gigi is guiding her by shaking the tail ends of her scarf and he drops the tasselled ends between her shoulder blades as if they are reins. With a smile, she gets up the three steps he has fashioned from the pallets, so simple, natural, clever. From up there, she says it's time, that she wants to share something. As she starts to tune up the orange guitar, they are ten deep in any direction, cinched around her. I remain at the bar. Gigi returns to a stool close to me and offers me a cigarette. I go for the one with diamonds in biro but Gigi sharply draws back the pack and I take a plain cigarette and wait for it to be lit. He pats his groin then his chest then as a last resort gives me his own cigarette with which to light mine. Pushing too hard, I knock the lit tip to the floor and begin sucking furiously. Astrid is warming up her crowd, saying something about how the heat brings out the worst in those who weren't born to it, fanning her face and looking around with a half grin. The crowd are happy to have her to themselves, she is stoned, a little drunk and they cheer in clusters at the mimes she makes that imply that this is so. The Swede hands her a different guitar and she thanks him and strums them to silence, the whole almond tree canopy above them catching wind of the loving sigh before she begins. She tunes the guitar a little more and turns for her gaze to dock at mine. The cigarette burns unsmoked in my hand as she reaches into her boot for something, and even at distance, I recognise the squares of my paper.

As I stand the stool falls heavily but silently in the sand and I lunge forward with a flat hand toward strangers' backs then, realising this is impossible, I start to burrow between people, burning someone with the cigarette that I thought wasn't lit. They yelp, abusing me in Greek, looking for the mark on the back of their arm, but I have to push on. 'It's something that someone wrote for me,' she is saying to them. They throng round her and I don't recognise the urgency in me – I am unaccustomed to this kind of indignity. They seem to condense as a crowd as I push: they are not vicious but they have waited for this and they will not be moved. The cigarette has snapped and hangs at a dangerous angle, and I hurl it backwards out of the crowd so that I can seek out the gaps between these strangers in earnest. 'Something called *Greek Stars*.' She gives her interrogative lilt to the title. Shrugs. Everyone laughs and I push wantonly with my shoulder now but at the first line of the song I drop to the floor to squirm through legs on my belly. She is singing it and I stand again, unhinging a couple from each other, swiping at a straggler at the front of the crowd to get a foot up on the back of the dais where I step back pushing the crowd behind me, then hunker down to lever up the corner of a pallet. Someone pushes me backwards when I am down but I have gained enough leverage and she tips and they gasp, hands framing their faces as, mid-song, she leans forward dangerously on the legs of the stool. She falls slowly then is saved by their hands but sways, tottering counter to the original lurch, and some behind her skitter backwards on tiptoe in readiness for her while others thrust up hands and she takes it: a hand thrust from the crowd to right herself. An almighty cheer goes up and she steadies, laughs incredulously and starts the song again.

FIRE

How light you were without the *Zoot*! Did you know the past was just a sandbag waiting to be dropped? You felt you owed it to Ray to catch the kiss he blew you as you ducked into the cab for the airport. You practiced being upbeat on the plane, because it was easy to be optimistic without any challenges. Henry was going to be delighted when he saw how you had grown. Paris, miles below, might not have happened. You see it now: the *Zoot* had become a drag.

And the second you crossed the threshold into your apartment, you longed to tell him how different things were with you now but you were not fool enough to ruin these first moments with all that. You hadn't meant to mention Gigi. When Henry returned to the living room, you put your arms out and hugged him with tragic restraint, noting that he had removed all the things that ever made the apartment yours: the window gawped now the velvet drapes were gone; your Nina cushion was easy to spot through the strip of space into the bedroom but that was certainly not where it belonged. And where was Laddie? You didn't ask.

'You miss me?' Your arms remained stiff, straight blunt knives at the base of his neck. You had already spotted the notebook which had also gained the dumb threat of a weapon.

'They want my book,' he said solemnly.

You would kill to know his plans but you flopped to the sofa and breezed: 'I'm going to need a week to tell you about Ray's alone.'

'Please do!' he called out. Glasses clinking in the kitchen.

You looked around for the absence of more of your things: *he is un-remembering me*, you said to yourself. *I exist too much for him*. This thought slowed to a stop, balanced, immobile for a second before slowly spinning on a different axis that you hadn't known was there until this moment but here he was with a very full glass, no ice, though it was still light out, commanding, 'Tell me everything about Hypno Ray.'

Tasting the potency at the first sip, you lost heart, just how he liked you. Henry let you kiss him, your last, but only after you gave him details about Baskets then the whole bloodhounds spiel but he was probing for details only of that world, not your experiences in it. You made no difference to the story he wanted and the story he would get. You took a couple more gulps of what you thought was Long Island iced tea, remembering again the benefits of pleasing him, and you began to feel more magnanimous, more willing to reinvent him rather than reminding yourself of what he was, but there was something new under this, something seismic, a juddering invisible harm that animals are good at detecting. Two big gulps more and you felt a strong urge to sing, and in the same way you needed to rub hard against Henry's leg when he kissed you, you experienced a three-way between past, present and future, all wounds active, itching and threatening to open, like when you rubbed your very hardest. The thought of freedom, like the never-broached thought of orgasm, had grown without your attention and had become a blast space, a living obliteration in which you could be set permanently adrift, recognizing nothing.

After the second drink you draped yourself off him, hoping he too had softened. He slid something in your back pocket, his eyebrows demanding a reaction that you gave to him because you were so used to letting go of rules you could not live up to. But if this was relief it had lost its flavor. You accepted his first stand-in to please him without mentioning that Lucien had also taken care of you on the flight, nor did he know that you drank on the plane; you weren't going to spoil his surprises for you. The mix of what you have taken melts down exposing something grotesque: the thought that a new you might be incapable of the old joys. You watch dusk and dark begin their negotiations, waiting as always for him to start acting the way you wish he would.

When the stand-in rudely introduced itself, a WAY OUT appeared for you right there in the room. It was as big as a hallway runner: a giant asphalt tongue that beckoned you with frilly undulations along its edge. You wonder if you can get rid of it without him noticing. Out the window? Even if you were strong enough to lift it up it would crump back on itself like thick, black gingerbread. You stood quickly to cross to the window, but it slid into your path and got under your feet easily and had you standing smartly in the middle of it. An aggressive muscle of a thing pulsing under your feet. You forced the window up, quickly letting air and noise rush in. Switching strategies, you pretended it wasn't there, and this pretense radiated a small zone of control. The path hummed with threat to lick you out of the window but you stood fast. Your gaze lassoed the park, kept it there, drawing the tips of the trees together, and all the longing that you had ever packed into him threatened to atomize. Or return to you. You quelled this with a double gulp.

'Come over here and tell me more Ray stuff,' said Henry. 'I've saved the papers for you. I hope there's more Ray stuff?'

You showed him your Nudes certificate. Henry didn't want to be bothered by how Ray had been the turning point and you started here to hail Sinead, now safe behind you, as your unlikely four-wheeled savior. You deftly filleted the Nudes story, trying not to be too enthusiastic, launching humiliating details of Ray's place and the meetings with a pyrotechnic dazzle so you could retreat behind them, compose yourself, plan a different retreat, but he drew you out into describing the fighting, the peril, and you were dismayed that you felt safer, that this brought you closer to him. This mutual nastiness, a confluence of decay. Could you give this up, this receptiveness only ever there for the appreciation of soul-blackening gossip, a miserly need that seeped out of Henry at moments like this? Only these have been your intimacies, these the only times you could ever satisfy him, with meanness about others, or a carving up of yourself. Henry wanted a brutal butchering of Hypno Ray. You refused to be insufficient to the task but your puppet hands tried to sacrifice Ray and when your wooden fingers and liquid wrists tried to dig in with the blind knife, the slackness of your grip meant that Ray survived, Ray stood. His slanted little legs dithering in a jig. Sinead slackening to a similar orientation. You made childish, cheap fun of Ray's hair – he straightens it now – and you even described his puckered balls, but where was your heart in this? Henry could taste the change because all of a sudden Henry was putting on a jacket, scouring for keys, the notebook that was sulking against the wall.

'But I just got back!' you cried out.

'I told you, I have a meeting with Greg's publisher.'

'Told me when?'

'Watch an episode. I'll catch up when I get back.'

The betrayal in your face set him howling with laughter. 'Relax!' he said but you had never seen him so happy. The apartment door banged, the notebook shuddered.

Three nights later, he sat on the opposite end of the sofa from you and took up the remote.

'Now, where were we?' But you were too injured to feel complicity and of course, neither of you had the slightest idea what was coming. Maybe Adriana's death was a curse on everyone who watched her shimmy on her knees out of the picture, as if she dragged along the forest floor our denials that it was us, that we enabled those motherfuckers to kill her. It could be said that Adriana's death made way for you to finally slip out into the rest of your life because she meant something to you and not having her meant something even bigger.

Lucien had come by in the night with a package but you had avoided the hall because the newspaper that Henry had left was open at your picture. Henry was at the clinic, leaving you a chance to examine the degradation he was so great at inducing. You turned off the cruel news to hunt for anything that would help you survive today. You held the package but didn't open it and the burden of anticipation began a slow crush forcing you to look at your picture in the paper, which in turn sent you to the window, grasping for comfort and scared of photographers. Stories below, there stood a hot dog cart pushed by a woman in a see-through poncho with greasy straps of pewter-colored hair hanging from her beret. You gazed at the tops of the trees in the park, testing what you had left in you. Returning to the woman to smile at her just as there was a knock. Lucien had a key. Who then? You went into the hall, quickly hid the package and opened the door a crack, looking out with one eye.

'Telephone,' someone said from the darkness. You didn't move.

'Dr Sinclair? Your business line?' said a voice, revealing an eye of its own.

'This is my apartment,' you said.

'You want this or no?'

You opened the door a little more. A black hand held up a champagne-colored wall-mounted telephone in Saran Wrap, just like the one you used to have.

'Where you want it?' He was breathing heavily.

'There,' you said, pointing at the lighter patch of paint and the screw holes.

He held the phone at the wall for a few seconds, looking for your appraisal before he fitted it. He was a heavy man and you didn't want to pity his efforts but whichever room you moved to, you could still hear him struggling and puffing. Catherine rang on your cell. She was touchy since Burning Man but you felt you must do something to get over Ade's death. Though she warned you off it you decided you would go out on your own. You chose a scarf alternately edged with quills and inkpots. You gave the phone guy more tools.

He was swearing when you returned and still holding one edge of the telephone set against the wall.

'Do you have anything to pack this out? Paper. Cardboard? These walls are *old!*' You put down season six on the green glass table. In the kitchen, you pulled out the plastic recycling box from next to the wall under the table. Henry ate crap when you were out of town. Mini cereal boxes, unopened newspapers, a stack of cardboard tubes and there was a box for a brand of tea you didn't recognize, but you kept with the task and burrowed.

'Not too thick,' the phone guy cried.

'OK,' you shouted back.

'Not too thin,' he yelled.

You ferreted under the papers and boxes until you grasped something flat against the bottom, a pliant square of card about the size of your palm. You picked it out and you stared at it and you assessed the thickness with your finger and thumb. It was white and stiff and looked unused and instinctively you bowed it open slightly to see if the CD was in there before you opened it out and saw written *For Astrid Love Sandy*, in a rounded teenage style, the hole of the second d was a heart. 'Cheroot Girl' was track number one.

Every day when my mom left for work, my heart would strain to contain the longing I had for her. It didn't take much of her pity to make you feel you could light up and stay lit. You survived years on next to nothing; you could count those rare soft moments when she said, *Come on baby, it's a bush fire but it'll go out* or *Ain't nothing can't be be shifted if you get your back into it.* I had no idea that letting go of my mother was the only way that I would find myself.

Then one day my mom came back at midday and surprised me with fried chicken. The overdose of what I had always wished for threw me for a loop. At first, I was ashamed of her for giving in to me. The day before I had hallucinated weevils in the Lucky Charms and had spent the whole day in one corner, knees tucked under me. She said that was nonsense but there had been black fly the summer before. Even so, her coming back, this unexpected dreamed-of rupture was unbearable, because my distantly cherished mother was untouchable up close, repulsive even. I want to make that little girl say, *Don't take any notice of what I am doing, I'm just looking for someone who can see through me, make me not terrified of love.*

I didn't want to see my mother's false teeth making hard work of the chicken anymore. After breaking apart my pieces, she went to wipe her hands so I floated across the yard to knock on the Campbells' trailer. The Campbell kids were all freckled: two boys and a girl. All three silent. They looked at me blankly, standing on the bent step with a tray of spiced meat. In the dim of their trailer, their mother said 'Let's straighten things up a little' – they too had just started eating. The herbs and bell peppers which she had grown herself perfumed her trailer and even as a little kid, I sensed the fat from my chicken was ruining the atmosphere. She cherished her own kids and drizzled on their lunches her knowledge of them, balancing uniquely what was wanted by each of the three. I offered my lunch to each family member by sliding it around under their chins before devouring it myself standing up. From their faces, I don't think these guys ever chomped bones. Their Ma singing nervous and high at the small metal sink and its single faucet, to let everyone know she was there if they needed saving from me and my melancholy. She never needed no man. It was in this trailer where I learned that silence sucks the sass out of you. They had never waited for their mother outside an abattoir by a creek, playing with bulls' ears. Not one of them spoke because if any of them did they would have to ask why the hell had I come over to stink out their fresh wholesome lunchtime with my gristly chicken knuckles?

'How you know that ain't a squirrel?' one of them said finally.

I point to the tray. 'It says *Chicken Shack*.'

When I should have been burned by it, I didn't lay shame down, I was bulletproof right on through. How can these waves of shame gain on me with such force now? Maybe nine-year-olds have force fields. Maybe I never earned the right to be a kid. Or never let kid-dom fit me (cuz it didn't) or because it fit me so well I knew I'd never be able to live without it so I thought hell, let's just be done with it before I put it on.

I didn't know that it was humiliation that changed me; I only felt I had less to lose.

It's how I knew what I must do. The changes in the Campbells' clean, blank, well-loved faces when I sang behind the dumpsters. The staggering fluctuation in what they thought of me, how I could make them think of things out there worth feeling about, connecting with them even among the garbage. And I see just as clearly that when the singing stops the signals change. Everyone could ignore me again and they'd shuffle off, betraying none of what I'd changed in them, puzzling mad to know how I did it.

I calmly hand the square cardboard CD case to the phone guy. He talks but I don't hear him or answer. Crying seems an abomination, I should have cried when it mattered. The phone guy holds the CD case and holds his breath as he packs it between the phone and the wall, he fixes it tight with screws. I move toward him, my flesh needs other flesh, and out of the blue he wheezes that he likes my songs. I offer him a drink. Of course he can smoke in my apartment; half of the package turns out to be clean senior-level weed from Lucien. I roll a joint, and with trembling lips, I let the poison out of myself to this stranger and tell him that I am done fooling myself. When I tell him about my reasons for returning to New York it feels like it is news to me and we are silent for a long time. I still do not cry. He gets up effortfully, goes to the bathroom, returns, tests the phone mount to see if it has decided to become steady.

'You need more paper?' I ask him.

'Maybe one piece.'

I get up and rip a page from the notebook at random and he folds it, slips it behind the phone. I ask him to dump the notebook and he nods, sure thing, slings it under his armpit.

'Stay open to bewilderment,' he reminds me.

I jag my hand in a stuttering arc over his head. 'Be-wild-er-ment – my next album.'

The engineer squeezes my fingers before he leaves and I pull him back, kiss his cheek.

I pack my scarves in my bag first then I unwrap the phone book and flick to subsections of the University Hospital. Professor Leary is charming, sounds rational, he agrees to what I ask and he gives me Bradley's number without question. I crawl on my hands and knees and I take out the last disc of season five from the machine. With the sun setting over the park, I skim the DVD high above the alley, wincing at the thought of it connecting with the hot dog woman's grubby beret and in the last of the light, I feel hacked in two, but cleanly.

I call Catherine to tell her I'll do it. I give her the title. No I am not high I tell her. I am wide as a river mouth. I step to the window, look out. I am every inch the distance between here and there. I am looking down at myself, the way I flare at the bottom and I can see what I have to do and I know I will make it. I hang up.

I lock the door to my apartment.

I put my cushion where it should go.

In goes season six.

I press play.

228

ACKNOWLEDGEMENTS

This book started out as a short story and its growth would not have been possible without the patience of Stella McKinney and the love and encouragement of Tina and Graham Siddall; the vision and advice of Laurence Piercey, Conor O'Callaghan and Susannah Gent; the friendship of Mary Peace, Suzanne Higgs, Kathy Towers and Antonia Boothman; the generosity of Arts Council England, The Reckitt Trust and Arvon; the warm embrace of Manchester Writing School, the stimulation of Bookklub (Tom Stafford; Harriet Cameron; Laurence Piercey; Eleanor Kent; Charlotte Foster; Joe Shrewsbury); the hospitality of Joanna Walsh (Oxford) and Jessica Weetch (Cornwall); the heart connection I have with Amanda Ravetz, Sally Anne Wickenden, Jennifer Hodgson and Noah Nazir (also God, Sheikh Nazim, Sheikh Mehmet and the Sheffield Naqshbandi Sufis); the perspicacity of Tara Tobler's editorial advice and the risk-taking of Stefan Tobler. I am particularly grateful to Kate Smith who has given me unlimited support throughout this protracted endeavour and who makes me laugh regularly to the point of tears.

Declan McKinney, you remain my number one.

And to my daughters, Esther and Ingrid, what life before you?

Dear readers,

As well as relying on bookshop sales, And Other Stories relies on subscriptions from people like you for many of our books, whose stories other publishers often consider too risky to take on.

Our subscribers don't just make the books physically happen. They also help us approach booksellers, because we can demonstrate that our books already have readers and fans. And they give us the security to publish in line with our values, which are collaborative, imaginative and 'shamelessly literary'.

All of our subscribers:

- receive a first-edition copy of each of the books they subscribe to
- are thanked by name at the end of our subscriber-supported books
- receive little extras from us by way of thank you, for example: postcards created by our authors

BECOME A SUBSCRIBER,
OR GIVE A SUBSCRIPTION TO A FRIEND

Visit andotherstories.org/subscriptions to help make our books happen. You can subscribe to books we're in the process of making. To purchase books we have already published, we urge you to support your local or favourite bookshop and order directly from them – the often unsung heroes of publishing.

OTHER WAYS TO GET INVOLVED

If you'd like to know about upcoming events and reading groups (our foreign-language reading groups help us choose books to publish, for example) you can:

- join our mailing list at: andotherstories.org
- follow us on Twitter: @andothertweets
- join us on Facebook: facebook.com/AndOtherStoriesBooks
- admire our books on Instagram: @andotherpics
- follow our blog: andotherstories.org/ampersand

This book was made possible thanks to the support of:

Aaron McEnery
Aaron Schneider
Abigail Walton
Adam Lenson
Adrian Astur Alvarez
Adriana Diaz Enciso
Aifric Campbell
Ailsa Peate
Aisha McLean
Aisling Reina
Ajay Sharma
Alan Donnelly
Alan Simpson
Alastair Gillespie
Alastair Whitson
Alecia Marshall
Alex Fleming
Alex Hoffman
Alex Lockwood
Alex Pearce
Alex Ramsey
Alexandra de Verseg-
    Roesch
Alexandra Stewart
Alexandra Stewart
Ali Smith
Ali Usman
Alice Morgan
Alice Smith
Alice Toulmin
Alice Tranah
Alice Wilkinson
Alison Hardy
Alison Layland
Alison Winston
Aliya Rashid
Alyse Ceirante
Alyssa Rinaldi
Amado Floresca
Amalia Gladhart
Amanda
Amanda Dalton
Amanda Geenen
Amanda Read
Amanda Silvester
Amber Da
Amelia Lowe

Amy Benson
Amy Koheeallee
Andra Dusu
Andrea Barlien
Andrea Reece
Andrew Lees
Andrew Marston
Andrew McCallum
Andrew McDougall
Andrew Reece
Andrew Rego
Andy Corsham
Andy Turner
Angelica Ribichini
Angus Walker
Ann Menzies
Anna Dowrick
Anna Gibson
Anna Milsom
Anna Zaranko
Anne Carus
Anne Craven
Anne Guest
Anne Kangley
Anne-Marie Renshaw
Anne Ryden
Anne Sticksel
Anne Willborn
Annette Hamilton
Annie McDermott
Anonymous
Anonymous
Anonymous
Anthony Brown
Antoni Centofanti
Antonia Lloyd-Jones
Antonia Saske
Antony Pearce
Aoife Boyd
Archie Davies
Arthur John Rowles
Asako Serizawa
Ashleigh Sutton
Ashley Cairns
Audrey Mash
Audrey Small
Aviv Teller

Barbara Bettsworth
Barbara Mellor
Barbara Robinson
Barbara Spicer
Barry Norton
Bart Van Overmeire
Ben Schofield
Ben Schroder
Ben Thornton
Ben Walter
Benjamin Judge
Benjamin Pester
Beverley Thomas
Bhakti Gajjar
Bianca Duec
Bianca Jackson
Bianca Winter
Bill Fletcher
Bjørnar Djupevik
    Hagen
Brendan Monroe
Briallen Hopper
Brian Anderson
Brian Byrne
Brian Smith
Bridget Gill
Brigita Ptackova
Briony Hey
Caitlin Halpern
Caitriona Lally
Cal Smith
Cameron Lindo
Camilla Imperiali
Campbell McEwan
Carla Ballin
Carla Carpenter
Carla Castanos
Carolina Pineiro
Caroline Jupp
Caroline West
Cassidy Hughes
Catharine Braithwaite
Catherine Barton
Catherine Fearns
Catherine Lambert
Catherine Williamson
Catie Kosinski

Catriona Gibbs
Cecilia Cerrini
Cecilia Rossi
Cecilia Uribe
Chantal Wright
Charlene Huggins
Charles Dee Mitchell
Charles Fernyhough
Charles Raby
Charles Tocock
Charlie Cook
Charlie Small
Charlotte Briggs
Charlotte Coulthard
Charlotte Stoneley
Charlotte Whittle
Charlotte Woodford
Chelsey Johnson
Cherilyn Elston
Cherise Wolas
China Miéville
Chris Blackmore
Chris Holmes
Chris Köpruner
Chris Lintott
Chris Maguire
Chris Potts
Chris & Kathleen
  Repper-Day
Chris Stevenson
Christian Schuhmann
Christina Moutsou
Christine Bartels
Christine Hudnall
Christine and Nigel
  Wycherley
Christopher Allen
Christopher Homfray
Christopher Mitchell
Christopher Stout
Ciara Ní Riain
Claire Adams
Claire Brooksby
Claire Hayward
Claire Mackintosh
Claire Potter
Clare Young
Clarice Borges
Clarissa Pattern

Clive Bellingham
Cody Copeland
Colin Denyer
Colin Matthews
Colin Hewlett
Collin Brooke
Cortina Butler
Courtney Lilly
Craig Kennedy
Cynthia De La Torre
Cyrus Massoudi
Daisy Savage
Dale Wisely
Dana Behrman
Dana Lapidot
Daniel Gillespie
Daniel Hahn
Daniel Jàrmai
Daniel Jones
Daniel Oudshoorn
Daniel Raper
Daniel Stewart
Daniel Venn
Daniel Wood
Daniela Steierberg
Danny Millum
Darcy Hurford
Darina Brejtrova
Dave Lander
David Anderson
David Ball
David Cowan
David Gould
David Hebblethwaite
David Higgins
David Hodges
David Johnson-Davies
David Key
David Kinnaird
David Leverington
David F Long
David McIntyre
David Miller
David Musgrave
David Reid
David Richardson
David Shriver
David Smith
David Thornton

Dawn Bass
Dean Taucher
Debbie Ballin
Debbie McKee
Debbie Pinfold
Deborah Banks
Declan Gardner
Declan O'Driscoll
Deirdre Nic Mhathuna
Denis Larose
Denis Stillewagt & Anca
  Fronescu
Denton Djurasevich
Diana Digges
Diane Humphries
Diane Salisbury
Diarmuid Hickey
Dina Abdul-Wahab
Dinesh Prasad
Dipika Mummery
Dominic Nolan
Dominick Santa
  Cattarina
Dominique Brocard
Drew Gummerson
Duncan Clubb
Duncan Macgregor
Duncan Marks
Dyanne Prinsen
Earl James
Ebba Aquila
Ebba Tornérhielm
Ed Burness
Ed Tronick
Ekaterina Beliakova
Elaine Kennedy
Eleanor Maier
Eleanor Updegraff
Elena Galindo
Elif Aganoglu
Elina Zicmane
Elisabeth Cook
Eliza Mood
Elizabeth Braswell
Elizabeth Coombes
Elizabeth Dillon
Elizabeth Draper
Elizabeth Franz
Elizabeth Guss

Elizabeth Leach
Elizabeth Perry
Elizabeth Seal
Ellie Goddard
Emeline Morin
Emily Armitage
Emily Paine
Emily Webber
Emily Williams
Emma Bielecki
Emma Louise Grove
Emma Morgan
Emma Page
Emma Patel
Emma Perry
Ena Lee
Eric Anderson
Eric Cassells
Eric Reinders
Eric Tucker
Erin Cameron Allen
Esmée de Heer
Eva Oddo
Eve Corcoran
Ewan Tant
F Gary Knapp
Fatima Kried
Fawzia Kane
Felix Valdivieso
Finbarr Farragher
Finn Williamson
Fiona Mozley
Fiona Davenport White
Florian Duijsens
Forrest Pelsue
Fran Sanderson
Frances Spangler
Francesca Brooks
Francesca Rhydderch
Francis Mathias
Francisco Vilhena
Frank van Orsouw
Frankie Mullin
Freddie Radford
Friederike Knabe
Gabriel Colnic
Gabriel Martinez
Gabrielle Crockatt
Garan Holcombe

Gareth Tulip
Gary Clarke
Gary Gorton
Gavin Collins
Gavin Smith
Gawain Espley
Gemma Fitzgibbon
Genaro Palomo Jr
Geoff Thrower
Geoffrey Cohen
Geoffrey Urland
George Stanbury
George Wilkinson
Georgia Shomidie
Georgina Norton
German Cortez-
    Hernandez
Gerry Craddock
Gill Boag-Munroe
Gillian Grant
Gillian Spencer
Gordon Cameron
Gosia Pennar
Graham R Foster
Graham Blenkinsop
Grant Rintoul
Gwyn Lewis
Hadil Balzan
Hamish Russell
Hanna Randall
Hanna Varady & Mikael
    Awake
Hannah Freeman
Hannah Mayblin
Hannah Procter
Hannah Vidmark
Hans Lazda
Harriet Stiles
Harriet Wade
Haydon Spenceley
Heather Gallivan
Heather & Andrew
    Ordover
Heather Tipon
Heidi Gilhooly
Helen Brady
Helen Coombes
Helen Moor
Helena Buffery

Henriette Magerstaedt
Henrike Laehnemann
Henry Bell
Henry Patino
Hilary Barry
Holly Barker
Holly Down
Howard Robinson
Hugh Schoonover
Hugh Shipley
Hyoung-Won Park
IKE Lehvonen
Iain Forsyth
Ian Hagues
Ian McMillan
Ian Mond
Ian Randall
Ian Whitfield
Ida Grochowska
Ilona Abb
Ingunn Vallumroed
Irene Croal
Irene Mansfield
Irina Tzanova
Isabel Adey
Isabella Garment
Isabella Weibrecht
Isabelle Schneider
Isobel Foxford
Izabela Jamrozik
Jacinta Perez Gavilan
    Torres
Jack Brown
Jack Hargreaves
Jacob Blizard
Jacob Swan Hyam
Jacqueline Haskell
Jacqueline Lademann
Jacqueline Ting Lin
Jacqui Hudson
Jacqui Jackson
Jadie Lee
James Attlee
James Beck
James Crossley
James Cubbon
James Dahm
James Kinsley
James Lee

Kirsten Ward
Kirsty Doole
Klara Rešetič
Kris Ann Trimis
Kristen Tcherneshoff
Krystale Tremblay-Moll
Krystine Phelps
Lacy Wolfe
Lana Selby
Laura Batatota
Laura Clarke
Laura Ling
Laura Zederkof
Lauren Pout
Laurence Laluyaux
Laurie Sheck & Jim
   Peck
Laury Leite
Leah Zani
Lee Harbour
Leon Geis
Leona Iosifidou
Leonora Randall
Liliana Lobato
Lillie Rosen
Lily Blacksell
Lily Hersov
Lily Susan Todd
Linda Jones
Lindsay Attree
Lindsay Brammer
Lindsey Ford
Lindsey Harbour
Line Langebek Knudsen
Linette Arthurton
   Bruno
Lisa Agostini
Lisa Dillman
Lisa Fransson
Lisa Leahigh
Lisa Simpson
Lisa Weizenegger
Liz Clifford
Lorna Bleach
Lorna Scott Fox
Lottie Smith
Louise Evans
Louise Greebverg
Louise Hoelscher

Louise Smith
Luc Verstraete
Lucia Rotheray
Lucile Lesage
Lucy Beevor
Lucy Gorman
Lucy Greaves
Lucy Huggett
Lucy Moffatt
Ludmilla Jordanova
Luise von Flotow
Luke Healey
Luke Loftiss
Lydia Trethewey
Lyn Curthoys
Lynda Graham
Lynn Fung
M Manfre
Madeline Teevan
Mads Pihl Rasmussen
Maeve Lambe
Magdaline Rohweder
Maggie Kerkman
Maggie Livesey
Marcel Schlamowitz
Margaret Dillow
Maria Ahnhem Farrar
Maria Hill
Maria Lomunno
Maria Losada
Marie Donnelly
Marijana Rimac
Marina Castledine
Mario Sifuentez
Marisa Wilson
Marja S Laaksonen
Mark Harris
Mark Huband
Mark Sargent
Mark Sheets
Mark Sztyber
Mark Waters
Marlene Simoes
Martha Nicholson
Martha Stevns
Martin Brown
Martin Price
Mary Byrne
Mary Heiss

Mary Ellen Nagle
Mary Nash
Mary Wang
Mathieu Trudeau
Matt Davies
Matt Greene
Matt O'Connor
Matteo Besana
Matthew Adamson
Matthew Armstrong
Matthew Banash
Matthew Black
Matthew Cullinan
Matthew Francis
Matthew Gill
Matthew Hiscock
Matthew Lowe
Matthew Warshauer
Matthew Woodman
Matty Ross
Maureen Cullen
Maureen Pritchard
Max Cairnduff
Max Garrone
Max Longman
Maya Chung
Meaghan Delahunt
Meg Lovelock
Megan Taylor
Megan Wittling
Meghan Goodeve
Melissa Beck
Melissa Quignon-Finch
Melissa Stogsdill
Meredith Jones
Meredith Martin
Michael Aguilar
Michael Bichko
Michael James
   Eastwood
Michael Friddle
Michael Gavin
Michael Kuhn
Michael Pollak
Michael Roess
Michael Shayer
Miguel Head
Mike Turner
Mildred Nicotera

Miles Smith-Morris
Miriam McBride
Moira Sweeney
Molly Foster
Mona Arshi
Moray Teale
Morven Dooner
Muireann Maguire
Myka Tucker-Abramson
Myles Nolan
N Tsolak
Nan Craig
Nancy Jacobson
Nancy Oakes
Naomi Morauf
Naomi Sparks
Nathalie Adams
Nathalie Atkinson
Nathan Rowley
Nathan Weida
Neferti Tadiar
Neslihan Yegul
Nicholas Brown
Nicholas Jowett
Nicholas Smith
Nick James
Nick Nelson & Rachel
    Eley
Nick Sidwell
Nick Twemlow
Nicola Hart
Nicola Sandiford
Nicola Scott
Nicola Todd
Nicole Matteini
Nicoletta Asciuto
Nigel Fishburn
Nina Alexandersen
Nina de la Mer
Nora Hart
Odilia Corneth
Ohan Hominis
Olivia Payne
Olivia Turner
Órla Ní Chuilleanáin
    and Dónall Ó
    Ceallaigh
Pamela Tao
Pat Winslow

Patrick Hawley
Patrick Hoare
Patrick McGuinness
Paul Cray
Paul Daintry
Paul Jones
Paul Munday
Paul Robinson
Paul Scott
Paula Edwards
Paula McGrath
Paula Turner
Pauline Westerbarkey
Pavlos Stavropoulos
Penelope Hewett
    Brown
Peter Edwards
Peter Goulborn
Peter McBain
Peter McCambridge
Peter Rowland
Peter Taplin
Peter Wells
Petra Stapp
Philip Herbert
Philip Scott
Philip Warren
Philip Williams
Philipp Jarke
Phillipa Clements
Phoebe McKenzie
Piet Van Bockstal
Pippa Tolfts
PRAH Foundation
Prakash Nayak
Rachael de Moravia
Rachael Williams
Rachel Dolan
Rachel Gregory
Rachel Matheson
Rachel Meacock
Rachel Van Riel
Rachel Watkins
Rachel Watkins
Ralph Cowling
Rebecca Braun
Rebecca Micklewright
Rebecca Moss
Rebecca O'Reilly

Rebecca Peer
Rebecca Roadman
Rebecca Rosenthal
Rebecca Servadio
Rebekah Hughes
Rebekka Bremmer
Renee Humphrey
Rhiannon Armstrong
Rhodri Jones
Rich Sutherland
Richard Ashcroft
Richard Catty
Richard Gwyn
Richard Mansell
Richard Priest
Richard Shea
Richard Soundy
Richard Stubbings
Rick Tucker
Rishi Dastidar
Rita O'Brien
Robert Gillett
Robert Hannah
Roberto Hull
Robin Taylor
Robina Franko
Roger Newton
Roger Ramsden
Rory Williamson
Ros Woolner
Rosalind May
Rosalind Ramsay
Rosanna Foster
Rose Crichton
Ross Beaton
Rowan Bowman
Rowan Sullivan
Roxanne O'Del Ablett
Roz Simpson
Ruby Kane
Rupert Ziziros
Ruth Deyermond
Ruth Morgan
Ruth Porter
S Italiano
Sabine Little
Sally Baker
Sally Bramley
Sally Hall

Sally Hemsley
Sam Gordon
Sam Reese
Sam Southwood
Samantha Cox
Samuel Crosby
Samuel Wright
Sara Kittleson
Sara Nesbitt Gibbons
Sara Quiroz
Sara Sherwood
Sarah Allman
Sarah Arboleda
Sarah Boyce
Sarah Duguid
Sarah Elizabeth
Sarah Farley
Sarah Forster
Sarah Jacobs
Sarah Lucas
Sarah Manvel
Sarah Pybus
Sarah Roff
Sarah Strugnell
Sasha Dugdale
Scott Astrada
Scott Chiddister
Sean McDonagh
Sez Kiss
Shannon Knapp
Sharon Dogar
Shauna Gilligan
Shauna Rogers
Sheila Duffy
Sheila Packa
Sheryl Jermyn
Shira Lob
Shona Holmes
Sienna Kang
Simon Pitney
Simon Robertson
Simonette Foletti
SK Grout
ST Dabbagh
Stacy Rodgers
Stefanie Schrank
Stefano Mula
Stephan Eggum
Stephanie Lacava

Stephanie Shields
Stephanie Smee
Stephen Pearsall
Steve Chapman
Steve Dearden
Steve James
Steve Raby
Steven & Gitte Evans
Steven Vass
Steven Willborn
Steven Williams
Stu Hennigan
Stuart Snelson
Stuart Wilkinson
Subhashree Beeman
Sue Gordine
Susan Bamford
Susan Bates
Susan Edsall
Susan Ferguson
Susan Winter
Susie Sell
Suzanne Devlin
Suzanne Kirkham
Tamara Larsen
Tania Hershman
Tara Pahari
Tara Roman
Tasmin Maitland
Teresa Werner
The Mighty Douche
    Softball Team
Thom Cuell
Thom Keep
Thomas Fritz
Thomas Mitchell
Thomas Smith
Thomas van den Bout
Thomas Andrew White
Tian Zheng
Tiffany Lehr
Tim Kelly
Tim Scott
Tim Theroux
Timothy Cummins
Timothy Pilbrow
Tina Rotherham-
    Winqvist
Toby Halsey

Toby Hyam
Toby Ryan
Tom Darby
Tom Doyle
Tom Franklin
Tom Gray
Tom Stafford
Tom Whatmore
Tony Bastow
Tory Jeffay
Trevor Wald
Tricia Durdey
Tricia Pillay
Val Challen
Vanessa Baird
Vanessa Dodd
Vanessa Fuller
Vanessa Heggie
Vanessa Nolan
Vanessa Rush
Victor Meadowcroft
Victoria Eld
Victoria Goodbody
Victoria Maitland
Vijay Pattisapu
Wendy Langridge
William
    Brockenborough
William Dennehy
William Franklin
William Mackenzie
William Richard
William Schwaber
William Wood
Yaseen Khan
Yasmin Alam
Yoora Yi Tenen
Zachary Hope
Zara Rahman
Zezinha De Senha
Zoë Brasier
Zoe Taylor

RACHEL GENN is a neuroscientist, artist and writer who has written two novels: *The Cure* (2011) and *What You Could Have Won* (2020). She was a Leverhulme Artist-in-Residence (2016), creating The National Facility for the Regulation of Regret, which spanned installation art, VR and film (2016–17). She has written for *Granta*, *3:AM Magazine* and *Hotel*, and is working on *Hurtling*, a hybrid collection of essays about the neuroscience, art and abjection of artistic reverie. She's also working on a binaural experience exploring paranoia, and a collection of non-fiction about fighting and addiction to regret. Genn works at the Manchester Writing School and the School of Digital Arts, both at Manchester Metropolitan University, and lives in Sheffield.